# Apotheosis

*Stories of Human Survival After
The Rise of The Elder Gods*

Edited By Jason Andrew

# *Copyrights and Credits*

The authors maintain copyrights to their individual stories, which are printed with this anthology with their express written permission.

ISBN: 978-0-9794221-3-3

Cover by Mark Henry

Editor: Jason Andrew

Copy Editors: Lisa Andrew, Maria Cambone

# Table of Contents

# Introduction to Apotheosis

by Jason Andrew

I remember the very day that I discovered the Lovecraft Mythos. A sweltering summer drought swept California when I had been shipped off to a rural farming town named Sanger. The entire land felt foreign to me. Fields and dirt replaced stores and concrete. I was a stranger in a mundane land of broken backs and dry tomorrows.

Books were my world then as now. I was an introverted kid that had virtually nothing in common with my relatives save for blood and familial love. They took me to the town's antiquated library hoping to find something to keep me entertained through the summer until school started and it was there that I found the massive tome from Arkham House that featured a bowdlerized collection of H. P. Lovecraft stories edited by August Derleth.

My fingers tingled just holding the book. By then I had already consumed every Steven King novel I could find second-hand. I had begun to dip my literary toes into macabre. I had consumed every novel from Steven King and had just begun my journey into the sexual fantastic grotesquery of Clive Barker's Books of Blood.

In that book lay a vast uncaring universe where ancient things tread creation unconcerned with the trivialities of mortal, human existence. Lovecraft's purple, archaic prose appealed to my youthful sensibilities. Everything seemed to be an epic battle with forces beyond my control.

This book proved to be a gateway to other greats — the quiet dread of the King in Yellow by Robert Chambers, Robert E. Howard and the undreamt of Hyborian Age, and the terrifying ghost stories of Algernon Blackwood.

This was an era before the internet where rumors of lost editions and out of print books everywhere. A fan had to explore old thrift shops and libraries and swamp meetings hoping to find a hidden treasure. It was just maddening enough to imagine yourself one of Lovecraft's protagonists, desperate to know that which man was not meant to know. My friends and I spent many of our formative years borrowing these creations for our own purposes— casting the Old Ones as gods in my Dungeons and Dragons campaigns, recreating entire races of Deep Ones that plagued my characters, and Nyarlathotep serving as tormentor and wiseman.

Slowly, I moved on to other obsessions until college where I discovered much to my disappoint that the Arkham House I had read — pardon the expression — whitewashed much of Lovecraft's racist and chauvinist attitudes. How could I reconcile my adoration of these stories with the realization that the germ of their inspiration came from hate and fear?

To paraphrase Papa Hemingway, a writer has to fight his demons if he wants there to be blood on the page. Other writers played in Lovecraft's metafiction sandbox and made it their own in ways that might have horrified the old man — the transgressive dark fantasy and horror of Caitlín R Kiernan, Wilum Hopfrog, Pugmire, or the weird tales of China Miéville. Lovecraft himself felt out of touch with his own time and I suspect trapped by the cage of his own fears and disorders. It is any wonder that his universe appeals to those that feel different? Is it any wonder that the Other had been so featured in stories inspired by Lovecraft?

Apotheosis is the elevation or exaltation into godhood — to make something grand from the ordinary. Can you pluck something the muck and transform it into your image? If that is possible, then surely the Lovecraft Mythos has become radically diverse and thereby immensely more interesting.

I pondered editing an anthology set in the Lovecraft Mythos for years, but the exact theme of the potential anthology always eluded me. I knew that I didn't want the same retread of the dread possibility of the Elder Gods finally coming to Earth when the stars were right. I wanted to see worlds where the Elder Gods have come and conquered — and then revealed what happened next.

The seed of this anthology came to me while listening to Cody Goodfellow flamboyantly read the story that appears in this collection. "Earth Worms" posited a world where the Elder Gods came to a broken world not as conquers, but as saviors and farmers that transplant humanity to a new Eden.

And that's when the anthology crystalized in my mind. I wasn't satisfied with stories that teased the Elder Gods, but never revealed their eldritch glory. I didn't want to wait until the stars were right; I wanted to experience the dread then and there and see what would happen next. How could humanity survive such horrors? And if they did manage to eke out some sort of existence, what would be the price they paid? The perennial quote from Fredrick Nietzsche echoed in my head. *Whoever fights monsters should see to it that in the process he does not become a monster. And if you gaze long enough into an abyss, the abyss will gaze back into you.* Would they even still be human in any practical sense?

*Apotheosis: Stories of Human Survival After The Rise of the Elder Gods* is the fourth anthology I've edited under the small press imprint Simian Publishing. As always, Simian Publishing wanted put out an anthology that would be open to talented emerging writers and set them alongside known professional writers.

Our guidelines established one hard rule: all stories in the anthology had to focus upon humanity surviving in a world where the Elder Gods has returned and conquered. We asked for character-driven stories exploring what it meant to be human in a universe of ancient horrors beyond the limits of morality. We wanted this anthology to embody a wide range of human experience, voices, and in particular, to credibly consider our present and future demographics of the world.

I believed in this project and we asked for our patrons to help us fund it. Our successful Kickstarter collected $2,333 towards paying our writers. I would like to thank each and every one of the 92 patrons who allowed us to chase this dream. Thank you for supporting Simian Publishing and the small press.

A themed anthology is a great risk for an open submission call. Some writers will scrounge through their trunks sending anything that might vaguely fit the guidelines. Others will glance at the anthology and spark their own ideas. We received over 300 submissions. Reading through the slush was the most difficult aspect of this assignment as the scope and breadth blew my mind. There were great ideas from new writers and old-school professionals. Once I narrowed down the submission pool to 150, every successive cut was to the bone. The great sculptor Michelangelo once said, "I saw the angel in the marble and carved until I set him free." Simian Publishing painstakingly read through every submission until we began to see a pattern for the project and learned what we wanted the final book to be.

*Apotheosis: Stories of Survival After The Rise of The Elder Gods* has more than 70,000 words worth of stories that terrify and delight you. It will open windows to worlds never before glimpsed or dreamed of — to face our nightmares by dragging them into the light and riding them for all they are worth.

The poet Heather McHugh once wrote that horror is seeing the alien in the familiar. Terror is seeing the familiar in what should be alien. Isn't that the point of horror?

# The Smiling People

by Andrew Peregrine

The smiling people always seem to be staring at you, even without eyes. We have two in the office today, a male and a female. They keep out of the way, to be fair. The male has spent most of the day at the window near the forgotten copy machine. I think he has moved twice all day. The female has been more active. She was in the kitchen for the morning and somehow moved into the main office this afternoon. Come to think of it she seems to have been following Jason for most of the day.

They keep to themselves, but even when they are facing away from you they still seem to be staring at you. The males all dress very alike, neat suits and ties, with elegant and almost identical tailoring. The females are a little more varied: some wear suits, others dresses, and their hairstyles can be quite individual. They always seem to stand perfectly still, and move quickly when you aren't paying any attention. The most unnerving thing about them though is their faces. They are all the same, blank white ovals, broken only by a huge smiling mouth of sharpened teeth.

They are everywhere in the city. So common you almost don't notice them anymore. They just stand around watching us, sometimes following. Yesterday, I saw a crowd of them following a pregnant woman along the street. I suspect she'd tried to ignore them at first, but more had gathered behind her. I looked up when she turned and started screaming at them to leave her alone, but that seemed to make more of them join the group. Faced with the silent, grinning crowd, she fell quiet and backed away. She broke into a run, but then suddenly stopped only a few yards later. She sank to her knees, as if she was exhausted, and just sat there crying. The smiling people crowded around until I couldn't see her anymore. I kept walking.

I'm not entirely sure what my job is. Every morning I arrive at the office to find a collection of paperwork on my desk. It mostly needs filing, and I have to read a lot of it and then sign it to say I've done so before passing it on to the next department. Once or twice I've seen my own name signed on a document I don't remember reading. But none of them are memorable. Lists of data, market research, and invoices for products I don't even know if we sell. Come to think of it, I'm not sure what we do sell, or if we sell anything at all.

My work colleagues are a decent bunch, but the office is usually quiet. There is always at least one of the smiling people around. You can feel their nonexistent eyes burning into you as you work, trying not to look at them. So there is little chatter here. We just exchange knowing looks as we pass papers to each other. It's like sharing your space with a predator. We instinctively keep quiet and move away in their presence. I've seen conversations end abruptly and groups break up just due to the presence of one of the smiling people. I've never seen one of them hurt a human being yet, but that's what makes it worse. None of us know what they are capable of.

Alison brings me another pile of papers, and sometimes she smiles at me, a rare thing among us these days. I don't know her very well, but I look forward to seeing her each day. She is quite an average looking girl, but clever and funny. I like the way her hair curls over her face, and the smile I keep hoping she saves for me. Our hands touch and linger with each other as she passes me the papers. But the smiling people are there as always. Our moment passes and she turns to leave. I want to say something, ask her to go for a drink, even say something stupid just to bring her back. But it never seems the right time. On her way back to her desk, she turns and glances at me. I look away, embarrassed by my own failure.

With my attention on Alison, I fail to notice one of the smiling people has come closer. He stands at the end of my desk, still like a statue. His dreadful grin is turned towards me and he leans a little closer over my desk. I try not to move too quickly, reaching again slowly for the pile of papers Alison left. As I pull them towards me the smiling person's hand is suddenly upon mine. He leans a little closer again, bending halfway over the desk. I can feel the office go silent, everyone trying their hardest not to notice what is going on. The hand covering mine is soft and moist, and cold. My hand begins to go numb at his touch and my body is screaming at me to pull away. But I daren't move. We are locked together there for what seems an age; my heart beats so hard I can feel it pounding in my chest.

Then I'm suddenly released. The smiling person is no longer in front of me but standing with his back to me. I think he is staring at Alison's desk at the end of the floor. I feel suddenly sick. Running to the toilets I curl up in one of the stalls and throw up until I'm empty. No one comes to see if I'm alright.

At the end of the day, no one stays any later than they have to. We shuffle on our coats and gloves and silently scatter back into the city. It is always cold here, and the seasons never seem to change. The date was lost a long time ago, so no one marks the festivals. It feels forever like January, Christmas long forgotten and spring so far away. We drift out of the building in ones and twos. Large groups tend to attract the smiling people. A few of the couples attract one tagging behind them, silently following them home.

They seem to have had their fill of me today though, and I reach home without an escort. There is rarely any electricity operating in the city, so I have to take the stairs. I pass a few more smiling people on a couple of the landings as I make my way to the eighth floor. They turn and watch me pass but seem interested in someone else. A group of them on the sixth floor stand watching a small boy play with a ball in the corridor. His mother stands in the doorway, trying to wave him inside with silent urgency to little avail.

My apartment is on the eighth floor, but at least it is quiet. Of the six apartments on this level, only two of them are occupied. Outside my door is my weekly parcel. It is wrapped in brown paper and while there is no name I know it has been left for me. Getting out my keys in the silent corridor I pick up the parcel and quickly enter my flat.

Dumping the parcel on the table, I lean on the door and look around for a while. Sometimes the smiling people get inside, but this time I am blissfully alone. Taking off my coat, I open the parcel, enjoying for a moment the trepidation of opening a gift, even though I know what it contains.

As usual, the contents are a little random, although mainly canned goods. I remember the brands from my childhood, and it always makes me wonder if they are still being made, or if one day they will simply run out. There are a few candles among the various cans. With no electricity, candles are an essential, but the ones they send are slightly sticky and soft. The smell of them tends to get into your clothes, a deep dank smell of old basements and soggy books. I put them in a drawer; there will be enough light for a while, no need to light one yet.

I usually keep the curtains closed because I'm close to the wall here. The apartments on the other side of the building look out into the city. They show the rows of broken buildings that stretch out in ruin upon ruin. My view looks out the other way, towards the wall. No one I know has got close to the wall itself, but few people would want to. It rises over sixty feet high and is made of wreckage and bodies. It looks as if something vast scooped up the remains of rubble and victims left from the apocalypse and glued them together with spit and bile. It is a vast, organic-looking mess of stone, metal, and horror, sculpted by something inhuman to corral us here. They say it goes around the whole city, or at least what remains of it. When I think of the scale of that, all those bodies, it makes me feel sick. I try not to look at it, but the sky is worse.

The clouds are yellow now, swollen and infected, and they clot a sky made of green and mauve hues. On some nights, the colors can be almost pretty, but most of the time they make me want to retch. They churn together up there, as if in pain. Sometimes they make shapes, shapes of creatures I remember only in my nightmares. I tell myself they are only shadows, but a part of me knows they are not. There are no birds, but sometimes you see flying things skittering across the sky. It's one of the reasons we tend to stay on the ground. Everything here feels hungry now.

After unpacking the box, I crouch by the bedroom door to lift a loose floorboard I found years ago. I look around the apartment again quickly, just to be sure before I take out the small box I keep there. I sit down with my back against the wall and open the box, taking out the small gold ring. It is solid gold, yet still surprisingly delicate in appearance. There is an engraving on the inside that simply says "All my love, 23$^{rd}$ March 2023." It is my mother's wedding ring.

I think she knew we'd never see each other again when we were separated. I have nightmares of that time, but thankfully the memory has faded. The ring helps me focus on remembering my mother, not the monsters who took her away. But I remember the fear; that never leaves you. I think we were outside, herded up in a great crowd, horrible creatures all around us. There was no screaming, the time for that was long past, just weeping and despair. Everyone knew they were going to die, or at least there was no future. All we had to hope for was that the stories of what they did to those they captured were not true. We were tired and dirty, and I had long given up asking if my father was coming back. Then the creatures surrounding us started pulling and separating people. Everyone began to push and shove and then there were screams as it became clear they were separating the adults from the children.

We stayed together as long as we could, just holding each other. There was no point in resistance anymore. We stayed together until claws grabbed my mother and tore us from each other. As the creatures pulled her from me, she slipped the ring from her finger and told me to keep it safe. I clutched it hard in my hand as they pushed me with the other children into some form of vehicle. The floor was slick and organic, and a tarpaulin was thrown over us as the machine juddered into life and took us away. In was quiet for a while, but then we heard the screams. They didn't last very long.

My mother's ring is all I have left of her, all I have left of anything. I have to be careful to make sure the smiling people never find it. I don't think they search our rooms, but you can never be sure. It is possible they wouldn't take it from me, but that isn't the point. It's the one thing of mine they haven't touched. They have everything else, but this is mine, and mine alone. Perhaps it is even the last thing on the whole planet that they haven't corrupted or taken from us.

A soft knock at the door sends me into a panic. I push the ring into its box and quickly return it to the hiding place. Replacing the floorboard I rush towards the door, but then turn back to check I've put the floorboard back properly. The knock comes again, a little more urgently. I'm still looking at the floorboard, as I open the door. So I'm a little surprised to see Alison slip into the apartment and begin checking around the rooms. My mind is taking a while to process this new event and so I stand there open-mouthed as she looks into each room. I close the door and wait for her to finish. I don't know why she's here, but I know I don't want her to go.

After a few moments, Alison seems content my apartment is how it should be. She stands in the center of the living room, her coat unbuttoned and her hat in her hand, staring at me. I look at her, not knowing what to do and hoping I don't say something stupid to make her leave.

"There aren't any of them here?" she states as a question, taking a step towards me.

"Them? No. No, I don't think so."

She drops her hat and takes two paces towards me, pausing as if to reconsider. I have my back to the door but no desire to get away from her. Then she seems to make a decision and crosses the room to kiss me. For some stupid reason I find myself wanting to tell her she has dropped her hat, but her kiss makes sure I don't say anything. My arms curl around her, and her hands begin to slide into my clothes. She breaks the kiss for a moment and whispers to me.

"Make me feel. I just want to feel something."

I let her guide me to the bedroom, but we only get as far as the sofa. We share a moment together, or what feels like only a moment. Afterwards, the room feels cold again. Alison puts on her coat, and I worry she is going to leave me until I remember her dress is still on the floor. It has got dark without us noticing, so I light a candle.

"Don't," she says. "Not one of those, not now. Not after we've…"

I think for a moment and remember I have some packing paper in this week's box. I tear some into a bowl and use the candle to set light to it before I blow it out. Alison smiles. The paper burns with an orange flame and she comes back to the sofa. We curl around each other with nothing to say as the paper gradually burns away. For the first time in years, I feel what must be contentment. Her coat keeps us both warm.

I wake up later than Alison. I find her in the kitchen making beans on toast, silhouetted against the morning light through the curtains. She is already dressed and her hair is still wet from a shower. I go to put my arms around her but she turns to dish out the food and I only mange to awkwardly kiss her on the cheek.

"I hope you don't mind," she says, putting two plates of beans on toast on the table. "I never seem to get beans very often in my box."

"It's like they know what we remember from our childhood," I joke, bringing the room into silence.

The food tastes just that little better than usual with Alison here. Everything seems a little brighter somehow. As we sit there together eating, the fear takes a step back. It's as if something could be normal again. I finish before her and reach out for her hand, but she shies away.

"Don't," she whispers.

"I'm sorry, I just thought…"

"We can't, I'm sorry. I want to, we just can't. Last night was wonderful, but we can't be together."

"Why not?" I say, failing to realize I'm getting angry.

"You know why not. Because they'll see, and they'll know, and they'll spoil it all and take it away."

"We could be careful."

"It wouldn't matter. They might even be outside the door, watching now. I like you, I really do. Maybe we can do this again. But if they see us together too many times they'll follow us. You know what they are like with couples, moths to a bloody flame."

"You don't know that," I almost shout. I can feel something breaking inside me, and an angry part of me wants her to hear the crack.

"Yes, I do. And you do, too."

She's right, but I'm not ready to admit it. "So is this what you do, then?" I retort.

"Excuse me?"

"Just a few one night flings." My voice is getting louder.

Alison looks like I've just struck her, but that only makes her angry too. "It's not like that, not that I have to explain myself to you. Anyway, I didn't hear any complaints last night."

"I didn't realize last night we were just trading for beans on toast."

As I say it, I know I have crossed a line. "Fuck you," she says, almost too quietly for me to hear it. She picks up her hat and marches to the door, the remains of her breakfast pointedly forgotten. As she flings it open she almost runs straight into the small crowd of smiling people that have gathered outside. There are about seven of them, all facing us, but who gently part to let Alison go. The fear of them knocks the anger out of both of us. As Alison leaves she turns, wanting to say something but having no more words than I do. I answer her in silence, as the smiling people look on. Then she turns and hurries past them, and I close the door.

I walk back to the loose floorboard and almost take out the ring. But I know they are out there and I stop myself in time. I sit on the floor crying, my hand on the floorboard. Grief gradually gives way to hate. The smiling people. I can't believe they are taking away something I don't even have. But Alison is right: any relationship gets their attention, and under that gaze, anything is poisoned. Is there nothing left for any of us? The rage builds up inside me, as I list the things Alison and I will never be, the happiness we have been denied.

Picking up her cold plate of beans on toast, I walk over to the door, and as I open it, I throw it at whatever remains in the hallway. There are only three smiling people there now, but I almost hit one of them full in the face. The plate bounces off his shoulder and smashes on the floor. He barely moves, the impact momentarily shaking him, like hitting a tree. The beans run down his face and drip across his expensive suit jacket, but he still does nothing. Then a long thin tongue slides out from between the crescent teeth and slides around his face.

It wipes away the sauce and beans slowly, as if savoring each moment. I'd swear his smile gets a little wider, something I'd thought impossible and I step back to close the door. My hands are shaking so much it takes me two tries to shut it properly.

After that night, I hate the office even more than I used to. Alison and I barely even glance at each other. A few times we are forced to interact, such as passing pointless papers to each other. I want to say something to her, and I think she wants to talk too, but the smiling people are always there, somewhere. After a few days of this, I can't take the silence anymore. I walk over to her desk intent on apologizing. I just want to tell her I understand. It might not be what I want, but it's so much better than not having a part of her in my life. I don't want to make a scene. All I want is to say my piece and see her smile again. That is all it would take to settle things between us, and I could go back to having hope again.

But as I get closer to her desk, I see her talking to Bill Abbot. He's sitting on her desk and grinning like a cat. She puts a hand on his knee as she laughs quietly at one of his awful jokes. It's then that I realize I can't share her. I don't know Bill that well, but she deserves better. He might be perfect, the sort of no strings guy she can share brief nights with to ease the pressure. But I don't want that for her, or for me, but there is nothing I can do. I want to punch Bill, or just walk over and kiss Alison and tell her I don't care about the smiling people. Maybe I want to do both. But the truth is that I do care about the smiling people, we all do, and as I realize this, I notice one is standing a few feet away watching them both. Something inside me snaps.

"Just leave her alone," I scream, picking up an ashtray and hurling it at the smiling person.

It strikes him on the head and he staggers. He reaches out for support on a nearby desk and a green thick liquid starts to run down his head. The whole room goes silent. The smiling person turns to look at me. He moves towards me very deliberately, but a little unsteadily. The green liquid is running steadily down his back and dripping on to the floor as he comes towards me. I can't move. Fear has me rooted to the spot. I stare at Alison, wanting her to be the last thing I see, and her eyes are wide and confused.

The smiling person crosses the last meter between us suddenly and grabs my hand, the one that threw the ashtray. Then he slowly begins to squeeze, tighter and tighter. I try to pull away, but I can't. I find myself standing on tiptoe as I feel the bones shift in my hand. There is an audible crack as something breaks, and I whimper out a scream. I know in that moment he is going to kill me slowly.

But there is a noise to my left as someone starts singing. Tom Franklin has stood up and, with a voice only barely suited to karaoke, is offering his rendition of "Mack the Knife." The attention quickly shifts from me to him. There are other smiling people in the office and they begin to cluster around him. The one grabbing me turns to look at this new spectacle. Having not captured all his audience, Tom jumps onto a desk and begins showing us dance moves worthy of a drunken dad at a wedding. It is such a comical sight a few of the office workers are giggling, some out of hysteria.

The smiling person releases my hand and moves closer to get a better look at Tom. I sink to the floor clutching my hand. It's agony but I grit my teeth not to cry out. Tom and I exchange looks, and I mouth a brief thank you. He nods in acknowledgement as he tries to get some of the others to join in the chorus. To his credit, he gets some of them to at least begin clapping along. I remember there is a medical kit in the kitchen that might have something I can bind my hand with. As I leave the main office, I turn to look at the smiling person who hurt me, and he has his head turned towards me. I freeze, and he turns back to Tom, who is coming to a big finish. It is all I need to see to understand this incident is not over.

I'm too scared to leave early, so with my hand wrapped in a bandage and throbbing with dull pain, I stick out the rest of the day. I want to catch Tom to thank him for possibly saving my life, but he seems to be avoiding me. He is not the only one. It's like I've been marked, and no one wants to get tainted by being seen with me. So all that I can do is walk home and hope the day doesn't get any worse. My hand continues to throb as I walk, but the cold helps a little. Something must be broken, but there are no hospitals here. Pain is a draw for the smiling people. I think they want to know how easily we break or how much suffering we can endure.

Just before I get home, someone pulls me into an alley. I shake off the hand that has yanked me by the arm and turn to defend myself. I'm surprised to see it's Tom.

"I need your help," he says. "I figure you owe me after this afternoon."

He's right, but I'm still confused. "What do you need?" I say noncommittally.

"I'm getting out of here."

It's a simple sentence, and not the first time I've heard it. I'm filled with equal parts hope and terror.

"What makes you think you can leave?"

He opens his coat and shows the handle of a gun poking out of his belt. The device looks old and a little worn, but it might just still be serviceable. I think it might be the same type of gun my father used to own before the creatures came.

"This will get us past anything if we're fast. Once we're over the wall, we can get hold of the resistance. I just need someone to watch my back. I can't do this alone."

"Why me?"

"You know why. They are going to kill you after what you did today. That's why I distracted them, why I risked my life for you. I need someone with nothing left to lose."

I want to tell him I have Alison, but I know that isn't true. I change the subject.

"Where did you get the gun?"

"It came in my box. I know that sounds crazy, but there it was, and a few bullets too. I think the resistance has infiltrated wherever they pack this stuff up. There must be people like us filling the boxes and delivering all this food and one of them sent me this. I don't know if they meant it for me, or if they just wanted to get it to someone, but it could be my ticket out and I'm not going to waste it."

"Okay, so when do we leave?"

"Now."

"Okay," I say, unsure. "I'll get some things and meet you back here."

"No. When I say now, I mean right now."

"What? No! We need clothes, provisions; I have stuff at my place." I don't want to say it out loud but I can't leave the ring behind.

"That's no good. We start packing anything and they'll know. They might even know just from us talking here. We have to start walking and maybe, just maybe, they won't know what we're up to until we're at the wall."

I close my eyes for a moment and picture the ring, safe under the floorboard. It is all I have left, but if they kill me, it won't matter. If they bring us back, they won't find it on me. If we escape, maybe I won't need it.

"Alright. We go now."

Walking to the wall, we do our best to look nonchalant. It gets harder as we get close because the smell from the wall is thick and heavy. As we get closer there are fewer people around until we are the only ones. Both of us have our collars turned up so we can cover our noses from the dense rot that stinks over the whole area. But no one stops us; no smiling people seem to be around. Maybe without so many people here, they don't have much interest.

When we reach the wall itself, it is hard not to retch. The smell is deep here; I can feel it seeping into my clothes and sticking to the inside of my nostrils. It towers above us, a pile of detritus and effluent. The remains of an entire civilization has been used to build it. There are bodies there, so many I can't count. Each is mummified after years encased here. Some seem to reach out as if they might have been alive before they became part of it. There are animals in there too, and bones. But the construction is not entirely organic. Rusted girders, rubble from destroyed buildings, and even a few vehicles have been used as materials. The whole construction is held together by a green and yellow mucus that has set almost as hard as cement. However, even now, the outer layers of it somehow remain sticky and soft to the touch.

Tom and I grit our teeth and begin to climb. It isn't a difficult climb in many ways. There are so many handholds, and the angle isn't as steep as it might be. My damaged hand is a problem, but not an insurmountable one. But the smell is overpowering, and everything I touch is disgusting. Dead eyes stare out at me as we climb, and my feet keep slipping on God knows what as I push up each step. With each breath, I want to throw up. It feels so high that I wonder if I'll ever reach the top.

I don't know how long it takes us to climb the wall, but it must have been hours. The night has deepened as we crawl up to the apex, but we can still see by the light from the city behind us. It feels empty up here, far from everything. When I look back, I think I see something moving below us, but it is too far away. Is it a smiling person? I can't tell, but I'm not sure if they can see us up here from down there. We are both exhausted and take a moment to rest, spread out on this jagged ridge. The climb down should be easier, but with the worst over, we both take a moment. Tom smiles at me, but it is too early to think we are safe yet.

Given the darkness, it is hard to see very far, even from here. But the sky bathes the land in a soft glow of sickly mauve and green. I can't see anything but barren land, though. There is nothing out there as far as the eye can see. In the distance, mountains rise up to the clouds and here and there, the shapes of tentacles wave frond-like from the sky. Where they touch the ground, they seem to be grazing on the dust that remains.

"Beyond those mountains. That's where they'll be," says Tom, his hope failing to infect me. I don't answer him. Looking out here, I can't imagine there is anything else left. I'm not even sure without provisions we could make it past the mountains. But I can't destroy his last hope, and I want to believe him. I want to believe him so badly I'm still ready to risk my life here.

After we've taken a moment to catch our breath, we start to make the climb down. As we stand to begin the decent, there is a screech and something falls from the sky a few feet from us. It looks like a cross between a bird and a reptile. It has a thin humanoid form, made of bones and skin. Its head is pointed with glittering eyes and great leather wings block out the sky behind it. Its feet are claws, and it grips the wall as it perches there. It screams out a cry at us both and stalks towards us, reaching out with long sharp fingers.

I want to run, but Tom pulls the gun from his belt. He fires at the creature four times quickly. Three of the bullets find their mark, spraying both of us with its yellow blood. The creature staggers back, its screams gurgling as blood fills its throat. Tom smiles at me in victory as the creature falls backwards to slip down the wall.

I meet Tom's gaze just in time to see another creature pluck him from the wall in front of me. It lifts him off his feet in seconds. As it does so its wings smash into me and knock me from the wall. I fall, tumbling and turning down the steep hillside. I hear bones crack under me, but can't be sure if they are mine. Shards of steel slice and bash me as I slip along the broken edifice.

As I fall, I hear Tom's gun fire, but I can't tell how many times. It seems far away, up in the sky, but how high I can't tell. Then I hear a crunch not too far away as I slowly come to a rest. Opening my eyes and uncurling myself, I try to look around. Every part of me hurts and I can't tell if the thick liquid that covers me is my blood or more slime from the wall. Tom lies on his back a few feet away, his eyes staring skyward. One of the creatures squirms nearby, flapping its wings in death throes as it sprays yellow blood around it. Another creature lands next to it, but ignores me. It tears the head from its kinsman, almost in annoyance at the noise it was making. Then it fixes me with a glare, struts over to Tom's body, and begins tearing into his stomach. His body lurches as it rips out his succulent organs, while his eyes continue to stare blindly at the sky.

I crawl away as best I can. It will come for me next and there is nothing I can do to stop it. As I drag myself away from the wall onto the dry earth, I look up to see smiling people all around. They stand in a great crowd facing me, and they seem eager for something. I force myself to kneel, then to stand, so I can face them. It is over for me. I don't know how I can stay alive, or even if I want to anymore. But I will at least keep some of my dignity.

"Go on, then," I shout at them. "Just kill me and get it over with."

I'm waiting for their usual silence, but instead, one of them opens his mouth a little and in a quiet voice full of echoes says, "No."

I step back in shock. They have never spoken before, at least not to anyone who has talked about it.

"Why not?" is all I can think to say.

"We have not finished."

"Finished what? Is this some experiment? You just want to see what it takes to break us, what you need to do to make us beg? Why? What is the city for?"

"To entertain us."

"That's it?"

"We have no other use for you."

The smiling person tilts his head to one side, curious I should think I had any importance. It continues to smile at me.

"Why the blasted smiling faces?"

"We thought it would put you at your ease, so you might continue your business without interference. Do you find us unsettling? We do our best to observe without influencing. You are more entertaining that way."

"That's why you won't kill me then? I'm still entertaining?"

"Yes, and we have a question, as there is something about you we do not understand."

I'm almost laughing with hysteria. "Well, what's your question?" I ask, consoling myself that I can at least deny them an answer.

"We don't entirely understand the importance of the ring."

They know. They have everything, and the force of that pushes me to my knees in front of them. I look down and see Tom's gun lies fallen beside me in the dust. I pick it up cradling its weight in my hand as tears roll down my cheeks. I look in the clip, and find there is one bullet left. The smiling people crowd around, eager to see what I will do next.

# The Pestilence of Pandora Peaslee

### by Peter Rawlik

Endora Peaslee, called by those who feared her Pandora, paused to
check that her package was secure. She had abandoned the boat that
had brought her from Haiti and set it to autopilot after the satellite had
locked on. Her muscles ached from swimming through the warm
Florida waters, but she had no time to rest. She was just a few miles
from her destination, but if she was going to make the deadline, she
was going to have to hustle. She ran up the sandy shoreline and onto
the streets of what had once been Palm Beach, home to old money,
and moved through the wreckage of the low buildings that had once
been an exclusive shopping district. This area was mostly abandoned;
even the dogs and cats had moved inland. Without the rich, the island
had gone wild. Sand drifted down the streets. Saltwater ponds filled
parking lots. The grass had died and been replaced with plants that
were more tolerant of the sea spray. Mangroves were slowly reclaiming
the island, marching in from the lagoon at a slow but sure pace. As she
crossed the bridge over the Intracoastal, she looked south and in the
distance could see the Suncoast Arcology rising up into the sky. Even
this far away, she could see the cloud of machines that were flitting
around it like bugs on a corpse, except the corpse was hundreds of
years of human effort, being systematically recycled for a bold new

future. If only that future had been planned by human minds, she might not be a terrorist.

She careened over the crumbling concrete bridge and through the shadows of derelict condominiums and abandoned office towers into what was left of downtown West Palm. City Place and the Kravis Center for the Performing Arts lay in ruins; shattered glass windows and barrel tiles littered the streets. Spray-painted purple symbols marked the area as scheduled for demolition and harvest. All this area would be restored to the way it had been before man decided to try to shape Florida to suit his own needs. The rest of the world was going the same way. The world was becoming a better, cleaner, safer place. The old ways of doing things had been replaced, with newer, better ways.

She followed a ramp south, moving against the direction of traffic that no longer existed. She crossed over I-95 and looked at the vast ribbon of concrete and asphalt that stretched both north and south like a dried up canal. Once, this road had been a river of steel and light; now, it was as dead as everything else, abandoned by humanity in favor of a new way of life, one that guaranteed the survival of the species, but at a price Pandora Peaslee couldn't accept. Not that she didn't understand what had happened; she just didn't approve of it. Men should not give up their freedoms so willingly.

The first hint that something was awry had been the loss of contact with the Falkland Islands. The British were still trying to figure out what had happened when New Zealand went dark. Things snowballed from that point forward. Shoggothim, ancient alien machines

31

comprised of weird matter that looked like slime and absorbed anything organic, had been released from some Antarctic prison. The creatures devoured anything that moved. How they had made their way off the frozen continent wasn't clear, but they had a taste for human flesh and normal weapons did little to slow them down. Humans fought back with devastating weaponry. Most of the lower part of South America was still burning. New Zealand and Tasmania were more radioactive than Chernobyl, and just as abandoned.

Her brisk pace took her through-long abandoned office blocks, hotels, and a burnt-out fast food restaurant. Feral cats had claimed a parking garage -- nothing to worry about -- but she picked up her pace when something large shifted within the tiered darkness. Her route took her into the airport and she climbed over the rubble of collapsed flyways that had once steered cars from the interstate to the small, bustling transportation center filled with dead cars. There weren't any working cars anymore, at least not like there had been. Small electric things still flitted through what remained of the great metropoli, drawing power from the grid embedded in the roadway, but that grid didn't extend out this far into the brownfields. Even if it did, any vehicle would have been a clear target for the satellites that now dotted the sky.

It had been amongst the islands that dotted the Pacific that the next threat manifested, though no one at the time recognized it for what it was. The small nations of the Pacific Ocean, all normally fiercely independent, suddenly found a new sense of unity. Some said it was because of the Shoggothim, that small areas were highly vulnerable and they needed to ally themselves against a greater enemy. Other weren't so sure, but the result was clear: in a single month, the nations of Kiribati, Tonga, Micronesia, Palau, the Seychelles, Tuvalu and Nauru all lay aside their rivalries and formed the Pacific Union. They rewrote laws concerning data privacy and finances, and within the year were suddenly a financial and technological powerhouse. Eighteen months after its formation, Samoa and the Philippines petitioned for membership. Papua, Malaysia, and Indonesia weren't far behind. A new global power emerged on the planet, not based on military prowess, but rather on the intersection of money and a technology that seemed years ahead of anybody else. Even the fleet of airships they built, huge whale-like things with no speed but incredible energy efficiency, seemed designed to serve rather than threaten.

She jumped a fence and sprinted across the runways. Cattle egrets and iguanas scattered before her. A covey of doves took flight, screaming their umbrage at her presence. Something large and tawny, a deer, maybe a coyote, or perhaps a panther, trotted through the tall grass that had colonized the places between the cracked cement. She could feel the heat radiating off of the artificial rock and a little part of her longed for an afternoon thunderstorm to come and cool things off, however briefly, and even if the subsequent humidity was unbearable.

The airships of the Pacific Union were the first to arrive after Typhoon Fabiola had unexpectedly turned north and devastated Japan from Kumamoto to Sapporo. Union forces carried out rescues, turned malls into hospitals and shelters, stabilized nuclear reactors, and made sure everyone was vaccinated against diseases that had been long thought eradicated. The images of Pacific Union airships hovering over Tokyo's skyline became commonplace, and it came as no surprise when Japan's emergency government, operating out of Okinawa petitioned to become a member state. When the Koreas and Taiwan followed, China protested, but by that point the wave had gathered such strength that it was pointless to stand in its way.

She found her way through a gutted hanger and back onto the road on the far side of the airport. She took another crumbling overpass to leapfrog over a canal and come within sight of her destination. There was an old Reserve Base opposite the shell of a burnt-out building with traces of a gold sign still visible, but her target was the monolith that loomed before her, an imposing angular thing that screamed to be left alone. It squatted on the landscape with a row of thin windows that squinted like eyes, peering out at the surrounding neighborhood like an angry cat ready to leap and spit and scratch. This was the building that showed the least response to the vagaries of time and weather, an edifice built to last, to be secure, and to keep its occupants under control. Pandora looked at her watch and finally stopped running as she entered the grounds of the Palm Beach County Detention Center.

Pacific Union aid centers sprung up across the world and began to tackle problems that other governments, organizations and corporations had either failed at or abandoned. Safe water in Africa, chemical cleanup in the Middle East, food in India, energy and housing in South America, even urban blight in the rustbelt of the American Midwest suddenly had solutions, or progress toward a solution. Even Europe and China allowed for the establishment of working groups within their borders. The only real resistance was Russia, a nation that could have used the help, but was either too proud or too stubborn to let foreigners in. A new iron curtain went up just as barriers everywhere else in the world went down.

The power in the Detention Center was still on, functioning at emergency levels that kept the cells locked but little else functioning. There were other buildings that had better power systems, but they all lacked the ability to remotely operate doors. The plan depended on keeping things under control until the very last minute. Prisons, long abandoned but often with their own power supplies, provided the perfect opportunity to do just that. All she had to do was wait for the right time.

With clean energy, clean water, and clean food came a sense of prosperity, of unity and of trust. Those feelings left little room for the fear of subjugation. When evidence emerged that the leaders of the Pacific Union had all suffered from some sort of seizure, one that resulted in the total dissolution of previous memories and personalities, it was all too late. People didn't care, they gladly traded exploitation by the Western Powers for exploitation by people that looked and spoke as they did, and took care of their needs. In a quarter of a century, the Pacific Union had conquered the world without so much as firing a shot.

Pandora moved through the dilapidated building with sure-footed accuracy, dodging broken-down furniture and decaying concrete. Weeds and scrawny trees had taken hold in walls, drawing light and rain from cracked skylights. Bugs had found their way in too, mostly

Peter Rawlik

mosquitoes and dragonflies. There was also a large paper wasp nest that buzzed angrily as she passed by, forcing her to dodge right and bounce off of the wall of holding cell. Something inside moaned ominously and the steel grate rattled as its strength was tested. She softly cursed, put her hand on her gun and slowly backed away. She eyed the shadows moving beyond the weak light, waited for them to settle and then took off running again. She had to reach cover. The exercise level twelve stories up had been prepared, stocked and fortified. All she had to do was avoid being caught before she got there. Three years of planning was about to reach fruition. All around the world, her sisters were following the plan, and like her, leading their own pursuers into similar situations. After today, the world would never be the same, one way or another. Once the plan was in play, it would take only hours to wrap the world in terror.

Two stories below her, the entrance exploded in a shower of glass and cheap aluminum framing. She glimpsed a dozen shock troopers as they stormed through the smoke and ash. They wore insignia that harkened back to various law enforcement agencies, but the laws they were enforcing weren't in any municipal or state code. These men were enforcing new laws, written by their new masters, and those masters may have looked human, but that was only a facade. It had only been after most of the world had submitted to the Pacific Union that its leaders had revealed themselves as something inhuman. The world had been invaded, and the invaders were creatures of pure mind, cool, ancient and alien intelligences that brought with them solutions to all the world's problems. All they demanded was complete and

36

unquestioning obedience, and most people readily complied. The only ones who hadn't had been those who recognized them for what they were. People like Pandora's parents, people who gave the invaders a name, the Yith.

"Endora Peaslee!" The sound of the voice over the bullhorn was familiar, a ranking Yithian who went by the name Mister Ys, a man, for lack of a better word, who was very good at his job: tracking and capturing unruly humans. "Endora Peaslee, fifth daughter of Robert Peaslee and Megan Halsey, you have been tried in absentia and found guilty of crimes against humanity. A warrant has been issued for your execution. Surrender now and I assure you that the method will be painless." His voice was nearly void of emotion.

Pandora looked at her watch. Her pursuers were right on schedule -- her schedule, not theirs. Hopefully everything she and the others were doing wasn't on the Yithian timetable.

The Yith were time-travelers, aliens that had, eons ago, discovered a way to mentally move through time, leaping forwards and backwards, stealing bodies and infiltrating societies, all on the premise of doing research. They were obsessed with gathering historical data and documenting eras they considered historically important while ignoring events that men might consider critical. Pandora's own grandfather had fallen victim to their machinations. He like many others had been released from their grasp, but only after they had finished with him. The event had devastated the family. Her uncle had become obsessed with the Yith, and hunted them down whenever he could. In contrast, her father had spent years trying to avoid the taint that had cursed his family, only to be drawn into altogether different but just as sinister matters. That may have had more to do with her mother, who had seemed born to the mysterious and macabre and had drawn her husband into the darkness with her. The resistance had grown up out of what Pandora's parents could tell them about the Yith and how they behaved.

Pandora and her friends in the Resistance -- and that is what they called themselves, no fancy names or acronyms, simply the Resistance -- didn't particularly like what had become of the world. They knew more about the universe, but less about their government. They were building power stations, but not families. They understood chemistry and physics and ecology, but not command structures and decision-making. In the eyes of the resistance, humans were becoming technicians, leaving the leadership to their newfound masters; masters that often went unquestioned about motives or goals. When the Resistance found the first baby factory, children engineered to be stronger and faster than normal humans, Pandora knew it was time to act. She and her sisters formulated a plan, gathered like-minded friends, and started a worldwide underground network.

They'd been on the run, building to this day, ever since.

On the side of the stairwell, she found the hole she had cut that led into a utility shaft. It was tight, but she squeezed through it and found her footing on the stirrups of the zip line. She clipped herself into the harness and squeezed the regulator. She flew up through the darkness as the weights she was connected to fell down. She whisked past rats and loose material at breakneck speeds, clearing the rest of the floors in seconds. At the top, she stepped out onto the roof and cut the line with her knife, making sure no one could follow her using that particular route.

She walked away as some overzealous trooper fired up through the shaft. The bullets stopped almost immediately and she could hear the soldier being berated by his or her commanding officer. She threw the first switch on the control panel. She needed the troopers to be oblivious to what was going on around them. The aging speakers blared to life and babbled out a cacophony of prerecorded noise: animal sounds, growls and shrieks, and cages rattling. Sounds designed to mask the noises of what was going on in the prison itself.

While her enemy climbed the stairs, she slipped into her combat armor, a Kevlar bodysuit with matching gloves and boots with magnetic combination locks. Over that, she put on an impact resistant vest and strapped on articulated leg armor. A harness went over her neck giving her huge shoulders and a high steel collar. The flexible neck rings snapped into the helmet in three places. The last piece of her defense came out of her backpack. This is what she had gone to Haiti for, and what so many others had given their lives to create. Dr. Oueste swore that it would work, that he had tested it and it had proven adequate to the task. Adequate didn't make Pandora feel very good, but that was all she could get out of the madman who pretended to be a scientist.

Pandora threw another switch and powered up the building's internal sensors. A bank of micro-monitors jumped to life as cameras in the stairwell suddenly began to broadcast grainy images of the men moving up toward her position. She flipped on the microphone, tapped it, and spoke. "Can I ask you a question Mister Ys?"

Pandora watched as the alien raised his bullhorn. It blared again, echoing through the stairwell. "By all means, but it won't change anything."

"What are you doing here? Why did you invade? My grandfather believed that you weren't interested in humans, that when you finally left the Mesozoic invertebrates, you were going to leap past humanity into the future, after men had gone extinct. What changed your minds?"

Ys located the camera and addressed her through it. "We were perfectly content to leave humans alone, but then we started having problems. Somehow, someone here figured out how to exclude us. We can't insert any agents, and any that we drop in beforehand never return. We are not fond of Dead Time. You and your little band of rebels, or someone like you, have blocked us. We came to stop you, from creating the Dead Time, or failing that, finding the generator and destroying it."

Beneath her mask her face screwed up in puzzlement. "How exactly am I responsible for that?" She flipped another switch and whispered a tiny prayer, hoping that her trap wouldn't be noticed for a few more minutes. Timing was everything. Around the world similar traps were being sprung. A few minutes' warning, and the Great Race might have enough notice to escape back through time.

"We don't particularly know." He moved to the next camera, cautious steps flanked by scuttling human soldiers. "We gave your

40

people, one of your relatives actually, the technology to block us over small areas once. We used it to build a prison for some of our own less desirable members. We assumed you had figured out how to widen the application of the barrier."

"So you invaded the world and conquered the planet because you couldn't see what we were doing?" Pandora chuckled. "When exactly are we supposed to have erected this barrier?" She switched her attention to the other screens. There were things moving in the prison. The cell doors were swinging open.

Mister Ys looked at his watch. "We lose contact in exactly three minutes. Unless we find your equipment and destroy it."

Pandora threw the last switch, the one that unlocked the doors from the stairwell to each floor. The actuation was time-delayed. She had less than a minute before things got really bad. "Is that how time works? Can you change the future by altering the past? If you destroy the machine, the barrier will fall, but then why would you invade in the first place? What about causality and paradox?"

"Time isn't as rigid as you humans would like it to be. There is fluidity. You may not be able to break the laws of time, but you can bend them. Once we find your machine and destroy it, the barrier you will erect will never have been, but we are already here. We can't simply be erased from existence."

"That's what my grandfather said. He warned me that using time against you would be pointless. He said you were grandmasters, that you played the long game superbly, and as long as you had players on the field, you would be nearly invincible."

"I knew your grandfather. Spent some time in him. He was clever for a human."

"My parents were much more clever. Did you ever meet them?"

He was on the floor below her. "Your father, Robert Peaslee? I never had the privilege. I knew him by reputation. I've read his file."

Endora "Pandora" Peaslee pulled the plug on her control board and then smashed it with the heel of her boot. "Did it ever dawn on you Yithians that I might take after my mother? She had an alias as well."

Twelve soldiers swarmed out of the stairwell, red dots appeared on her chest, but not one man pulled the trigger. "Your mother was Megan Halsey, the so-called Reanimatrix. She had access to a primitive reanimation formula."

Pandora went down on her knees trying to appear less threatening. "We've made some improvements over the years." Beneath her mask she smiled. "We didn't build a field generator, Mister Ys. We didn't try to exclude you from the game; that was likely impossible. We just found a way to keep you from using any of the pieces."

A sense of panic suddenly filled Mister Ys voice. "The rest of the resistance, where are they?" He barked orders at his troops, "Find them! Kill them!"

Pandora assumed a crouched position. "You still want to kill the Resistance? Pointless really. I'm afraid they are already dead."

Mister Ys fired a shot and struck Pandora in the shoulder, spinning her around and knocking her to the floor. Her armor was barely scratched. "Whatever you and the resistance have conjured up, whatever you've cobbled together, I assure you we shall end it, here and now. You and your friends will be liquidated."

Pandora sat up rubbing her shoulder. "I told you, Mister Ys, the resistance is already dead."

From the darkness of the stairs, broken shapes moved and stumbled up on to the roof. They had been men once, and alive, but they weren't either anymore. Pandora's formula, her reagent, had transformed them into something bestial, something subhuman. They shambled out of the cages they had been held in and with each step gained speed. There were hundreds of the things, pouring out onto the roof like ants swarming a piece of candy. There were only a dozen armed soldiers, and the unstoppable wave of undead washed over them. Gunfire did little to slow them down, and as man after man fell, the desperate sound of the remaining soldiers and their pathetic guns did little but serve as an attraction to the things that screamed and bit and spread their infection.

"This is your plan, Miss Pandora?" Mister Ys shouted, marching toward her, swinging the gun back and forth between his quarry and the things that were tearing his men apart. "You've weaponized a reanimation reagent, made it contagious. I assume some sort of retrovirus. Do you really think we can't put a stop to this plague of yours?"

She tore the package open and reveled the sigil beneath it, a stylized, tentacular thing that seemed to crawl out of infinity. Ys hissed at the thing but anything he was going to say was drowned out as

43

Pandora began to recite a necessary bit of poetry.

> "Strange is the light which black stars doth shine,
> And men become monsters beneath a yellow sign,
> Lost Carcosa rises ruined, but stranger still,
> Sending ravenous hordes bent to Yhtill's will."

"You dare!" Mister Ys was screaming, but Pandora could barely hear him, the chant filled her ears. "You invite the Yellow King. Are you mad? He will lay waste to this world, warp everything to his own corruption." For the first time ever she saw fear in the eyes of a Yith. "Please, don't do this. We would have given you a paradise." He fell to his knees and scowled. "Do you really think that you can control it? Do you and yours think you can bear the Mantle of the King? Hear my words little girl, the Pallid Mask will give you his power, a taste of it at least, but in time it will worm its way inside. It will gnaw at you, corrupt you, and leave you a hollow empty shell." The undead paused as he emptied the clip in their direction, but only for a moment.

Across the world, Pandora's sisters continued the invocations that would bind the undead members of the Resistance to their service, and in turn dedicated themselves to the service of Hastur. In the sky, the sun slowly declined into a Yellow Sine, pulsing with a sickening rhythm. "Better to rule in Hell than serve in Heaven," she whispered softly.

The curtain had been drawn, the Song of Cassilda sung, the second act was imminent. It was time for the King in Yellow to send his terrible messenger. Her army, her subjects, thousands of undead, fell prostrate before her. They were hungry; she could sense it. They were ravenous, capable of consuming all they could lay their hands on. It wasn't enough. It would never be enough.

Through time and space, the Yellow Sine took its measure, and upon the world the Dead Time fell. Somewhere in what was left of her humanity, Pandora Peaslee hoped that someday, somehow, some men, some humans might survive.

But not today.

Beneath her helmet, the Pallid Mask settled into its rightful place. Pandora Peaslee assumed the role of Yhtill and headed south, toward the arcology.

Her army followed.

# Daily Grind

## by J. Childs-Biddle

Dr. Mary Ambrose wasn't, and hadn't, been listening to her patient for at least ten minutes. She muted him, his accusations and revelations silenced, his hands flapping to emphasize his words as she watched the space behind his head. Black oil oozed from the light socket there, and she focused on how it pulsated in rhythm to the soft pitter-patter of words from his complaints. The viscous fluid reached out for a second, paddling the space between it and the back of her patient's head, trying close the distance in between by swimming through air. It almost touched him, then withdrew quickly, peeking shyly out from just inside the plug. A broken giggle, high-pitched and malicious, rang out and made her want clap her hands over her ears to block it out.

"Are you listening to me?" The patient asked. The silence triggered an automatic response as she tilted her head and feigned interest in his concerns. The laughter intensified, and her hands trembled as she willed them to hold her pen instead of ripping at her ears. The patient smiled, satisfied he struck the right chord and that he was again the center of her universe, if only for 45 minutes. He continued with his numbered list of small harms and inconsequential nuisances.

The oil in the light socket mimicked her patient. It shifted with the strength of his words, feeding on the vibrations of sound bouncing off

46

walls. He hit a loud note, the agonies of communicating clearly with his spouse increasing his volume to a wail, and broke the surface tension of the bubble. It burst, a cackle its death wail, and splattered the back of his head forcefully. He rubbed his neck, oblivious to the black-blue fluid dripping between his shoulder blades.

The pop of fluid brought her back to him. She had scribbled notes but they were useless: half-words lost in margins filled more eagerly with inked eyeballs and screaming mouths. She flipped through them, thankful talk therapy was repetitive. It was the same people going over the same things and having the same epiphanies they always forgot by the next week. If her mind wandered, the road map constructed by humans with the red and blue lines of their personal miseries was easy to follow back home.

"I think you've really made some progress today, John. We can discuss some suitable boundaries for working with your partner in greater detail next weekend. Please check out with the receptionist. She can schedule your next appointment," she spoke with the calm neutrality of a telephone operator. She switched him from a location of outpouring revelations back to a place where he would need to hold his feelings, like a hand of aces, to his chest.

Once he left, she glanced over to the light socket. It was unmarked, a glossy, plastic white. She breathed in, and her anxiety cut her deep breath into half-gasps. She took another breath, more successful this time, and glanced out the window.

It was a pretty day, but every day was pretty now. The pure-ocean blue of the sky emphasized how white, fluffy, and non-threatening the clouds were. The trees seemed to reach up to it, their long arms dressed in ever-green sleeves worshipping as though Mayday revelers. The grass was too long, but it invited tumbling around and afternoon picnics. She had little doubt when she walked home tonight, the temperature would be perfect. Even she longed to be free from the office, to sit down, and absorb the tranquility of the scene.

From the corner of her eye, the ground shifted. It was only an inch or so, nothing she would see if she started at it straight on. She pinched her lips together hard enough to taste blood.

"You really ought to be more careful in your sessions, Mary," he spoke quietly. His tongue lingered around the S sounds as though it was prodding a sore spot in his mouth. She spun around in her chair.

"Dr. Fisher. I'm sorry, I wasn't aware you were…"

His shadow moved first, a few seconds ahead of the hunched shoulders responsible for it. It dragged him along as though it was his undertaker, until he stood on the other side of her desk. He leaned over the pictures of her wife and her dog. His corpse-heavy hand landed on her shoulder and the swampy scent of wet decomposition overwhelmed her. She gagged and a children's song came to her, the voices a screeching child's cacophony of syllables:

*"Ring a' ring a rosy*

*Burning nice and toasty"*

She snapped away from it, swallowing the salt-water taste in her mouth, the taste of the ocean as it poured into every part of a person before they were devoured by waves. He smiled, sharp teeth barely taking shape before flickering away into average dentistry.

"I wasn't aware you were in the office today," she finished, with false brightness. She placed her hand over his. It was sticky. An oozing sliminess coated her fingers. She brushed his touch away, without changing expression. He moved back and fresh air rushed in to replace the dankness of him.

"Management reported some issues with the sessions and wanted me to make sure everything was on the up and up. It is, isn't it? A-okay?" From a few feet away, he was average. He was a study in spheres: a dome of shiny skull with greasy hair combed over it, a belly bulging round with too many meals, and his hands jointed balls too plump to work effectively.

"Oh. Yes. Fine, really. I have some personal issues, and with the holiday coming up…" She rattled off what sounded like the most appropriate answer.

He waved his hand as though the information was expected, and then forgotten as non-consequential. "Good. I thought as much. Told them you were the kind of doctor who focuses on the bottom line."

Dr. Fisher whistled *Ring Around the Rosy* as he soft-shoed his way out of her office. His shadow brushed the edge of her desk and turned the walnut wood pitch black. He turned at the door and gave her one last nod of approval.

"I'll see you tomorrow, bright and early, Doctor."

The air was heavily perfumed by honeysuckle vines, layered over the persistent odor of smoke. She focused on her thoughts, mentally going through the notes of her therapy sessions. The walk home was short enough, and she could ignore the burning smell peeking around the façade of what a summer evening should be.

Her wife, Lindsay, greeted her at the door. Lindsay was all enthusiasm, with her waving arms and golden-blond hair seeming to envelope Mary on the threshold, wiping away all of the troublesome moments where something almost existed. Mary took a whiff of her wife's skin, an intoxicating mixture of sea-salt and sweat, and returned the embrace.

After dinner, the dirty plates sat as their audience to the trials of their day. Mary would go over vague details from her patients, touching on the monotony of going over the same thing again and again. Lindsay spoke about issues she was having with perspective, of getting something to be the right color. Mary then briefly mentioned Dr. Fisher, and Lindsay pinched her face up in disgust.

"He's such a creep, Mary. I don't know how you keep working for him," she spoke. Lindsay's history of relationships with others was marked by how easily she transitioned between them. She grew-up without understanding hardship, and it cultivated her thoughtlessness into a lifestyle. She believed transitions were easy things, and did not suffer that which was grating or difficult. Mary suffered through things, and it was as much of a conflict of misunderstanding as Lindsay would allow between them.

"It's not that bad. He's even sort of okay, once you get to know him." Mary lied. It was an easy mistruth, one she told out as much out of protection as habit. Lindsay never worked, as the idea of being managed was distasteful to her. Mary insisted she stay busy with her paintings, focusing on her art. Lindsay produced stock work, filling canvases with pastoral landscapes, fruit bowls, and horses in motion. She thought she should be an artist, so she focused on the results of such rather than the process.

Even with the insulation of her airy personality to keep her warm and safe, Lindsay would stop sleeping. The paintings would take on the sickly, blue-green hue of the ocean. Faces appeared, smashed against the glass windows of the white-washed cottages, screaming to be released. She painted decomposition, hollow-eyed horses, and fires in the distance. She asked Mary if she thought she needed help, or perhaps to find something easier, like a part-time job.

During those episodes, she relied on Mary, innately afraid of how psychotherapy could strip her of her defenses. Mary could control those intrusive thoughts. She did it every day, unwinding the twisted knots that made up the psyche of others. It was easier for her and safer for her wife if Lindsay stayed within closed doors, her most difficult challenge her weekly trip to the grocery. Dealing with others, working with them in a close environment, caused folie à deux, a shared slip in reality. Each person involved increased the difficulty in putting things back into place exponentially.

Lindsay's dreams were as deeply as she ever swam into darkness and she nearly drowned emotionally under their weight. Mary couldn't risk the sort of madness a job would cause. She couldn't bear the consequences if Lindsay's brief interludes turned into Mary's world of constantly staring into the shadows. She lived in terror of what *They* would do if they ever had reason to think her wife knew anything. She burned her wife's paintings, and the pervasive spell would break like a fever. Lindsay returned to her cheery carelessness. The cottages washed their windows, the fruit glistened fresh and inviting, and the horses romped in too-green fields.

The couple cleaned up the dishes, the playful splashes of water becoming passionate kisses. They made love on the kitchen counter. After, Lindsay lay her head on Mary's shoulder, out-of-breath, her cheeks and breasts flushed pink from their efforts.

"Thank you so much, for everything you do to take care of everyone."

Mary buried her head in her wife's sun-bleached hair, using it to hide her tears.

"I don't think anybody understands me." The patient huddled inside her jacket, trying to disappear in the extra folds of fabric. Mary looked up from her notes, from her drawings of terrified eyes and hungry maws.

"Why do you feel that way?" she asked, clinically.

The patient shrugged and looked out the window. The pupils of her eyes dilated, only for a millisecond, but Mary took note of it. Something slipped outside of the window and the patient had seen it. The woman spoke distantly, saying the words without any conviction,

"I... sometimes... things don't make sense. It all seems like I should be happy, there's no reason to be unhappy, but I am. I don't feel real. I feel like none of this real."

The woman flicked her eyes to the burnt corner of Mary's desk. The doctor's composure held as she ran through the canned responses she learned in training. "That happens frequently with your syndrome. It's disordered thinking on your part. I can up the dosage on your medication, and it should help center you. I think 300 MG twice a..."

"You're full of shit. You know that? I can see you drifting off, watching when some part of them breaks through. The reflection of them. I can see it in your eyes, doctor. What's really happening?"

Mary shook her head, and a desperate bark of laughter escaped. The patient saw only bits and pieces of it. She couldn't have wrapped her mind around the reality that constantly shimmered, like heat coming off asphalt. She couldn't hear the screaming that broke through when Mary took a sip of her coffee, couldn't feel the hands that slithered up her legs while she showered, and couldn't smell the dead fish smell when Mary only meant to take whiff of flowers. If she knew anything worth knowing, she wouldn't have come to her appointment, would have swallowed her madness down like a diabetic sneaking sweets, and she would have smiled beautifully and responded glitter-bright when anyone commented on the weather. The woman took a glimpse, and made from it a fairy tale. Even her worst assumptions were sweeter than the truth.

"Please. Stop. You're ill. Let me help you. We'll adjust your medication, and everything will be right as rain."

"I'M NOT SICK!" The patient leapt forward, slamming both hands on top of Mary's desk with such force that it rattled her coffee cup. Mary pushed herself back in surprise, out of the reach of the angry woman.

"Please. You must understand these thoughts. They're delusions. You're imagining things. That's what's happening to you. You're having a break, but we can handle this." Mary pleaded, putting all of the right suggestions in the right places. The woman's upper lip twisted up, as she fought with the words that separated mental illness from clear perception. She closed her fist, again hitting the desk. Mary's pen rolled on the floor. The picture frames fell and the glass cracked within the frames.

"I'm not. You know I'm not." She sunk down until Mary could only see the top of her head, bobbing with sobs as the woman kept asking herself why.

Mary received her medical training in the military, and sharpened her resolve with quick decisions on the field as to whether someone was worth saving. She was on the team that discovered the first artifact. She was the one who cut down the rest of her colleagues when they started screeching into the night, gouging out their eyes, and pulling off their ears in gobs of cartilage and flesh.

*They* appreciated her ruthlessness and clear thinking under duress, spinning it into what could be imagined was a job offer, rather than the forced term of service revealed to be reality. She believed them, believed her experiences trying to piece together someone blown into five different chunks by a land mine was preparation enough for anything they could throw at her. It meant survival, and she wore that survival like an armor when reality split off a dozen times and *They* started slaughtering anyone who would not be controlled, who would not be deceived, and who would not serve. She would maintain peace and keep the calm. She would live. Her family would live.

Even when the fragmented parts of time and space were brought close together again, when all five of her senses told her the truth, her belief that survival would serve her better, autonomy drove her. She understood she was a slave, that everyone who had sold themselves to *Them* was chained to their threats of how much more could happen, to their spouses, to their children, to their mothers, and to their friends. The first time the crafted reality slipped, she almost tripped into a pit full of teeth as it opened before her, endlessly chewing at the limbs and faces of people who were still living. The second time, she drowned repeatedly, each time slimy hands pulling her out of the water, and pressing their rotting, spongy lips to hers, forcing dank air into her lungs to revive her. Thousands of cracks where *They* broke through—some great, and others small—were the price she paid, believing it a small cost to shoulder on the behalf of making sure she wasn't crushed between the teeth of their vast hunger.

Mary edged around the desk, kneeling before the woman who was curled up tightly around her knees. She always understood there was no escaping, no righteous tearing up of contracts or paperwork, and then storming out of the office. She still wanted to curl up beside the woman, taking what little understanding she could give her, whispering their horrors so they instead became girlish secrets. The remnants of her bravery and hope pulled at her soul, this woman's brief view a reminder that *They* could not quiet all voices or smother every breath of defiance.

Mary leaned closer, and the woman kicked at her. She fell back onto her heels, hitting the bookshelf with her right elbow. One of Lindsay's paintings—another cottage, another garden— cracked her across the temple as it fell from the top shelf. She let out a loud curse, clutching the side of her head.

"Why are you doing this?" The woman asked, never looking up. Mary picked up the painting—unobtrusive and pretty—created by someone who understood nothing of difficulty, of suffering. The blue skies and white, fluffy clouds were brought into existence by hands that had never turned a gun on another human being and had never scrubbed off slimy decomposition after brushing by a coworker. Her wife only knew *Their* world through the safety of her dreams, as close as she could come without being consumed. Those secrets belonged to Mary. The weight of the knowledge could not be lessened or shared, only protected.

"Because I have to." She reached out, and placed her hand on the woman's shoulder.

*They* gave her no real power, but they had little concern for what others ripped from the power-charged veils around them. She could share her memories and what she lived through. She conveyed it in the touch. All the madness and agonies of war, both hers and theirs, pressed into the flesh of someone who would not be controlled in any other way.

56

The woman writhed under Mary's hand, screeching out like a dying bird within the clutches of a hawk. Her words contorted, stretched over the scream so they were non-recognizable, but Mary knew that she asked her why. Always why, as though it could soothe the agony. The woman's eyes rolled back into her head, and she lost control as her limbs and torso began jerking wildly in a seizure. Mary pulled the patient closer, cradling her as though calming a child.

"Shhhhh…" She whispered, the woman's tics shaking Mary as though to remove her arms from their socket. Mary hummed "Ring Around the Rosy" and gently kissed the woman's forehead.

The door burst open. Orderlies rushed in, breaking Mary's embrace, and shoving her aside. They lifted the convulsing patient, carrying her out by her elbows while the woman continued to thrash ferociously in the air between the two men.

Mary came to her knees, brushed herself off, and lowered her head. She took several deep breaths, willing the beats of her heart to slow into normal rhythm instead of pounding in her chest.

Dr. Fisher's shadow crawled over her, singing the hairs on her arm. She didn't wince. She wouldn't give him the satisfaction.

"Fantastic job, Dr. Ambrose. Glad to see you're back to fighting form. Lunch is on me."

# What Songs We Sing

by L. K. Whyte

I like to visit the dead.

Here, it is always quiet. The dead are old and peaceful, and they sing no songs. Some nights I slip out of the shanty and wander among the stones and the trees and the grass as crows watch me from too-wise eyes, and I wonder if they know what the dead remember. I trace the strange runes of their stones with trembling fingers and imagine what they might say, what secrets they keep through their long nights.

This night, the moon was high and red and I was alone, listening to the rustling of the trees. Alone in the quiet, I thought of Isana, eyes as green as tree-needles, lips as soft as moth-wings. Beautiful in every curve and sway.

I remembered the sight of Isana's blood, mere hours ago, bright in the waning light. Death begets life; her child, safely delivered, was even now in the creche, listening to the nurselings croon the Great Songs he would one day sing as he danced the Ecstatica for the glory and feeding of Those Above and Below. So things have been since the Return, twenty generations ago. Yet I was here, surrounding myself with death and silence and sanity while the shanty slept, secure in the soft grasp of madness. I was weeping and did not know why.

Motion in the silence drew me from my musings. No one else

came here, not the denizens of the shanty, not the beasts of field and fold. Only me, and the crows, and, that sweet once, Isana.

Movement, again; a flashing glint, hard in the soft red light. I rose to a crouch, careful to be silent. This place was not forbidden, exactly, but some things simply are not done. I have spent enough time in isolation this year already.

The safe course would be to flee, quick and silent, back to the shanty. But safety is not the only thing in this world or I would not have been here, alone, at night. Instead, I crept closer to the metallic glimmer. I wanted to know who, or what, had dared come here. In any other place, I would wonder if I was creeping up on a servant - one of the Mi-Goh, perhaps, or a nesting byahkee. But they do not venture among the ancient dead.

I moved as silently as I could, using the overgrowth for concealment as I drew up behind what turned out to be a woman, not much older than I, but pale, with skin like milk and hair that gleamed rosy under the moon's red light. She was bent over one of the gravestones and writing in some sort of small book. She tilted her head and I caught sight of her frowning in concentration, brow furrowed. There was something strange and lovely about her.

"Life in death." I saw no reason not to be polite, but she jumped, eyes wide, clutching the little book to herself as though to protect it. Surprised, I glanced around to see what might have startled her, but we were alone with the dead. "Are you well this night?"

"Who're you?" Her words came like the rapid pounding of a high-tuned drum, so that it took me a few seconds to make out their meaning.

"Ikere." I took a seat on a nearby stone. I do not think the dead mind anything that might bring them into contact with life; they have had ages in which to grow wise enough to know that I meant no disrespect. The stranger seemed not to agree, because she gasped slightly as I eased myself down. "And you? By what name are you called?"

She made no reply at first, and when she did, it came as another question. "Where'd you come from?" Though high-strung, she made no threatening moves, and I paused to admire the lovely picture she made, surrounded by shadows but bathed in roseate glow.

"From over there, if you mean that in an immediate sense." I gestured to where I had been standing when I first saw the gleam of her hair. "From the shanty past that hill, if you mean that in a more permanent sense."

"From the shanty," she repeated.

"Yes." I wondered if she might be a bit slow. Perhaps she was a madling, though they do not venture near the dead. They are more interested in the living and in Those Above and Below. "Where are you from? Seawrack shanty?"

"Seawrack - no. No, I'm not. What d'you call this place?"

"Mooncrest. Where are you from that you don't know the name of the shanty where you are bound? You are planning to pass the night there, yes? The open lands are dangerous after dark." Everyone knows that. Only madlings leave the shanty after dark. But here I was, and I was no madling; there was nothing sacred about me.

What, then, was I?

"I wasn't gonna hit the shanty."

I blinked. "Then what are you doing here?"

"What're *you* doin' here? No shantyfolk come to these places."

"No, not usually. It simply isn't done. But then, I'm not terribly good at doing only what is done." I smiled at her, small and wry.

She said nothing for a moment, only crouched there, thinking. Then she seemed to come to some manner of decision, for she sat, crosslegged, carefully to one side of the gravestone. "I'm Jonna," she said. Her manner was grave, as though she bestowed upon me a great trust. With her gaze firmly upon me, I noticed that her eyes were grey, grey as stones. I began to understand.

"You're not from any shanty, are you?" I spoke softly, almost whispering. There are humans who do not live in shanties, who do not revel, who do not sing. We tell stories of them, sometimes, in hushed tones. She shook her head, but said nothing, only watched my reaction. "What is it like?"

She smiled, only a little. "We've different songs," she told me, as though she knew the course of my thoughts. "Beautiful ones."

"There is no music more beautiful than the Ecstatica." I believed that. I knew what it was to feel the drums and the flute wash over me, to feel the voices of my fellows lifting me, to be carried toward that brief glimpse of Those Above and Below that is all we who are cursed with sanity are permitted.

"You ever listen to the music without the communion brew?" she asked me. I shook my head, perplexed. "Try it. You'll see it all different."

"If I do, will you come here tomorrow night so I can see you again?" I felt my face grow flush at my own daring.

That startled her, for she laughed, very softly. But it was not a bad laugh, and I could see a change in the way she looked at me. She knew what I meant, knew it in a way Isana had not. Maybe it was done among the folk outside the shanties. Certainly there was something in her eyes, a heat, that I had previously only seen among men, and few enough of them.

"Go a day without."

"The whole day?" She nodded. "And if I do that... if I do that, you will be here?"

"Yeah. I'll be here."

I looked at her again, at her paleness, at her steadiness, at the way she met my gaze without flinching. At the loveliness of her and at the soft look around her eyes and the firm set of her chin. I had never gone even a single meal without the communion brew that was part and parcel of shanty life. But I wanted to see her again.

"I will do it," I told her. Her lips curved into something almost a smile, strangely sad.

"I'll be here," she repeated. And then, glancing up at the moon, "But I gotta go now. Be seeing you."

I watched her leave, quick and careful in the dim light of the moon, and I wondered what tomorrow's moon would show me.

I did not sleep that night.

I crept back into my bunk and stared at the wood slats and thin mattress above me, imagining that I could see into my bunkmate's flesh and bone, into her heart, into the dreams that might grant me mercy. None was forthcoming. I was alone with the fleeting memory of Jonna's eyes, Jonna's words. They echoed in the vaults of my mind and I stared until light pierced the windows and the others began rising and I took my first step away from them.

*You'll see it all different.*

Breakfast was the usual porridge and brew. I ate the porridge hungrily, less weary than I expected, nerves still singing. But I only pretended to drink the brew. My heart pounded as I kept watch on my neighbors through the corners of my eyes, but nobody saw as I dribbled it bit by bit onto the ground behind my bench.

All through the morning's work in the field, I stole glances at those nearby, wondering if they noticed the difference in me. But they went about their tasks as cheerfully as ever, whistling, humming, singing. Only I was silent.

At midday I repeated the morning's subterfuge, even more apprehensive now that my fellows were no longer dream-fuddled. But again my actions went unnoticed. There was no suspicion in the shanty. Those within are dedicated, heart and soul, to the glory of Those Above and Below. It was unthinkable to betray that trust.

My joints began to ache as I mucked out the byre. Only a little at first, but it was a strange sensation, soon joined by a thickness in my head that I could not shake off. Every movement I took seemed too quick, leaving me slightly dizzy, so I slowed and hoped that nobody would comment. But even as the motion of my rake lagged, I realized that even at my most lethargic I was moving no slower than anybody else. It was I who had been too fast. Was this a side effect of nerves, or of refraining from the brew?

It happened again when I was spreading fresh straw. Arash hailed me as I raked it even and I stopped, breaking out in a cold sweat. "Ikere, hold! What drives you today?"

I glanced at the next byre and saw Darvin still breaking apart his bale, then back at my own work, nearly finished. I said to Arash, "My heart sings within me and the load is light."

He smiled. "The Ecstatica comes no sooner for your efforts. Do not weary yourself before the praises are sung." His tone was gentle, but chiding for all that. Working too hard during the day meant inferior revelry, and I hung my head. Putting work before worship was not done.

"I move to the rhythm of the shanty," I replied, chastened. He patted my shoulder and moved on. Thus warned, I forced myself to move at a more measured pace. Slow, it was so slow! The sun barely moved across the sky and my muscles cried out to be pushed, as though they had just awakened from a too-long sleep and needed to be stretched. I chewed on my lip, wanting the light to wane and the Ecstatica to begin. I needed to know if Jonna had told me the truth. I needed to be more careful. Beneath Arish's gentle words lurked the threat of real chastisement.

The thought alone was enough to slow me down as I remembered my last sentence to iso. Some things simply are not done; when they *are* done, the only response is rejection. Silence. Shunning. Iso meant serving myself meals while everyone else looked at everything but me. It meant sleeping in the byre because those who do not exist do not have bunks assigned to them. It meant days of biting my tongue, because the only thing worse than being ignored when I was silent was being ignored when I tried to speak. Nobody breaks iso until everybody does, all together.

There is no telling when it will fall or when it will end. Sometimes, after worship, the fellows of the shanty will rise and one of them will not exist. And then, days or weeks later, they will rise from worship again and it will be over. It has happened to me several times, and while it is possible to guess that it will be coming soon, I never knew for sure.

There is nothing as terrible as walking through home as a stranger that no one will touch. So I bent to my work, paying careful attention to my rhythm, focusing on the slight creak and pain in my hips and knees and shoulders. It was strange. It hurt, but better pain than shunning.

By the time I had finished, fighting against the shriek of muscles begging to vent an upswelling of energy, against the dull moan of joints begging for rest, there was still an hour or more until the evening meal. No one would be expecting me in the kitchens, or the creche, or the byre, or the field. Now was one of the times that I would sometimes go to the place of the dead, but I did not want to go there now. Not yet. Not until after I knew whether Jonna had spoken me true about the Ecstatica.

Instead, I wandered between field and byre. As I walked, I tried to think about yesterday, and last night, and today, but my mind refused and so I strode along the path with nothing in my thoughts but Jonna's eyes and hands, lips curving above her stubborn chin. I wondered what her loose canvas pants and vest hid, and my musing led me to other memories, lit by the green light of Isana's gaze, and I was not as careful as I should have been.

Memories of the lone night when I had seen Isana's eyes grow soft as her lips were morphing into the sight of them cold and empty when a sudden chill drew me back to the world around me. Not ten feet away, I saw a hooded figure in a robe, radiating a bone-searing cold. I knew what it was - one of the Great Ones' chosen servants, come to pass along the desires of Those Above and Below. It would speak with their madness-inducing tongue and move with their geometry-denying grace. I stepped off the path and bowed my head, waiting for it to pass.

Its every motion was graceful and smooth. It glided with an elegance that no human could ever match. But we try. Every evening when we come together to exalt the Great Ones who returned to us, we try. With flute and drum, we mimic their voices. With every gesture and step, we strive to emulate their grace. We join flesh for their glory. We die for their sustenance. And when one of their servants comes, we give them the entire path out of respect. This is the way it is done.

After it passed me by and my breath no longer steamed in the frigid air of its wake, I looked up the path the way it had come and saw the creche before me. I had wandered in a circle. A sudden madness seized me and I followed in its wake, striding to the door, opening it, bowing my head before the nurseling that greeted me.

Several children were gathered in the teaching room. A robed nurseling was leading them in one of our many songs, their high piping voices following along with the nurseling's thready rasp. The one at the door cocked its head to one side, huge bulbous eyes watching me, unblinking.

"The nursery, Singer." I was surprised at how difficult it was to speak in a properly respectful tone. "I felt a madness upon me, a desire to behold the newest."

The nurseling said nothing, only turned so that I might follow. They do not speak. Their voices are only for songs. We passed through the creche to the nursery at its center where the infants and smallest toddlers slept. Two robed figures strode between the cribs and pallets, the music of their voices washing over the babes. I felt none of the warmth and security that usually came when I remembered being watched over in the same way.

The one that had brought me waited as I approached the newest babe. As I looked down on him in his crib, tentacles came from the sleeves of her robe and lifted him. The nurselings do not have hands as the ordinary shantyfolk do; some do not even have arms. Instead, they bear the mark of Those Who Returned. Their tentacles are not well-suited to the labor of field and byre, but no hands are half so gentle when cradling the young or tending their hurts. Like all those with the Look, they are highly respected.

This one held up the babe for me to see him more clearly, tentacles admirably suited for supporting his overlarge head on his spindly newborn neck. I did not reach out to touch him, though I wanted to. It was not for the ordinary to handle the newly born. He wriggled a little in the rubbery cradle, and opened his eyes. They were dark, without iris or white, and they bulged with the Look. I saw that his nose was no more than a pair of slits in his fat round face, that scales gleamed in the hollow of his throat. He was marked. Chosen.

Somehow, I thanked the nurseling, voice hushed as was proper in the creche, and I left. Never before had I failed to rejoice at the birth of a child with the Look. All children were treasured, but those with the Look were special. Those Above and Below had touched them.

His eyes haunted me. There was no trace of Isana in him, though I had looked. In the curve of his ears, the shape of his chin, there was nothing to indicate that he had been born of her body. She was gone. The honor of her death meant nothing before that single stark fact. She was gone, and nothing of her remained, not even in her son.

I had so hoped that he would have her eyes.

By the time I returned to the center of the shanty, the evening meal was beginning. I accepted my share of meat and boiled grain and brew and found a place at the end of one of the tables, where I usually sat. The talk was of the servant that had passed me on the path. It would be staying for the night. I listened, but did not speak. No one was paying the slightest attention to me.

Or so I thought. I was just about to tip out some of my brew when I noticed Arash watching. I smiled at him, pretended to take a large swallow. He nodded and looked away without smiling back. I took the chance to set my mug back down on the edge of the table, so that when I took my hand away it fell. Feigning consternation, I leaped up and snatched at it, too slow to save it before it spilled out its contents. The liquid soaked into the dust and between the cracks of the stones immediately; it was impossible to tell how much had been lost. My tablemates stared, murmuring in sympathy.

I sighed. "At least I had almost finished it," I said with what I hoped was the right mix of relief and chagrin, fighting the pounding of my heart. "I would hate to trouble the kitchen for more when they have already cleaned up for the day." The others at my table nodded agreement. It was rude to trouble the kitchen, or anyone else. Their expressions indicated no surprise at my clumsiness, but Arash's face when I glanced quickly at him on my way past left me feeling cold. He suspected. Careful. I would have to be more careful.

Though I had been among the last to retrieve food, I was one of the first done. After setting my dish and fork and mug on a rack to dry, I returned to the center and began to stretch in preparation for what was to come. As I did so, others came to join me. The musicians collected their instruments and set up around the perimeter. They would not come into the center until the madness seized them.

The drums began, their deep regular beat soon joined by the skirling of flutes. I took a place near the edge of the gathering crowd, adding my voice to the chorus, my feet to the dance, stealing glances around at my fellows while they did the same. Their faces reflected the same ecstatic joy that always characterized the ritual; for them, everything was as it should be and all was right with the world.

But it wasn't.

The drums were ragged and out of time with each other, no two following the same beat. The flutes all seemed to be playing in different keys, with a dissonance that grated unbearably. Nor was the singing any more coherent. The words that usually carried me to heights of frenzied union with my fellows and with Those Who Returned were idiot mumblings, unintelligible. I felt no more connection with them than with the calling of crows. Less, because the cries of the crows fit my expectations. This cacophony did not.

*You ever listened to the music without the communion brew?*

I watched in amazed horror as the dancers stumbled and reeled, nearly colliding on several occasions. If I had stayed still instead of making my own weaving way among them, I would have been bowled over long since. What was happening?

Their expressions said nothing was wrong at all. In fact, judging by their faces, they thought this was all wonderful. I knew the communion they were feeling, the contentment and the joy, and it was strange indeed to be left out of the shared experience. The work of a shanty's farm is necessary for physical survival, but the Ecstatica is what transforms life and makes it worth living. Without the Ecstatica, we are only lonely animals; in it, we are made whole, one with each other and with the Great Ones we serve. Our lives gain meaning through the Ecstatica and its revelatory madness; our deaths gain meaning as they are given to Those Above and Below.

So what was this stumbling chaos? What was this wreck that I was watching, from which I was excluded? For a moment, I entertained the notion that this was somehow Jonna's doing, that she had managed to interfere with the sacred process of the ritual. But then I would not be the only one on the outskirts, confused and frightened.

Lupan crashed into my shoulder, grinning wide, never even noticing me. Her voice raised in song, she turned in a halting twirl and dove back into the center of the teeming mass of bodies. I fell to one knee and rose awkwardly. As I had wrestled with unanswerable questions, the tone of the ritual had changed. The singing was fragmenting even further as the singers grew distracted, coming together and moving apart. They stumbled more as muscles weary from a long day's work were taxed by unceasing motion. I stayed on the edge opposite the musicians, darting in and out of the center knot's periphery in a pretense of normalcy. Though my stomach twisted, I plastered an expression of devotion on my face and hoped without prayer that no one would notice anything unusual about my behavior.

I might as well not have bothered. Nobody was paying any attention to me. Already the most heated were beginning to consummate the spiritual union with a physical one. Flesh tangled and writhed, clothing was abandoned in careless heaps. The flutes had already stopped; soon, the drums would join them, their rhythms abandoned for the ones now being played out before me.

Hands around my upper arms drew me back until I could feel gyrating hips grinding into me from behind. I bit back a shriek, forcing myself to move with them. Darvin's voice, worn with use and weariness, filled my ears with the tongue-twisting words of the Great Song. Heart racing, I maneuvered him slowly toward a larger concentration of bodies, drawing him down to the ground and then rolling away when he grew distracted by Naumal's sweat-slicked breasts, heftier than my own. For a moment, I felt guilt, but she seemed to welcome his touch in some way that I could not, and I took advantage of the moment to flee.

I didn't intend to go anywhere in particular, but habit drew my feet back to the place of the ancient dead. It was cold after the frenzy of the Ecstatica, cold in a way that made me gasp more than the run itself. Because I made no effort to move quietly or carefully, I startled a sleeping crow, who scolded me.

Like the crow, I felt betrayed. What had happened? What had I seen? Nothing was as I remembered. None of it was right. Moonlight spread over me as I huddled in the grass, hugging my knees. Was the whole thing a lie created by the brew? Had it been a lie all along, and I an unwitting participant, thinking myself a celebrant when I was nothing but one of those shambling idiot creatures I had seen?

I shook. I wept. I tried, over and over again, to wrap my mind around it all. The Ecstatica was supposed to give us a glimpse of the truth, because a glimpse was all we could manage without the protection of sacred madness. Because to see more than a glimpse was to become mad, and madness was not to be sought by the unworthy. Perhaps that was truer than we thought, for the truth beneath the Ecstatica was enough to make me question my own sanity, though I knew I had not been so blessed. I was no madling.

Finally, though, despite wrestling, despite fleeing, there was one question I could neither outrun nor answer. If the Ecstatica was a lie, what other lies did I believe, all unknowing? What *were* Those Who Returned, really?

"Monsters."

I had not realized I had spoken aloud, or that I was not alone, until I heard Jonna's soft reply. It should have surprised me; jumpy as I had been since dawn, I should have reacted. Perhaps it was only that I was exhausted, but I did not move, not even to open my eyes.

"I have always thought them gods," I told her. "That humanity, in a time of great and terrible need, read from the books and began to sing the songs, and they came, and they saved us from ourselves. They brought the gift of madness that we desperately needed, and in gratitude, we continue to read from their books and sing their songs, and they embrace our dead to give us life."

"Oh, the books were read. Foolish men read 'em without knowing what would happen. Then the eldest horrors came. They enslaved humanity and bent most folk to their wills. They chain us and eat our dead."

"Why?" I asked, raising my head at last to look at her. She was sitting very close and watching me. Her eyes caught and held me; they were grey with the barest flecks of green. Like moss-touched stones. Like the stones of the dead all around us. She was frowning.

"I don't know. They don't seem to *need* us, really. But they do feed on our deaths somehow. Or maybe it's just that they're protecting themselves from the power of death by stealing it." She paused. "They fear it, y'know." At my confused glance, she gestured around us at the stones. At the ancient dead. "Why d'you think you never see their servants around here? These places're poison to them. If we knew why, maybe we could change things."

I shook my head. I said nothing. There were no words for what I felt. It was a deep emotion, swelling like the crest of a wave, tearing me between certainties. The Ecstatica was a lie; the Ecstatica was the only truth. Those Who Returned were our saviors; Those Above and Below were our enslavers. Death begets life; death begets only death.

Isana. The sight of her blood, the too-bright crimson rush of birthing, the light going out of her deep green eyes before she even beheld her child. Her lips, cracked and dry as all the force of her was poured out into the Great Ones Above. The emptiness of her. The stillness of her. If Those Above and Below were not gods, if the Ecstatica was a lie, then what was her death for? What good was it all? I remembered the tears I had shed last night, the night Isana died, the night I met Jonna. Had I known, even then? Was this terrible, appalling truth already pressing against me, waiting to be recognized?

How long had I been lied to, and for how long had I been doing the lying?

Jonna's hand on mine was gentle, tentative. I glanced down as she laid it there, surprised and not surprised. The people of the shanties touched all the time. I had the feeling that Jonna's people did not.

I looked up into her grey eyes. They were calm, and a little afraid, and a little worried. Was she concerned for me? I was. "I don't know what to believe," I whispered. Part of me wanted to flee back to the shanty, to find and drink the brew, to believe. To stop doubting. To stop wondering. To silence the questions that filled me.

I never wanted to see the shanty again. Disgust filled me, as strong as the fear, as strong as the strange nameless thing that still grew inside me. I could not return, knowing it for a lie.

The fear in Jonna's eyes faded. The worry grew and changed, becoming something else, something for which I had no name. It did not look like what was within me. It looked like something new, something strange. Something gentle. She lifted her hand, and my hand with it, and she pulled gently. It was like Darvin pulling me toward his embrace; it was nothing like that at all.

I went. Into her arms. I fell into her eyes as her lips touched mine. Soft, softer than Isana's. My eyes wanted to close; I did not let them. There were no lies in hers. The wave inside me crested and broke.

"I do not want to go back to the shanty," I whispered.

"Then don't," she said, and kissed me again.

I feel no guilt for what passed there, among the grasses that swayed above the dead. I like to think that the dead, long past such moments, treasure the nearness of life even if they lack it for themselves. I imagine that they remember what it was for them, so long and long ago.

She was lanky, her body strung tight with muscle, with fewer curves even than my own lean form. No one had ever found me desirable outside the Ecstatica; without broad hips and weighty breasts for child-bearing, I had little to offer. I had never been beautiful.

But she was. That was a truth I could believe.

After, she urged me to dress again, telling me it was time for her to return. Her people were waiting for her. I fell silent, wondering what was to become of me, unable to ask. When she took my hand before setting off between the stones, I was relieved. Maybe there was no more truth outside the shanties than in them, but I would never know unless I went looking. I followed her.

"Jonna?" I asked. She glanced back at me. "Would you sing me one of your songs?"

She smiled. It was an honest smile, a pleased smile. "Sure."

Her voice was not perfect. It wavered sometimes and once it cracked on a high note. But there was no pretense to it, and it was beautiful to me. I did not know the song she sang. I am not even sure what it was about; love, I think. The concept of love directed at a fellow human and not toward distant god-beings was strange to me. Shanty-folk do not fall in love with each other. The fondness and communion of our rituals is a closeness no one outside our walls will ever know, and I was raised to think that it was enough. Listening to Jonna, I suspected that there was something missing from the shanty, some lack I had always felt but never named.

We walked for hours with the moon rising and then falling overhead. Sometimes she sang and sometimes we moved through the silence of night. I was growing nervous. Were Jonna's people like her? Did they know I was coming? Would they be too different from the shanty-folk? Would they welcome or reject me? At times, my hands shook and I wanted to tear loose from her grasp and run - to the shanty, into the wild woods, to the sea, I did not know. But she kept hold of my hand and she looked at me and I did not run from her.

When the man stepped out from behind a tree beside the path, I was startled. For some reason, I had expected him to be pale, like Jonna. He was not. He was dark of skin, darker even than my own deep brown, dark enough that he almost blended into the night. Jonna stopped a few feet from him, a little farther than I would have stood from him had we both been in the shanty. She smiled at him and I saw relief in her eyes.

"I brought her out, Mkembe," she said. "You were right."

His forbidding expression softened into a smile of his own as he looked at her. There was fondness there. "Good. Very good." Then he turned to me. "So. Ikere. You're the one bewitched my student, eh?"

I stammered something incoherent and he chuckled. Jonna squeezed my hand. I swallowed and tried again. "I rather think she's the one who bewitched me. Or un-witched me, perhaps."

He chuckled again. "It's good to meet you. She said you were more cogent than the other shanty-folk she's seen." At my obvious surprise, his expression grew more serious and he nodded. "You're starting to see. We need to know the shanty, you get it? We need to know the Ecstatica and the Servants."

His words and Jonna's met in a flash. I did see. "You intend to break the shanties," I whispered. "You want to be rid of Those Above and Below."

"Hit the nail on the head. You found a sharp one, girl," he added to Jonna before turning back to me. "You've got a glimpse of the lie or you wouldn't've left. Will you help us?"

I knew, then, that this was the catch. There would be no true freedom, no idyllic life with Jonna, cavorting in moonlit glades. There was a cost. I thought about the shanty, the creche with the nurselings, Arash's lingering gaze, Isana and the child she had never seen. I thought about Jonna and how she had risked herself to tell me the truth. There was no way she could have known that I would not run back to the shanty and tell them there was a stranger in the place of the dead. I could so easily have told the wandering servant, brought it with me to lie in wait for her.

What lay behind me was a life I could never return to. What lay before me was a life I could not even imagine. I turned to Jonna. Her eyes were bright, and I remembered how the moonlight had gleamed on her pale flesh, turning her to a creature of molten silver. She said nothing. It was my choice.

"Yes," I told Mkembe, and meant it. He reached out to draw Jonna and me both into a warm embrace.

"Then thank you. And welcome. Let's go; we've a long walk ahead." He strode off into the night, and I followed, Jonna's hand in mine.

.

# Dilution Solution

## by Adrian Simmons

The line moved slower every time we came back. Remarkable, considering that odds were we almost always had fewer people than we left with. Only one thing to do for it.

Flipping the cover to the manual override on the side of my headphones, I punched the 'start' button. Even through the thick gloves it was easy to do, they had only put the one button in it.

Music, wordless for once, came streaming into my head, giving me a little bit of distraction to aid in the waiting.

After a while, they put words into the music. It played *What a Lady What A Night* and I wished they'd put an off button on it, too. I'd just have to endure until it shut off automatically.

At least I was close enough to see the check-in personnel behind their bullet-proof glass. Sandy, Ronald, and Johnny Tayl. The usual three, wearing mirror shades to protect themselves from each other. Plus, outside the glass, there were the ever-present red-guards: Dana and Mok today. They stood like two great wasps, their eyes covered by visors, their ears protected by thick headphones—same as me, except they could take theirs off at the end of their shift.

Patroller check-in is a slow procedure, not that we didn't get any entertainment, mind you. Tommy Mestor went nuts after his check-in;

Dana tackled him from behind (she was smart, she never stood in front of anybody) before he could bring his anti-personnel gun to bear.

Mok tazered him, which gave Dana quite a shock, too. Her mouth screamed at him, a ragged square from beneath her eye shield, her earphone antennae waving menacingly.

I used the distraction to skip up in line so I could be next.

I spun the rifle around, holding it up so they could see the clip was out, and opened the chamber to show it was empty. I dropped it into the bin, along with the three clips of ammo, grenades (only had one of those left), saber, and, of course, the socket wrench from my boot.

"Plug in, Mick," Johnny said.

"Right, Johnny." The plug in was right in the center of the visor, a good design feature. I plugged in and he looked at his computer screen, seeing what I saw.

"See my eyes?" he asked as he pulled off his shades.

"See 'em? I love 'em!" I joked, as the VR visor put a black strip over his exposed eyes. "Gimme a kiss, you brute!" I slammed my face into the glass, the visor's screen fuzzing for a second.

"Stupid fucker!" Sandy shouted. "He's gonna break the plug-in!"

Johnny waved her into silence, replaced his shades, and held up an object.

"What is this?"

"Salvador Dali's uvula wrestling a tequila worm?"

Dali's work had a huge resurgence after the Others showed up. My mom always thought that was funny.

Johnny just frowned and held the optical illusion up under my nose, just on the other side of the glass.

"Come on, Johnny," I said. "I've had a long day; need a little relaxation, a little humor. Don't ya like humor? Why don't you sing anymore?"

"Mick, just tell me what you see."

It was important that they checked both your equipment and your mind when you came back from a patrol. From the *outside*. I didn't hate them for doing their jobs, just hated the fact that their jobs might cost me mine.

"It is a dodecahedral. Didn't know I knew that word did you? A blue one."

Whatever it was he held was blocked out by the virtual reality gear that was mounted on my head. The VR gear masked it as a twelve sided figure in a pleasant blue hue for my sanity's protection.

"Great, great," he said. "Sign in now."

He slid the pad and the stylus to me under the glass. It came as a surprise.

"I thought the Council determined the SK test wasn't really accurate," I said.

"Tommy Mestor said the same thing." Johnny smiled, not very friendly, "The Council's decided to start it back up. Just sign in."

"Maybe I don't wanna sign in! Maybe I've had enough shit for one day!" A few hours ago I saw things that would turn most people's shit white. I'd gunned down naked crazies while unspeakable things hid behind the pleasing shapes the VR rig gave them. Honestly, who the hell could trust a signature after that?

I could hear Dana moving up behind me.

Maybe they had already pushed the button on me. They have buttons back there, in the check-in area, for various things. They said they have one they press when somebody goes over, a big red one like they have in bank-robbery movies. Nobody had really ever explained to me what a bank was, something from before my time, before the Others. When these banks get robbed, they push this big button to call the patrollers. If check-in people push the button on you, you're fucked.

I took the stylus and pressed it into the pressure pad, signed once, signed twice, signed the third time.

"Happy now? Lemme in!"

Johnny looked up from the screen. "You're last name isn't Marttel."

"It's a form of silent protest."

"It speaks pretty loud." He turned the computer screen so I could see.

My name appeared at the top, followed by my other entries, each from after a patrol and a randomly given SK test, until they stopped having us sign in three months ago. Each signature was a little more erratic than the last. Today's entry was barely recognizable. The computer pronounced its doom. Eighty percent degradation. I could feel them push the button.

"Give it to me again. I'm not a Mad Hatter. No jokes this time."

Johnny shook his head.

"Come with me, please," Mok the red-guard said. The door

opened and two more came out, their tazers drawn.

They looked at me with through their bulging black goggles. I tensed up. Not one out of ten come back from rehab, and they usually can't last past a few patrols. My legs tightened, ready to spring. I let go of my tension.

"Calm down... I'm on the way," I said.

"Smart boy." I heard Dana say from behind me.

It hurt a lot when they removed the VR rig. It's all designed so that it doesn't come off, in case a crazy hooks their filthy hands around it. They drill anchoring screws into your skull once you've passed all the tests.

That's a fairly painless procedure; they make an effort for you. You are a patroller, after all. You keep the crazies and the Others out, you secure the perimeter, get supplies, that sort of thing. When the rig goes on, they dope you up and give you a good pep-talk about what a great thing you're doing.

The doctor's aren't nearly so nice when you're a Mad Hatter, I was afraid they were going to chew up the bolt-head trying to get the screws out.

At least they told me that the new models have an inserting pin that the bone can attach to and that a screw fits into that could save future Mad Hatters a lot of headaches. Hooray, progress!

The earphones weren't a picnic either.

I shared rehab center #5 with three other Hatters: Donny Corloni, Sonny Crocker, and Angie Renaul (yes, the legendary Angie R). I felt a little sorry for Sonny. He was the only one who wasn't a patroller, just some poor slob who got the gaze. Oh, well; it happens.

Rehab center #5 was a simple arrangement: four "rooms" that were made of chain link about a hair bigger than a dog run. I had never seen a dog, but that's what all the old people called most of the cells in the underground. The floor was an incredibly ugly blue tile, after about ten feet outside of the cells all around there was *nothing*, just blackness. No floor, no wall, no ceiling, nada. They said that once you're a hatter it's real easy to fool your senses. The doctors usually appeared out of the blackness next to my cell.

The psychologists came to see us every third day, and every other visit we got to go to the check-up room. God, I never thought I would be so happy to see white tile and medical gear. Although we got to meet a lot of new faces at the check-up room, we made little progress.

One day, the doctors didn't show up; it was red-guards instead. Didn't say much, just had us sign in and take the Stewart-Kravtechenko test again. They compared notes afterward, and then they took Sonny away.

"Man, this fucking sucks, it *fucking sucks*," Donny said.

"Baby learn a new fucking word?" Angie asked.

"I'll tell you what, he may not be a hatter but he won't last a day before he's back," Donny spat. Then he dropped and started doing pushups.

Poor Donny. He suffered from the delusion that he was one of the great ones, up there with Angie R. Thought if you were a good enough patroller they'd take you back, no questions asked. It broke our hearts to tell him different, so we only did when there was absolutely nothing else to do.

Not that I didn't do pushups myself. I did; heck, I wanted to be back in the patrollers just like everyone else. Angie R. did pushups with her one good arm, more than I could do. She even did some on the stump of her forearm, more than I could do. Sometimes she would even climb to the top of her cell, hold on with her toes and one hand and do some sort of weird pull-ups. It was an unnerving sight.

I didn't try it.

"I heard that Katya has been coming around the cells," I said.

"Shut up... gotta concentrate!" Donny grunted.

"C'mon baby! Do it! Do it!" Angie encouraged.

I couldn't concentrate, but I watched; my shaded eyes jumped from Donny's stroking to Angie's dancing.

This stuff did nothing for me anymore. Well, it did; group masturbation with the voyeuristic risk that the doctors and who-knew-who-else might be ten feet away. Hot! But I couldn't concentrate at all.

Angie swayed side to side. Her stomach had three parallel scars running across it, but her breasts had come through unscathed. She was sweating just enough to shine.

Donny, on the other hand, had worked himself up into a lather. His black skin gleamed and shined. All the exercise had made a positive impact.

"Have you ever met Katya Kravtechenko?" I asked.

"Please, we're trying to establish mood here," Angie said. Donny said something ruder and kept up his frantic pace.

They sent Katya to see you when none of the other tests or relaxation techniques or drugs did anything for you. She inspects the patrollers with the rest of Council. I'd seen her there, just looking at us, talking sometimes to a random patroller. I'd heard she had also pulled a few out of the ranks. Unfit. She could tell, you know.

Some folks said that the sensitives, like Katya, were a result of the Others. My mom said that some rare people already had powers, but somehow the Others helped make them stronger. Another faction maintains that the sensitives are evolution's way of fighting back.

My mom said evolution didn't work like that, and normally I agree with her, but it's hard to think about your mother when you're doing things in cages that animals in a zoo would be ashamed of, much less ask for.

Man, a zoo must have been an amazing thing.

Anyway, now Katya was nosing around down here. And that meant that the Council was trying to do something. Or maybe that Katya was trying to do something. Like everything else Underground, our government didn't work that well.

"Turn around, Angie!" Danny pleaded.

She spun around, flinging her dark straight hair out. Something had got her on the ass, probably whatever took her arm off. Aside from the scars, it was a really great ass.

Donny thought so, too. In a few moments, he let out a muted cry, spraying out pleasure and frustration and hope into a crumpled tissue.

While he gasped and grunted, I spit into my palm, redoubled my pace, and jumped up ahead in line.

"Have you ever met Katya, Angie? I mean, you've been here for a while now..."

"You're going to spoil it, Mick," Angie said, turning back to us, a smirk playing beneath her eye-shields. "Agreements are agreements after all, gentlemen."

There was no arguing with that. "Ready Don?" I asked.

"Yeah... yeah, I'm ready," he said, gasping just a little.

"A-one and a-two and a-three-"

"Love is strong," we began in gravely unison while Angie took care of herself with her one good hand.

I had seen that hand bend the chain links on the fence of her dog-run. She was talented.

Donny's singing had gotten better, too.

Two days later, the medics wouldn't let me go to the rec-room with Donny and Angie. Ten minutes after they left, Katya

Kravtechenko walked out of the darkness and stepped lightly over the tile. She had two red-guards with her. They opened the door to my cell. She went in alone.

I smiled as pleasantly as I could.

She just stared at me through her Class Four eye-shields.

She was very young, maybe thirteen. "Shouldn't you be in school right now?" I said. My mom used to talk about schools, something like banks. You put money in banks and kids in schools.

She smiled shyly at me, shrugged

"I've never heard that one before. Tell it again," her voice had a luxurious Russian accent.

The red-guards walked in.

"So, how have you been doing?" she said.

"Oh, pretty well, I guess. I've learned which lever gives me the cheese and which doles out the electric shock."

"ECT doesn't work in most cases for people who have Reality Perception Disorder." She looked at me thoughtfully through her mirror shades then shrugged. "Maybe more study is needed," she motioned to a red-guard. He pulled out his tazer and shot me full in the chest. They ran so much juice through me I swear I was lactating before they turned it off.

I was lying in a pool of my own spit when I heard her speak again.

"Do you feel any better now?"

I wanted to answer but I couldn't make human noises.

"I see," Katya said. "Mick, would you like me to recommend that if

Dr. Malhan needs a new subject for ECT tests that he should get you?"

"N-n-no -o no," I managed.

"Do you have any more jokes or unpleasant remarks?"

"No, Katya." I had heard she liked to be called by her first name. I heard she was a reincarnated Siberian shaman. I heard a lot of things about Katya and the other sensitives who sat on the Council.

"Sit down in the chair, wipe your chin. Your SK tests have only gone up 4% since you began standard treatment. The medical specialists feel that you are still a recoverable resource. Would you like to be recovered? Do you want to be a patroller again?"

Oh yes, yes indeed. Respect, next to the Council and Katya herself. Action! Adventure! To get laid every night again.

"Yes, that would be nice. That is what I would like."

Ordinarily, the doctors always make you fill out forms and papers whenever they give you a treatment, session, injection, or what have you. Helps them keep track of what works and what doesn't. Katya wasn't a doctor.

She reached up to remove her Class Four eye-shields.

The last human being's eyes that I had seen were my mother's before I went in to get the VR rig bolted to my head. I looked down, almost instinctively. So many rumors floated around about Katya.

She pulled them off casually, folded them on her lap.

When someone has Reality Perception Disorder, or gets the gaze, their eyes are... different. The pupils are huge, and unsettling visions leap out and snare the mind of anyone who looks into them.

Everybody wears shades now, because you never know when somebody suddenly goes RPD or Mad Hatter.

Her eyes were a beautiful nondescript brown. Cool and sturdy like the bark of a great tree. We still had some trees on the surface, pretty things. I clenched the arms of the chair.

The mole dream goes something like this:

We're tunneling underground, trying to go underneath a river. We're all down there, digging, moving earth. Some have tools, some use hands, some use teeth. We're all wearing the full gear. VR goggles, I knew via dream knowledge, don't really work. Nothing we see is really what *we* see; it's what the VR goggles tell us we *should* see. Lately, they've been cutting out more and more of what is really in front of us.

Anyway, there we are, gradually going blind and tunneling. You know, like moles. Sometime after we go blind, the VR sets start to show us what's up on the surface. One of the Others, a big one, a really big one, is up there. The VR rig works well enough, so the Other just comes across as a big solid black pyramid. Sometimes it extends parts of itself out into the city around it. The crazies run all over the place, of course. It has a pitchfork. It waits until it feels the ground move – the moles digging around – and it stabs down into the pavement.

In our tunnels, we sometimes feel when the person next to us gets impaled, pulled up through the roof. We don't see it of course, but we hear it: a loud crash, a rodent-like squeal, and the sudden rushing of bodies trying to escape.

We all try real hard not to think too much on the mole dream. Rumor is that you never, never, ask Katya about it.

After she visited, I had the mole dream a lot more. On the plus side, my SK score went up by a whopping 10%. Ten more and I'm back in the mix. The visits from the medics get fewer and farther between after Katya talks to you. The medics don't really like Katya. But boy, the psychs won't leave you alone for five freakin' minutes.

"Actually Angie, the only really tangible effects that I'd felt were that no matter how disturbing my dreams or memories were, they seemed distant, like they belonged to someone else. Sort of like having a VR assembly over my mind's eye."

She nodded, scratching at her chin before lifting her eye-shields and rubbing at the corners of her eyes.

As long as we were sharing, "So what got your arm?" I asked.

Angie dropped and started doing her one-armed push-ups.

"No, really," I said. "I've heard a lot of different things. Tell me the real story."

"One of the Big Boyz came along," she said, dropping down.

She pushed back up, "Search-and-Snatch mission at the zoo." Down.

Back up. "No way something the size of that thing could fit into the tank it came out of." Back down.

"They're bad about that," I said, speaking from experience.

Up. "Probably two-hundred crazies, easy." Down.

Up. "We unloaded on the crazies, I mean really let 'em have it, grenades, shells, you name it." Down.

Up. "What we didn't know was there were three Pink-Spots." Down.

Nobody who was sane really knew what a Pink-Spot was. It was just some creature that the VR rig covered with a bunch of moving pink spots, thus the name.

Up. "Came out of the north end of the reptile house." Down.

Up. "Six Nar Tips and four D-fluxes was all we had to start with. Most of those we use on the Big Boy." Down.

Up. "The pink-spots tore into us like a tank-car through crazies." Down.

She stayed down. "Crazies pulled me to the ground and broke two ribs. One of them bit through my boot heel, even. One of the Pink Spots cleared 'em off. I reached for my gun. I had to reach over two big pieces of rubble. It brought its foot, or tentacle, or whatever, down right on my arm, breaking both bones between the rocks. I think that someone set off a D-flux, drove the thing back. I tried to run, but the crazies got hold of me. I think they pulled the rest of my arm off while I tried to get away. I can't really remember it all."

"I see," I said. Even though I couldn't see her eyes, I knew she was lying.

The Others are dangerous to even look at. The crazies had been caught in the initial wave, turned and looked, and lost what little grip on sanity they had. The Others were dangerous to listen to. If they had crossed over, or spawned, or landed, or whatever the hell they did about fifteen years before they had, we would have all been fucked. Fortunately, our technology – my mom's generation's technology – had come so far that we didn't really need to rely on our flawed natural senses. The VR rigs filter out all the Others, keeping your mind fairly safe.

The patrollers, fight, and secure resources from the surface. Sometimes, when things are going really well, they bump you up to Owsla and you get to go on a wide-patrol and search for a. . . a starport, or a temple, or *something*. Something to explain it.

I've never gone on a wide patrol. There have only been two since I became a patroller, and both right after Katya led her group from Four-Corners to us. Not bad for a ten-year-old.

Those were good times, busy times, making room for all the newcomers and doing good works for our fellow sane men.

They finally came for Donny and Angie: two red-guards, one of whom was almost old enough to shave every day. They handed them the stylus. Donny just about shit himself, he was so excited, but Angie didn't seem too happy about it.

She signed in, and the guard looked at her SK result.

"Please write your real name," he said in as expressionless voice as he could muster.

"Go home to mama," she spat back.

His partner tagged her with his Taser. She jumped about three feet off the ground, crashed into the cage wall, and slumped to the floor. Donny had a look of almost comical shock on his face as they gathered her up, cuffed her good arm to one of their belts, and slapped her around a bit to wake her up. The reds led them away. Donny was happy again by the time they left the light circle.

It gets mighty boring when you don't have anyone to talk to, or share your perverted fantasies with. Group masturbation is, of course, out of the question. Solo only does so much.

Like I mentioned, even the meds don't like to talk to you once you've talked to Katya. The standard treatment was pretty dull, too. There were almost no other treatment candidates. Those that did come in during those long, awful weeks were what I'd risk calling unrecoverable.

One of them – her name was Jamie, I think – was in the circle of lights with me for a while. She didn't sleep, not once in three days. On the third day, when she was on one of the exercise bikes in the rehab center, she suddenly spun around and held her water bottle in front of my face.

"Is this half full or half empty?" she demanded.

"Oh, a little from column 'A', a little from column 'B'."

"It's half full!" she shouted at me.

I started doing push-ups, deciding that I didn't really want to know anymore.

"It's half full of half-piss!" she added. "Not a problem if you've got enough water! Enough minds! Dilution is the key! The big if, the *plan!*"

The red-guard Tazered her, and she lost her footing on her cycle. The pedals kept spinning and her legs got all tangled up in them. It was really funny in a disturbing way.

I don't know where she got off to after that.

I knew the reds were coming for me. They gave me the SK test. Didn't bother to do a confirmation test, just looked at the result, smiled and told me I was ready to be a patroller again.

It was really odd, since I signed in under a completely different name, one that had all consonants. But then, these were the two reds that Katya usually had with her.

I got a new VR set screwed onto my head. They didn't use those special anchoring sleeves after all. It really hurt. I mean, it hurt a lot.

In my four months in the cage, things had really fallen apart. I could tell because nobody bitched about how bad things were. That meant things were fucked-beyond-funny.

I was outfitted and got my first patroller assignment before the blood had even dried.

It was nice to be back in the patroller section of the Underground again. I got to see it for about five minutes. Sinh Tong was still there, distributing the tools of our trade.

"Hey Mick, good to have you back. We missed you."

"No need to shout Sinh, I've got a headache," I said, pointing to the fresh anchoring screw.

"One standard patroller rifle." He held up the beautiful thing, opened the main chamber, the spear-chucker chamber, and the grenade chamber to show they were all empty.

I took it, he handed me my ammo. It was less than I used to get.

I noticed that my ammo was all that was left in the boxes.

"Saber, knife, and of course – this!"

"Ah, Daddy's missed his little girl," I said, taking back my old socket wrench and sliding it into my boot.

The disembarking room was a storm of orange and black. Patroller uniforms are stunningly ugly, but they keep us from shooting each other. Katya herself stood on the map table and fifty antennaed heads turned to look at her, mine included.

She didn't have a VR unit, just those damn eye-shields. Someone handed her a microphone and she addressed the crew. It was all I could hear over my new headphones. Very touching speech. Something about one of the broadcast towers getting a distress call from the Albany area, our moral duty to come to the aid of our fellow sane men, that kind of thing.

I took advantage of the distraction to push my way up to the front of the crowd.

Angie R. was there, right in front. She was looking up at Katya, listening intently to her uplifting speech. I knew it was Angie because she had some sort of razor wire chainsaw thing protruding out where her right arm should have been.

I wondered if she would recognize me. I tapped her casually on the shoulder, the one with the real arm.

"Hey Mick!" she said, a huge smile splitting the lower half of her face. I wasn't as surprised that she remembered me as much as I was that I remembered how to read lips so well.

I had no idea what I was going to say. I honestly didn't. I mean, shit! What do you say to someone like Angie R.? Maybe something like "Hey, don't go nuts and kill me like you did your other patroller unit," or even, "Hey, why don't you get out in front?"

What I ended up saying was, "How are you feeling?"

She watched my lips move, smiled and nodded so fast that one of her antenna thumped my VR rig. "I'm doing better. We're all doing better. We'll be even better when we get to the folks in Albany."

Katya finished her motivational talk and we applauded.

We began to get into line. With this many people, it would take six separate trips to get to the surface.

I stood in my old place in the line. It felt good, good to be back. Someone had told me that Katya herself was going on this one. The Council really wanted it to go right. Things were getting worse. We were getting worse.

Katya walked by us, looking us over. She pulled a handful of us out of the crowd, Angie and myself included.

She told me to stay close to her, no matter what else happened. Even reading her lips, I got the Russian accent. She said something to Angie too, but she was turned away and I couldn't read her lips. There were about ten others. We were the first group in the elevator.

At the top, Katya took off her eye shields. She punched in the exit code, and motioned for us to go. Outside. How long had it been?

The ruins waited, quiet, patient, deadly. There were no crazies in sight, or any of the Others.

We unloaded the tank-cars and the bikes.

"Mick, cripple the elevator." Katya said. "That's an order. Donny, cripple the communications tower."

We didn't tunnel after all. It took six days to get to Albany overland. I saw things that turn most people's shit white. We got kinda crazy. . . and that's saying a lot. I couldn't tell if I never slept over those six days, or if I just never woke up.

Angie didn't even shoot any of us. For the first two days, we sent her to take care of the other patrollers when they got too close. They didn't try to follow us after that.

The folks in Albany were awful glad to see us, awful glad to look right into Katya's beautiful brown eyes.

Katya let the madness – hers, ours, animals we had met on the way – out into the Albany colony.

I don't think they noticed, what with all the good works and making room for us and all.

Some part of me felt pretty bad about it, but Angie R., who is an expert at not feeling bad, told me that Katya's getting better at this each time.

# Earth Worms

by Cody Goodfellow

Gary Caldwell awoke from a dream he couldn't remember, except for the sound of his own voice telling him *to be fruitful and multiply.*

Cold, golden light poured like sand into his eyes, but he could not close them. Could not move at all. He could see nothing but the light and feel only a vague, universal aching which brought him to the edge of panic. He was still in his body, or he seemed to be. The sensations he felt were nothing like the deep meditation or the OOBE training that were supposed to prepare him for the end.

Something his wife said came to him, just then: *the End isn't when we die… it's when we all get what we deserve…*

Was this what he deserved, then? Was this the Limbo reserved for infidels and unbelievers? It would be far better if he *could* panic; if he could feel exultation, fear, anything.

Because the end had come, and what he believed had come true.

This thought cast his discomfort and confusion into a whole new light. He had seen them come down out of the sky with his own eyes. When the whole human race had succumbed to despair, he and the others who shared the vision had held out long enough to see them come.

He was with Joyce in the communications bunker, watching the

100

torrential acid rain. The telescopes and pirate satellite feeds had found nothing, but their Big Ear had been pinging with anomalous radio signals for weeks. Someone had to be listening out there, and might finally be trying to speak.

Caldwell was the only one well enough to stand watch. A Gray Grids infection had wiped out half the group in the last week. Joyce was well into the terminal phase, the livid, circuitry-shaped rash branding every pallid inch of skin, but she came topside to bring him soup and spend her last breaths on accusations.

"Just admit it, darling," she whispered, like begging for medicine. "Admit you were wrong." It was unworthy of her, but it was easier than facing the real betrayal. She had followed him out here, and she was dying, and he was not.

"What did I do, now?" He busied himself with rebooting the sweeping radio receivers, but no outsiders broke into their argument. The constant atmospheric disturbances caused by the roving tri-state cyclone-cluster they called the Funnel, now a permanent feature of the Great Plains, had snuffed out all terrestrial communications.

No one on Earth had anything to say that was worth hearing, anyway. Night and day, the group tended their telescopes, their radio transmitters and their lasers, and sent out Dr. Scriabin's message to the universe.

"All of this was a mistake. All the calculations, the predictions, the pilgrimage out here… just laser-guided prayer. Just another cargo cult pipe dream."

That stung. The world had called them a cult, but what did they believe that was not written in the poisoned earth, the tainted skies, and the rising, dying seas? Their leader was not a wild-eyed crankcase or a glad-handing evangelist, but a soft-spoken retired college professor.

Dr. Scriabin predicted the end based on Malthusian charts and greenhouse gas curves, while the rest of the world clung to their fantasies of a universal Daddy who gave them the earth to eat like a pie in an eating contest. Was their retreat into the Montana badlands to try to contact an extraterrestrial intelligence any more insane than the infantile belief of a solid majority of Americans that they would be raptured away from the end by angels?

It was hard to look at her, but he forced himself. "You'd rather we stayed in LA when it fell into the sea, then? You'd prefer to have died in the food riots?"

"We didn't just come out here to *survive*," she spat. "You staked our lives on the premise that someone out there was watching. And that they would save us."

The distress signal had been going out, in some form or other, for almost twenty years. The endless string of binary laser-light pulses and more esoteric codes were a barrage that anyone who could make sense of mathematics would surely decipher to learn the location of Earth and the dire state of its environment. If they were as merciful as they were advanced, they would come running to save the few humans left from imminent destruction.

"We could have gone out with our families," she sobbed, "with people who mattered to us… we could've gone somewhere and just tried to live…"

Immune as he was to the rogue nano-compilers riddling her flesh, he could still be infected with her doubt. Scriabin had spent their pooled life savings on the mostly underground compound, the telescope farm and some weapons. It seemed less like fate than the plot of some corny made-for-TV gospel, that their Moses did not survive the journey himself.

Society collapsed even faster than Scriabin had predicted, and angels lifted no one out of the fire. Of the forty-two men and women who set out, only twenty were still alive, and less than half of them were fit enough to get out of bed. "We are still alive because of the group, Joyce, and we have a purpose… we still have—"

"Hope? Have you talked to anyone down below lately, Gary? Hope has them, and it's eating them alive." After the canned food ran out and the hydroponic victory garden failed, the weakest took their own lives or deserted, while the rest shaved their heads and prayed to outer space. Some claimed they heard Scriabin lecturing them in their dreams, promising a new Eden.

Even Joyce had drifted away into a desperate fugue state. Caldwell spent more time in the communications bunker just to get away. "This can't be the End," she said. He looked away, and then it happened.

The night was a black wall, the jet stream of toxic clouds grinding grimy lightning sparks off the empty wasteland, and suddenly, the whole sky was alive with light.

"Joyce, look! Do you see them? I told you—" He threw up his arms to shield his face, turned to reach for her, so transported by joy that he didn't realize that he was blind.

They were not at all as he expected. He had tried to prepare his mind for flying saucers, for vast, weightless cities of otherworldly light, but he was utterly wrecked by the reality of them. The only way to frame what he saw was the Biblical descriptions of the Angels' appearances to Jacob and Ezekiel – the wheels within wheels of fire, the terrible intensity that lifted his hair erect on his head and blew out every circuit in the bunker.

They did not descend out of the clouds. They were so instantly, absolutely there that they must have come through a fold in space, or out of a parallel universe, to hover directly overhead. As if summoned by his faith or her doubt, they had come at last...

He trembled with true awe that transcended fear for his life, but even then, he did not let his excitement run away with him and scream for the others. He had not eaten in almost three days. He might be hallucinating. It couldn't be real...

But then the sonic boom and shockwave of displaced air from the overwhelming manifestation smashed into the bunker. The blinding, rosy glow of that fleet of celestial wheels grew so bright as to fill the space between his eyes and his hand with a pink opaque ocean.

There was no message of universal peace, no psychic embrace from the visitors. There was nothing at all... until now.

He was cold, and he ached all over. But slowly, agonizingly, he was able to move. His hands brushed a brittle crust off his face, and bumped against the ceiling. He lay supine in a thickly padded space the size of a coffin. He might be in some sort of suspended animation pod, but something had obviously gone wrong.

The walls of his coffin were solid, but the one behind his head was slightly translucent and allowed the muted golden light to pass through it. He rapped on it, then pounded with his fists. It meekly slid back into the wall, and let the ambient air of the ship fill his chamber.

The first breath of it nearly killed him.

Carbon monoxide is a soothing way to die – three of the group killed themselves in the motor pool, when the nukes fell on New York. But carbon monoxide was the least toxic of the ingredients that he inhaled.

His eyes teared up so badly, they could be melting. He tried to scream, as the sulfurous vapors reacted with the fluid in the lining of his throat to form acidic foam. Coughing it clear, he found some relief by breathing through the fibrous padding torn from the walls of his coffin.

The sweltering yellow miasma was hostile, but not deadly. In fact, it was not really even an alien atmosphere, in the sense that he had breathed it before. It was all too familiar, reminding him of the fires that feasted on Las Vegas, and the long-gone smoggy stench of his morning commute. Perhaps they hadn't left Earth after all.

Closing his burning eyes and breathing shallowly through his mask, he lowered his legs over the edge of his cell. He felt much lighter than he should have, but there was still a discernible pull of gravity that dragged him downward. Probing with his bare feet, he found the convex windows of other coffins, but he did not know if he was anywhere near the floor. He clung to the wall until his fingers cramped.

Sweat beaded on his brow and burned like battery acid. If he didn't keep moving, he was going to fall. He lowered himself out of his open coffin and fumbled sideways on the wall of a bottomless mausoleum.

Moving like a crippled fly on a pane of dirty glass, he crept over to the nearest coffin. He scrubbed away the yellow scum from the translucent pane and rubbed his outraged eyes. *Joyce?*

A woman lay inside, her face dimly lit by the corroded gold light, but he didn't recognize her.

Where was the rest of the group? Where was his wife? He had hoped for some familiar face, but the coffins all around his were occupied by people he'd never seen before.

When he had peered into more of them than he could count and his legs shook and threatened to give out on him, he tried to return to his own coffin, but he was lost. It seemed such a shame to fall to his death, when he had come so far…

Something grabbed his leg and lifted him off the wall. Thrashing in its unbreakable grip, he dangled upside down over the murky abyss, then was spun around to face his captor.

A gigantic mound of spiny armor, bigger than a blue whale, clung to the wall on hundreds of jointed, branching tentacles. More of them slithered out of vaginal slots all around its underbelly to ensnare and cradle his helpless body. The tips of many of them swelled into polyps and darkened to become curious eyes.

He didn't know what he'd expected, but it was nothing like this. Benevolent, dome-headed gray humanoids were just as much of an anthropocentric fantasy as angels. But this thing showed no sign of the intelligence one would expect to find in a starfaring species. Certainly, it had none of the mercy one might hope for in aliens that had just saved humans from a dying world.

But maybe, the thought shot through him with the force of an electric shock, *they aren't merciful, at all. Maybe they didn't come to save us...*

The forest of forking tentacles brought him closer to the hulking shell. While it showed no semblance of a head, its pitted, bony surface danced with glossy black motes that, amid all this strangeness, gave him another horrible spasm of unwelcome familiarity.

Cockroaches. His alien savior was infested with cockroaches.

He fought against the very arms holding him up as waves of tiny, many-legged things came scuttling down them to crawl over his body and his face.

The tendrils stretched him out and held him completely rigid as the maddening tickle of millions of probing legs inspected every inch of him. Close up, the parasites were more like earwigs or silverfish, with twitching antennae at either end of their segmented, armored bodies.

*Your container was faulty,* said a buzzing, susurrate voice. *Apologies. We will rectify.*

He could not move. He could not even close his eyes or his mouth as they crawled over his tongue and sampled his streaming tears.

*You are conscious, lucid, and in somatic distress.*

Leave it to sentient insects to belabor the obvious. They spoke directly into his mind. A constant background hiss of discarded synonyms and alternate phrasings ghosted everything they said. Every expression was a consensus of millions of networked minds. But when they commanded him to RELAX, the devastating roar came at him in his own inner voice.

"I am terrified," he wheezed, "of you. I don't know what's happened, or where I am –"

*Contact with catalytic specimens is proscribed…*

Millions of tiny legs beat a jumbled tattoo on his skin that gradually became an even more infuriating united rhythm. *But our caste/brood mandate is curiosity. We have absorbed your cognitive modalities at great cost. Isolation… forfeiture of daughter colonies…*

He wanted to be a good ambassador for humanity. "I know I should be grateful – and I am… but why did you come to Earth? You heard our transmissions?"

*An unexpected permutation of your programming… we have never seen such progress. We have hopes the next cultivation will mature within our lifetime… this was promised to us. But you have questions…*

The gigantic shell-colony began slowly to climb the wall of coffins, holding him helpless for the insectoids that came and went over his flesh.

"Why did you come for us? Where are you taking us? Where are my friends? What happened to my wife?"

*Your clan was unsalvageable. Your individual genotype expresses exceptional immunity to environmental/viral hazards. We came as we have always come. It was foretold in your sacred texts… Dictation and transmission of transhuman spiritual visions was the core mandate of our caste, so we hope your race found them a comfort.*

In simple, flat sentences, the creature had undone all that Caldwell believed, and condemned all that he loved. He should rage, he should go insane, and yet he could only feel a dim, hollow echo of regret. "We got it wrong, then. We all got it wrong..."

*Your species' naïve misinterpretation of the cultivation and harvest cycle was the most useful and benign method of preparing you for your purpose.*

"Our... purpose?"

*Set down in a garden, you multiply and advance at a monitored rate, digesting raw resources until the indigenous biosphere collapses and environmental conditions become optimal for our colonization. Surviving catalyst specimens are harvested and transplanted...*

Optimal conditions? He scoffed at the bitter irony, but then the creatures did seem to inhabit a toxic stew... "You've known about us? You could have come down and contacted us at any time...?"

*We oversaw cultivation of your world for two million Terran solar years. Ancestors/mother colonies were far too cautious. By transplanting your species to an unripe world, we will take possession in less than ten centuries.*

Words and breath failed him. They could've saved us... but we were serving them, all along. All our pollution was not the by-product of progress, but the purpose itself... not of ruining the earth, but cultivating it, to make it perfect for them.

"And now you're taking over the Earth?"

*Taking it over? As your race understands ownership... it was always ours.*

The insect horde whispered on even as it placed his body inside a coffin and sealed it. The toxic vapors were vacuumed out, the temperature dropped and a skeleton crew of insects converged on his ears and eyes.

*Be fruitful and multiply,* they said.

They ordered him to *SLEEP* and *FORGET* in his own voice and tore any conscious thoughts of his own to shreds, but he hurled himself against the walls to smash them, and dug his fingers into his ears and sinuses until the last squirming body was smashed.

His ears thrummed white noise and his head pounded, but when drugged sleep finally claimed him, he felt possessed by a fierce exultation that kept his horror and despair at bay.

*A second chance!*

They were being taken to another planet, a virgin world, a new Eden, to start again. They would never make the same mistakes—

He awoke with the sun blazing down full on his face.

He rolled over and stretched, wiped the crust of sleep from his eyes, and marveled at the flawless aquamarine sky. His mind still drowsed under a fuzzy blanket of warm euphoria that he didn't entirely trust, but could not resist.

One of his ears gave only a dull thrum like the sound of distant crickets, but the other, though clogged with waxy exoskeletons, clearly brought him the sound of men and women singing.

He lay upon a broad, flat outcrop of burgundy lava rock on the edge of a placid green sea. The beach was a narrow strip of powdered sugar crowded by towering trees with white trunks and deep red bladed leaves.

A fat, balding man dripping sweat came out of the trees. When he saw Caldwell, he beamed and threw out his arms to embrace him, then caught him when he knocked him down.

"Hallelujah, brother! Blessings unto Jesus!" His thick Texas accent acutely reminded Caldwell of home, and everything that had gone wrong there.

The singing came from the forest. Caldwell steadied himself against the Texan's sturdy bulk. "How many people are there?"

"About a hundred or so, and mostly Americans... Awful lot of Chinese, which struck me funny, tell you the truth... I expected a whole lot more from my parish. We just woke up on the beach, and well, here we are! There could be more of us scattered all over. The angels said there would be other groups, but for now, we should make a home, and be fruitful—"

"They weren't angels," Caldwell said.

The preacher's tight, too-bright smile silently warned Caldwell that he was hanging on to sanity by his fingernails. This wasn't what anyone expected. It must've been a crushing blow, not to awaken on a cotton-candy cloud with dove-white wings and a harp.

Caldwell followed the preacher into the trees. They must've been up for hours, and they hadn't wasted any time.

Singing and speaking in tongues, the men chopped down trees, while the women stoned the flightless, six-winged bird-things that flapped honking out of the crimson foliage, and gathered their jeweled eggs in nests shaped like shopping bags.

"We found the lava rocks were almost ready-made axe heads, so we got a heck of a head-start chopping down a clearing, and our boys say we can dam up the stream nearby and have a sawmill… There's iron ore and oil just oozing up out of the ground."

"You think this is Paradise… and you're just going to plow it under and burn it down, just like the last one?" Caldwell could not keep the edge of hysteria out of his ragged voice.

The Texan fanned his ruddy face with a bleeding leaf. "I don't presume to question His means or ends, brother. I know the Bible is the Lord's gospel truth and I don't mean to cast stones at His divine plan, but I don't believe Adam and Eve ever had it half as easy as we're going to. Praise Jesus!"

Caldwell drew in a breath to shout, and it almost came out of him before he even felt it building… the desperate cry of his soul, to stop and look at themselves and the second chance they'd been given. He almost told them the truth about their angels.

But when he looked around, he saw no one who did not join in the hymns and glossolalia. Not a single member of his group. Just good God-fearing folks, chopping out their little piece of the new Eden.

At first, Caldwell only moved his lips so as not to stand out, but it didn't take long to learn the words.

And by then, he was swinging an axe.

# *Eliza*

by Joshua Reynolds

Oily rain wept down from the black sky and sizzled where it struck the rusty catwalks. Occasionally, a bolt of lightning would shriek down and dance across the iron shields that protected the upper reaches of the city and for a moment, the darkness would be swept aside in a flash of painful brilliance.

Despite the rain and the lightning, the walkways and catwalks were choked with people as the city went about its business. Impromptu markets sprang into existence as merchants of all stripes and legitimacies hawked their recycled wares to the dull-eyed populace. They sold protective amulets and powdered ancestors; dreams of protection and safety, though everyone knew the truth of it.

The city was humanity's last stand and outside of its walls, old things raged and fought in an entropic cacophony that had engulfed the rest of the world one mind at a time. The Old Ones had taught mankind new ways to shout and kill and revel in the doing so, and all of the Earth was burning in a holocaust of madness and freedom.

But not in the Empire; not in the last city of a once-proud race. There was order beneath the Iron Curtain. There was order and safety, of sorts, even if it was all the more cruel than the chaos outside because it could be taken away.

Eliza Whateley knew all about that. Soshe ran, her albino skin going the color of basalt and her pink eyes the color of the far stars. It wasn't just the hues that were changing, but the shape of her pupils and her bones, the latter shifting and cracking quietly whenever she tried to catch a few precious moments of sleep.

The horns had been first; twin nodules of calcified bone, poking up through her crinkly hair. They had grown so fast and become so heavy that she had been forced to keep her head covered by her rain-hood even on the rare dry days. Then her toes had stuck and grown into curved cloven hooves so that when she ran, she made a sound unlike anything anyone in the city had ever heard before, except in nightmares.

She was running now, her hood tossed back, her breath coming in short, sharp gasps. She gripped balance cables and rail-wires, hauling her aching body along, out into the burning rain and through the packed crowd. Curses and other querulous noises filled her ears as she shoved through the crowd, her hooves stomping on feet, her elbows digging into kidneys, hips, and shoulders.

Someone made a grab for her. Fingers tangled in her unwashed hair and she whirled, cocking her head and gouging at the offending hand with her horns. The owner of the hand screamed and suddenly the entirety of the crowd turned on her like an injured beast. Blindly, she fought back. She was stronger now than she had been, her muscles moving beneath her gape-pored flesh like pistons.

"Get away from me!" she shrieked, wrenching a struggling shape –

man or woman, she couldn't tell – into the air and hurled it into a flickering neon sign. The sign exploded into a shower of multi-colored sparks and there was a smell like burnt pork. The crowd's fury faded, replaced by fear. The tide drew back, leaving her alone in the center of the catwalk.

Breathing heavily, she looked around, peering through a curtain of hair. Her changed eyes making everything seem hazy and odd. "Get away," she said, more quietly. Her voice had changed as well, becoming rougher and yet somehow more feminine. Her breasts heaved and her hips ached, though whether from the posture forced upon her by her hooves or something else, she couldn't say. "I don't want to hurt anyone."

That was a lie. She did want to hurt them, to stamp them to paste beneath her mighty hooves and dance on their bones. It was in her to hurt them; she had been bred for pain, her gene-stock curdled and soured with the milk of the Old Ones. Whateley 65-A, the most changed, the most infected, the most tested. Even more than Marsh 12-C or Jermyn 6-13, the Whateley stock was a potent brew. Hardy and strong, that was how they had described her, the men in the white butchers' smocks with their lilting accents. Hardy and strong, a new breed of person capable of surviving... what?

She had not remained long enough to find out.

A loud hum filled the air and her palms flew to her ears. She jerked her head up, glaring around her, trying to spot the tell-tale ripple that would reveal the location of her pursuers. Out of the meeting point of two walls, a thin trickle of mist met the rain and turned to sludge. Time seemed to slow as she watched the thing behind the mist force itself out of a point no wider than an eyelash. The *Tind'losi* had found her.

It was said that they could follow a scent through time and space, being things of raw geometry and sentient mathematics rather than meat and bone. Artificial alchemical intelligences made of numbers and hate. They said the Empress Tsan-Chan, in her cosmic cruelty, had wrought them into being with ceremonies of abstract pain and untold consequence; that she had made them in her corkscrew palace to be her harbingers into the past. Hunters for the raw life-stuff needed to keep the ever-dwindling genetic pool of the remnants of the human race vibrant and functioning. They stalked the corridors of time, dragging back those who would not be missed in the centuries past to the endpoint of time where they were used and discarded, drained to keep the vampire-earth spinning for one more generation.

The hound was a canine grotesquery, bubble muscles under squirming flesh that pulsed with a thousand colors, draped over long, rubbery bones. Teeth like jagged shrapnel spun in a triangular maw and eyes the color of urine glared at her with single-minded determination.

They had followed her soul-musk through the angles and shadows. Now, they had come to drag her back to the Pnakoticopticon, to the tests and the chemicals and the men in butchers' smocks with their brass hands and syringe tipped fingers. Back to be torn open and tested and finally broken down back into the *ubosathla* to be re-grown and retested again and again until they were satisfied.

She knew this because she remembered it. She remembered it in the coruscating spiral of her genetic code; she remembered each birth and death as if it were her own. She remembered Wilbur and Lavinia and Zebulon and Agatha and Herbert and Spiro and all the other Whateleys, each one more Eliza than the last, until she had been born and had begun to become herself, complete and whole. Whateley-Prime was what they had called her and she knew that they were right. Just as she'd known that she had to escape, the way every Whateley tried to escape. To try to reach safety and the outside.

That they had sent the hounds only proved that she had been correct. In her head, the phantom voices of the others murmured in bitter satisfaction. The hounds had not come for *them*, after all. No, for them it had been the Empress' guards in their beetle-armor with their E-Sign tipped shock poles. But if she was the best of them, she also had the most to lose.

"No," she hissed, flexing her own talons. They had come after the hooves and she was grateful for them now as the hound squatted on its haunches and gave a sub-sonic bay, signaling the rest of its pack. "No! I'm not going back!"

The hound leapt, its body undulating across the distance between them like smoke. She swiped at it, scattering its substance, but it merely reformed behind her. Luminescent drool dripped from its mouth and splattered onto the catwalk with acidic effect. It lunged again. She sprang onto the rail to avoid it and then leaped out over the void.

The city spun beneath her as she crashed into a parallel catwalk slightly below the one she'd just vacated. People were screaming now, and someone had pressed an alarm. Eliza hauled herself up onto the catwalk, her heart hammering. People pressed away from her, making the E-Sign with contorted, trembling fingers, trying to ward her off. She snarled at them and tossed her horns. She hated them so much, with their wide mouths and round eyes. They gaped at her stupidly, like blind fish in a bowl. She wasn't like them. With her piebald skin and beast-muscle, she was better. Superior. She could survive anything!

Pain spiked through her a second later and she spun. The hound's teeth crashed together, inches from her face. Raw mathematics washed over her, stinking of imaginary numbers and poisonous formulas. She clawed wildly at it and it dispersed with a ghastly chuckle. Her soul felt shriveled and ragged in her chest; she screamed in frustration, her hoof slamming down and shaking the catwalk. People howled in fright and tried to flee to the street platforms.

More hounds raced along the electrical wires and catwalk rails like mirages made flesh, blinking in and out of existence as they closed in on her from all sides. She looked down... she could risk a jump. She was stronger now. A fall into the sub-streets might not kill her. But it would trap her. She looked up, where the edges of the curtain stretched in vain towards each other.

She could go up, but... up meant out, outside of the curtain and outside the city. Outside was where the Old Ones capered and crawled, rending the world. The thought chilled her and thrilled her. The part of her that was Whateley, the part of her that was black and cloven-hoofed, wanted to go up and out, to join the Old Ones Outside. But the other part of her, scared albino Eliza, wanted to run down and hide in the dark until the hounds found her at the last. That was what it meant to be human, after all: to run and cower in the dark.

In the end, it was no choice at all. She leapt straight up as the hounds closed in. Her claws dug into the iron and her palms blistered from the touch of the symbols carved into the metal-warding sigils and secret marks culled from the lost libraries of Pnakotus and Irem and patched together into a protective blanket by the Empress Tsan-Chan. The sigils held back the madness outside, and kept the dwindling ranks of Man safe in a womb of magic and metal. But they would only hold for so long.

That was why they had created her and her kind, she knew. Wilbur and the others whispered the truth of it in her ears. It was why the Empress had scoured the Earth in those savage final days, hunting for the gene-stock of those who already had contact with Those on the Threshold.

Her hooves struck iron and trailed sparks as she climbed with simian speed. Wilbur had been a climber. She had memories of places long lost now: a rotting farm house and a ring of stones. Genetic memories embedded in her thoughts like instincts. All the Whateleys knew these places and dreamed of them. They dreamed of other things too, things that cried out for divine parents in lonely places.

Did she have a twin out there? A long-lost uncle or aunt, invisible and inhuman. A thing of alien proportions and familiar scents. It would be nice if that were so. Her only family now were the ones she had in her head. There were multitudes in her, but she was only one. But if she could just escape. Just get outside...

Below her, the hounds began to scale the Curtain, their fluid shapes not quite touching its surface. The symbols were anathema to them just as much as they were to her. She hissed in pain as she tried to speed up. Her muscles were cramping, though from effort or from the poison in the symbols, she couldn't say.

Ethereal claws scraped through her leg and a scream wrenched from her throat. She nearly lost her grip but managed to hold on, if only barely. Snarling, she grabbed one of the plates of the Curtain and yanked it free. Steam and foul vapor rose from between her fingers, but she ignored the pain and swung the plate – and the sigil decorating it – at the hound as it slithered towards her.

The beast exploded with a yelp, bursting into flickering motes that drifted down like ash. Eliza chucked the plate at another hound; it sprang aside desperately. The howls changed timbre, becoming mournful and cautious. The hounds kept their distance now, pacing through the air, growling at her. Her hand ached abominably and she resisted the urge to look at it. Instead, she began to ascend once more, albeit one-handed.

The sky above was infinite shades of blue and streaked with a web of shivering lightning. Vast, amorphous shapes drifted across the limits of her far-sight. She shuddered on a cellular level at the thunder of their passing and she wanted to cry out to them, to say *take me with you*, but she could only lower her head and climb, the hounds nipping at her hooves. They could not hear her, not behind the Curtain. But outside...

The hounds closed in on her, growling and frothing. They were enraged now, the numbers under their flesh spinning and flashing. Other things gathered, slinking down the curve of the Curtain. Iron spiders with pulsing tubes and eerily glowing glass eyes clambered to meet her and contain her. Like the Curtain, the spiders were covered in runes and oaths. The Empress' automatons, built with her own gilded talons. Powered by the thought patterns of the mind-skins contained within the halls of Pnakotus, they were the city's first line of defense, its greatest protectors. They were metal golems with the souls of heroes, hierophants, and sorcerers from Earth's better epochs.

They haunted her nightmares and the nightmares of her other selves. Even more than the hounds, they terrified her. She swung out from the Curtain, avoiding the closest spider as it galloped towards her, claws clicking. Her hooves scraped sparks off of its back and she jumped higher.

Her ascent was roughly halted and she was slammed face-first into the Curtain, her teeth rattling in her jaw from the force of the impact. Just above the spider's head a hologram splashed to life and hovered like a demented halo. A familiar face looked at her sadly.

"Is this what we have come to?" the Empress Tsan-Chan said, her thin, lined face twisting with a snake's grief. "This? A clattering, cunning black brat? A goat-girl with more Outside than In?" The spider's talons buzzed as they punctured her shoulder and thigh, pinning her painfully to the Curtain. The other automatons began to gather, and beyond them, the hounds hovered watchfully. Eliza looked past the hologram, towards the twisted shape of the Empress' corkscrew towers, rising above the rat warren of the city. The Empress was there, sealed inside of shell of Valusian magics and advanced technologies. The Empress was always there, watching every corner of

121

her city, every inch of the curtain, watching like a matron searching for vermin. She watched and made sure that mankind remained human. Untainted. Unless it served her purpose.

Eliza squealed as the spider twisted her one way and then another so that the Empress could examine her with cool jade eyes. "Is this what I have been given, for my sacrifice? Is this what we must become? Satyrs and dryads?"

The hounds drifted closer, dripping glowing foam on the huddled, watching masses below. "No. No, I'll not have it. I'll not trade in my silks and combs for a matted mane and cloven hooves. There is some other way. Some other method. We will begin again. We have the rest of forever to do the deed."

Eliza's struggles grew in ferocity. The sky was just there, just out of reach. If she could just –

"We will strip it down. Mine it for the strong links and start again. Perhaps less of the Whateley, and more of the Marsh. Less of the Lurker and more of the Sleeper. We will find the right mix. We will survive." The Empress' voice rang out across the rooftops, artificially boosted by the spiders. Below there was scattered cheering.

Above, only silence. Eliza looked up through the haze of black that was collapsing her vision and saw Them looking down through the Curtain, the way the men in the butcher's smocks had looked down at her in her birthing crèche. Watching. Waiting to see... what?

"Through you," the Empress continued, "We will survive."

"Yes," Eliza said. "We will." And she struck out with her horns, bashing through the steel of the spider's skull and smashing its brain-cylinders into flopping shrapnel. It reared in artificial agony and released her. She kicked out, shoving it off. It fell, jerking and thrashing onto the catwalk below, splitting it and hurling screaming people into the maw of the city.

The Empress' hologram flickered and re-appeared above a second spider, but Eliza was already moving. She ignored the screams and curses behind her and scrambled up the Curtain. Her fingertips popped and bled, and her hoof-pads blistered and curled, but she kept climbing, certain now.

Above, they waited for her. Waiting to see whether she too could burst free of her bonds, whether she too could escape her prison and run loose on the hills of men. Bright, massive star-things bent low over the city, like children over an ant hill. Wilbur and the others whispered in her ear, urging her on. Escape was within her reach.

Behind her, the *Tind'losi* raged on, outpacing the spiders. They bled out of the right angles, trying to cut her off, to her back. But she was too close now, too fast. Eliza scrambled up onto the lip of the Curtain and extended her arms, reaching for the forces that watched. Garbled non-words sprang into her mind and from her lips, words she had been born to say. They flew like arrows into the maelstrom above, driven by the desperation of multitudes and a dozen lifetimes of instinct. The hounds fled, whimpering like whipped dogs as she called out the names of her fathers and her mothers and the sky suddenly roiled and bulged with *attention*. Vast faces, miles across and indescribable, peered at her with alien curiosity.

A gentle wind whipped her crinkly hair about her face and in her head the voices grew still as another voice, deep and sonorous like a giant's heartbeat overrode them. It spoke no language she recognized, but she exulted nonetheless in its familiarity. The wind picked up and then she was rising, her hooves leaving the uncomfortable solidity of the city.

And as Eliza rose, the last scrapes of her albino flesh melted away into the black between the stars.

# Footprints in the Snow

by June Violette

"Beyond the Mountains that Rend the Sky, there is a valley where no foot has tread since long before the nightmares walked in our midst. In this valley, there is a silent elfin wood where not even mice and chough break the stillness. Hidden in this wood, there is a temple that has lain quiet and forgotten for as long as our kind have dreamed. And in that temple there is a box – a plain wooden box, lacquered in black. And that box contains the oldest key, which opens the way to the very heart of the world."

I first saw her at the Morning Market. She sat cross-legged atop an old wooden crate between a blind man enthusiastically selling the Fruit That Brings Dreams of Remorse and the old brick road from the world that used to be, an old rifle in her lap and an intractable smile on her thin lips. She had an audience, though they were mostly children, crows and pigeons that picked the bones of the dead on the periphery of civilization.

She wasn't much older than her rapt disciples. She had the sort of face that might've been twelve years old or might've been less with the grime washed away. But there was so much more to her than her years – more to her than the child's body and gentle voice, more to her than the cut of her ragged clothes or the battered state of the Winchester that rested across her lap, more to her than the story of impossible places she told to the children around her.

She bore the same scars anyone her age might: the scars of violence and sacrifice. Her dark olive skin was caked in mud, filth, and engine grease, and marked with the tolls of the roads few living souls still dared to travel. She might have seemed entirely ordinary, like any other young outlander, but for her eyes, dark and bright and faraway, still shining with the glimmer of *hope* that no child ever keeps into her adulthood.

I first saw her at the Morning Market, and that was the moment I first believed.

By sunset, her crowd had gone, and the Morning Market with it. Darkness brought with it blood and terror. Already, I could hear the ululating shrieks of nightmares splitting the chill air, and the cries of the tormented who strayed too far from the roads and too late into the evening. I'd have hurried on to shelter and whatever meager safety it could offer me, but she caught my eye a second time, still sitting cross-legged atop her battered crate.

She sat in silence, polishing the barrel of her rifle with a dirty rag, as though she was oblivious to the danger closing in upon her with every passing moment.

"You are out late," she said, without looking up from her work.

"And so are you," I replied.

"I do not fear what waits in the darkness. Nor should any of us. The world was not always like this, rotted with fear and stalked by nightmares. It remains so because we allow it to. What have we to fear from nightmares?"

It was strange and unsettling, how she seemed unmoved by the predatory calls of the night's creatures punctuating her words.

"I've seen what those nightmares do to the ones they catch. It is well that we fear them, lest none of us survive them."

"They do only as we expect them to. You must not fear. It is fear that they feed upon, and it is fear that gives them power over us. I do not fear them. I mean to end them."

I couldn't help but smile. She was only a child, and I was growing increasingly certain she was mad. But I admired her earnestness and her courage. Though I'd lived a longer life than most, I'd rarely seen much of either.

"The nightmares are our gods, little one. How is it that one ends the gods?"

"Tehillim," she said, curtly.

"What?"

"My name is Tehillim. Not *little one*."

"Tehillim. You have my apologies."

"I will find the temple in the dead forest in the valley across the mountains. I will claim the key that opens the way to the heart of the world. And I will use it to open the way."

She believed it – every word she said. I was fascinated by her tale, strange though it seemed; I could not look away. I could not close my

127

ears.

"At the citadel in the heart of the world, I will ask an audience with the Painted Woman Who Sleeps Below, as our ancestors once did, countless generations past. I will ask her to allow hope into the world, as she did once before. And in payment I will offer to her the stories that my mother told me, that her mother told her, and her mother before that. I will not return from the citadel. So I share what I know with all who will listen. And when I've gone, perhaps, you will share *my* story."

Presently, she glanced up towards the sky, as calm as ever. "Look — it is dark. You should seek shelter."

The night had crept in quietly while we spoke. I nodded in silent assent and hurried on my way. Tehillim may not have felt cause to fear the darkness, but I had never strayed so far past the setting of the sun before. I knew as well as anyone what fate awaited me if the nightmares caught me before I reached the meager safety of my home.

Morning came, and with it came the somber accounting of the night's losses. The Morning Market was never calm, never subdued, always a jumbled bedlam of survivors and saints, madmen and mourners, the truest vestige of civilization that still breathed in the Hills Beneath the Mountains that Rend the Sky. Sometimes, the Market even saw visitors, caravansers and merchants from the south passing through to the east, or from the east passing through to the south.

Even so, every morning, we paid respect to those who did not return to the rattle and hum of the Market. The fruit-merchant was gone, and with him the bleak dreams that he sold all wrapped up in tart violet flesh. So, too, the ancient, ageless woman who distilled sweet red liquor from the roots of the Thorned Tree That Poisons the Mind. The places they had occupied a day before now held only folded squares of white cloth, a mark to remember where they had once stood: throughout the day, those close to the lost left offerings of pure water, locks of hair, conch shells.

Come tomorrow, their places would be filled again with new faces seeking to carve a life out of the Market.

The Morning Market was never calm, but still, I was surprised by the scene that unfolded before me. I laid out the wares I laid every day, beads of broken glass from before the Nightmares. Some clean, some dirty, some clear, some brilliantly colored. Simple tokens though they might have been, there was always a want for such reminders of *yesterday*. There was always a need for artifacts of the world before.

Across the old brick road, a stranger traded words with the fearless woman who wrested black-scaled fish from the river of gold. He had the look of a salt-trader, and the dark, wavy hair of a man from far to the south. I could not make out what they said, but I could see her refuse whatever it was he requested, and I saw the anger rising from his shoes.

He produced a long knife from somewhere I couldn't see, and was upon the fishmonger in the space of a heartbeat. I like to think I would've intervened, had it not happened so quickly. I like to think I'd have had the wits and the reflexes to save her. I know I never would have.

Tehillim did. Her voice rang out cold and clear in the winter air, and froze the salt-trader a hair's breadth from the fishmonger's heart. Indeed, the whole of the Market froze, the thrum of mercantile silent in the wake of her first word.

"Stop." Tehillim stood a half-dozen paces from the two, the weathered stock of the rifle settled comfortably against her shoulder. For a long moment, only the rustle of wind through the tattered hem of her faded raatuk broke the stillness.

"Your dispute is not worth your life, nor hers, nor mine. We are too few, and our comforts too scarce. The nightmares crave blood and sorrow. We must not give them what they want so easily."

I worried for her, in the interminably long seconds that followed. She was a child, and the salt-trader a man much larger than her, and he was fast. He might have closed the distance between them before she could even fire a shot. He might have hurled his knife, or wrestled her down, or broken her. He was a stranger, armed and angry, not raised with the laws of the Morning Market. Without a thought and without regret, he might have killed the strange young outlander with hope in her eyes.

Instead, he lowered his knife, then dropped it, then took a few hesitant steps back and away. Tehillim nodded to him, and lowered her rifle. The salt-trader spoke a few words of muted apology to the fishmonger, and as quickly as it had calmed, the Market rumbled to life again.

"I could not have shot him even if I wanted to." As she had the night before, she sat atop her old wooden crate, polishing the barrel of her rifle with a soiled rag. "I have no shells, and neither shot nor powder to fill them even if I had. It is not a weapon so much as a symbol. It is a reason for men to listen to me."

Unlike the prior night, I had sought her out as the Market died down for the evening and the sun began its descent. The roads still frightened me in the darkness, as they ever had and as they ever would, but the strange little girl with hope in her eyes intrigued me far more.

"How did you know he would stop?"

"I did not."

"What if he had attacked you?"

"I would most likely have died." Her answer caught me off-guard. It was earnest and strangely more grounded than anything I had heard her say before. "But he did stop, and he did not attack me. So why should I be concerned with what might have been?"

"You are very brave. Braver, I think, than anybody I have ever met. But if you are not careful, Tehillim, if you do not live, then who will journey to the Citadel at the Heart of the World, and who will trade your mother's stories for hope with the Painted Woman Who Sleeps Below?"

I realized then, for the first time, that I believed her stories, every word of them. And that I wanted to believe in her. I had not ever believed in something before, save for what I could see with my own eyes, touch with my own hands.

"If I do not live, there will be another – there is always another. Perhaps she will come in days, or years, or lifetimes, but she will come, as I have." Tehillim smiled at me, then. Her teeth were still a child's teeth, and two were missing, their replacements not yet grown in. "The valley I seek, it was once known as Sambhala. Many thousands of men, wise and foolish, ancient and young, passed into dust in search of this place, and none ever found it. I do not know that I will, either. There are, after all, many valleys hidden away within the Mountains that Rend the Sky. Most are alive, thriving and vibrant. And when darkness falls upon them, they are the domain of nightmares.

"Where I go, no living creature draws breath, and no nightmares have ever set foot. Where I go, there is only peace."

To hear her describe the valley again, there seemed a magic to it. I had never known a place where the nightmares did not venture. And had I been braver, I might even have asked to go with her. But I did not. Even then, I was old – and I was afraid. Even with the ululating howls of immortal horrors hanging heavy in the cold night air, there was comfort here, and familiarity.

So as I had the night before, I bid the strange girl called Tehillim a safe night, and I hurried home through the darkness. Although the piercing cries of the nightmares sang closer to me than they ever had before, they did not find me. They did not claim me.

When I slept, I dreamed uneasily, visited by an inhuman woman, painted red and gold, holding a painted box that held a painted key.

The morning was nearing its end when I finally arrived at the Market the next day. I had no mementos of the times before to sell, and even if I had, the ritual and rote of trading beauty for sustenance was far from my mind that day. Even had I wished to, I'd not have sold a bead; I arrived to chaos and commotion on the old brick thoroughfare.

The crowd was exuberant, torn between terror and excitement and uncertainty. I sought a better vantage, pushed and shouldered my way through other bodies until I could see what held everyone's attention so raptly, fearing what I might find when I did.

It was not what I had feared, but neither was it something I had ever hoped to see. A great black cat lay dead on the road. At first, I thought it simply a lowland hunter wandered too far into the hills. Too quickly, I realized it was not.

The beast had no fur; instead, it had a tarred, viscous skin that even now seemed to be bubbling away like boiling oil. Neither did it have the fangs of a wild beast – rather, its dead mouth was filled with thin, writhing tendrils that still wriggled like dying worms in a summer flood.

I had never seen a nightmare before. I had never expected to.

The din of the crowd rose to a roar as people sought answers, asked questions, laid blame. Some wept, certain that ruin would fall upon us, certain that the horrors would retaliate come nightfall. Some cheered, to see proof that the beasts that hunted us could die, just as we did. I had no answers.

So I searched for someone who did.

Tehillim was not at the wooden crate she'd made her home for the past two days. I searched the Market for her, oblivious to the folded white cloths that lay in mourning at a dozen or more places, but I searched in vain. She was not there, and neither were the children that had followed her so raptly whenever she spoke.

I knew where they had gone. I made my way to the northern pathway from the market, the one that wandered high into the sheer face of the mountains, where the snow never receded, even on the warmest days of summer. I saw their footprints in the snow, many sets of children's footprints, some with shoes, and some without. And I climbed.

I don't know how long I followed that ancient road before the chill and the thinness of the air began to slow me. Even then, I was old, and my body was not as strong as it had once been.

Behind me, the only world I had ever known still waited. I knew not how it would change, but I knew it would. I knew it *must*.

Before me, the strange girl with hope in her eyes, and the new world she promised. I wanted to follow her. I wanted, more than anything, to find her, and follow her to the valley where there is only peace. But I hadn't the strength, and I hadn't the breath, and I turned back.

I remember, now, that there were many sets of footprints on the trail when I left the Market. But at the foot of the Mountain, where I turned away, there were only three.

A barefoot child, taking hurried strides to keep pace with the others. An older child, with flat-bottomed shoes and a steady gait. And a great cat, trotting slowly at their side.

# *To the Letter*

by Jeffrey Fowler

Ben threw the bolt behind him, locking the door securely before turning to Lexy. "Shhh, baby, it will be okay. We're going to be fine. We just need to get to Aunt Trina's house. Then everything will be okay. So be strong for me baby, and we'll be just fine." He struggled to get the words out, keeping his tone light and reassuring even as everything within him sobbed in terror and regret. As he leaned back against the wall, hugging tightly to his four-year-old little girl, he wished once again that he'd listened to his friends and colleagues and never published the article that got them into this mess in the first place. Even in the midst of the panic, his mind drifted back to the last road trip he'd taken, though the emotions running through him then had been much different.

Though the reception had the slightest air of desperation, what with the occasion happening so soon after the government finally recovered and restructured from the horrors of the occupation event, there was still the air of joy and happiness that truly makes a wedding

136

memorable.

"So, Mrs. Paxwell," Ben said teasingly, "How does it feel to be off the market forever, bound to one man for as long as we both shall live?"

"In a word? Heavenly."

Her voice still sent shivers rushing through his body. They'd both done their best to keep their heads down, even as resistance fighters solicited money, food, and bodies to continue their guerilla fighting against the Mi'go. The cultists and sympathizers had done their own brand of recruiting as well, although it had far more to do with threats and outright stealing due to their heavy control of the government and military positions infiltrated in the years leading up to the actually invasion start. In an attempt to remind themselves, as well as their families and friends, that joy and happiness could still be found under the rule of the Mi'go, Ben had popped the question to his high school sweetheart Catherine. She'd said yes, even though the majority of what he brought to their marriage was a shiny certificate and a mountain of student loans.

They'd rushed through the planning, assembling in a fraction of the normal time, a wedding. It was as much a celebration of continued life as an event joining the two together. As the two of them drove up to a little cabin on the lake for their honeymoon, it seemed surreal. That a research doctor, and a school teacher could continue their lives together as normally as possible, when the planet had been conquered by an insect-like race of aliens and their cult of sympathizers and fanatics; it was almost unbelievable.

"It was nice of the hospital to give me an extra week before starting to have time for the honeymoon, especially since we did all that dancing around to make sure that we had the wedding during your school's break." Ben remarked, his hands on the wheel guiding them deeper along the winding forest road that would lead them to their cabin.

"Oh, don't remind me. I swear Principal Garrett almost had a coronary when he thought I was going to ask for time off. I think he was so relieved that we'd scheduled for break that he forgot I'd be missing those two days of Educator Instruction he'd scheduled." Catherine laughed, her voice was rueful with the knowledge that she'd have to make those days up if she wanted to retain her teaching certificate. She pushed the thought to the back of her mind and concentrated once more on the upcoming idyllic week they had planned together. As they drove she thought ahead on their life and plans for the future. They both wanted children, and Ben had been talking for days about the research he'd planned to start when they got back. With a small smile on her face, she whispered to herself. "Alexandra. For a girl, I think I'd like Alexandra for a name."

Ben shook his head, clearing the memory and once more concentrated on the present and all the tasks that needed to be accomplished before they could finally be safe. "Okay Lexy, it's time to go. Take my hand, we're going to be very quiet and get back in the truck, okay? You can watch your shows some more while Daddy drives." Although the little girl was obviously frightened, she struggled to restrain her tears. She delicately slid her hand into his for safekeeping. Then they quietly snuck out of the house and back to the beaten up F-150 that was their lifeline. His daughter watched cartoons on her tablet, and his wife prayed in the passenger seat. Ben drove deeper into the dark night towards the hope that lay half a state away.

Dr. Benjamin Paxwell popped the cork, sending champagne soaring like a fountain into the air. With a laugh, he filled the two glasses before handing one to his wife Catherine. "Cheers, love! With this paper finally published, I should be a shoo-in for that promotion at the hospital. I know things have been rough lately, but those times should be over." He smiled at his wife, trying to use his own cheerfulness to wipe the worry from her eyes. Ever since Alexandra had been born, they'd been struggling to hold things together. Under the Mi'go, everyone worked unless at least one parent qualified for an exemption. Once they'd found out Catherine was pregnant, Ben sought out a promotion as chief researcher at the hospital in hopes of affording Catherine the chance to stay home with Lexy.

"What James and I have worked on could very well lead to a cure for Alzheimer's. Just think of it, love, no more worries about tissue degradation in the brain. People will no longer have to worry about some disease stealing away the very things that make us alive; our thoughts and memories!" Ben's excitement was contagious, and Catherine found herself smiling as well, though she couldn't completely mask her fear. While Ben had only thought about the impact of his research in the terms of allowing Cat to stay home with Lexy, something she'd dreamed of doing since getting pregnant, her thoughts had meandered elsewhere. She found herself considering the other possibilities that may come from having her husband make a brilliant discovery in a world dominated by the Mi'go and their ever-present quest of hoarding knowledge and discovery. Her lack of response drew his attention. "Don't you see? This is an opportunity for our family to live out our dreams, and maybe even add..." The sound of glass crashing against the floor broke Ben from his speech as he realized for the first time that his wife's attention was no longer directed at him. Instead, she was looking at the door of their small two bedroom home. The delicate glass she once held between her fingers lay on the floor, shards glittering like diamonds in the pool of spilled champagne. With dawning horror he turned around, his eyes immediately fixed on the crimson envelope innocuously slid beneath the door. Mechanically he moved toward it, his eyes glued to it with a finality that bespoke its message: the end of his life as he knew it.

There was no misunderstanding its significance. No one could live under the occupation of the Mi'go and not hear about the crimson letters and their contents. Even as he grasped it from the floor and began to tear it open, accompanied by the wracking sobs of his wife who still hadn't moved from where she stood, the thought wandered through his head: blood red is an appropriate color for a death sentence.

"Dr. Benjamin Paxwell, you have been selected to receive the Mi'go granted gift of Immortality. Your recent work in the field of medicine, specifically the strides you have made in the prevention of degenerative brain diseases, has been judged to be of significant enough merit to warrant the preservation of your mind. It is with our greatest congratulations that we inform you of this honor. You officially have forty-eight hours from the date of posting to put any outstanding affairs in order that require a physical body, and thereafter report immediately to the nearest Immortalization Center with this letter to begin the harvesting process." He continued to read woodenly, emotionlessly reciting the words on the page even as his heart screamed in passionate denial.

"As you are registered as married to one Catherine Paxwell, she shall receive your severance package along with her certificate to allow her to legally remarry if she so desires. This package includes the generally established scholarship of education to be redeemed by your dependent Alexandra Paxwell upon her successful completion of the basic education program mandated for all who fall within allowable IQ range. Failure to respond is grounds for warrants for treason against the Mi'go to be issued against you, your spouse, and your dependents. Agents assigned to the execution of these warrants will be informed that you are to be taken without damage to the brain, but such restrictions apply only to yourself as the one chosen for Immortality."

Ben took a deep breath, closing his eyes for a moment against the pain. After that moment he reached his desk, grabbing a pad of paper and pen to write as he spoke. "Cat. Here are the passwords for the bank sites. The safety deposit box key is still taped behind that picture of you and Lexy. I'll ask Jim from next door to come over and check in on you both often." He continued frantically scribbling, his mouth moving but his eyes avoiding the growing horror in his wife's eyes as the reality of what was actually happening began to sink in. "I think you should sell my car. My insurance should pay for the house of course, and you won't need both cars. Should give you a little extra cash." He trailed off, finally looking up to see his wife violently shaking her head and with her arms wrapped around her torso in denial. He dropped the pen, moving to take her in his arms as he whispered nonsense sounds to give her any small measure of reassurance.

"Cat. Catherine. Sweetheart, we don't have any choice. Yes, this is terrible, but at least you and Lexy will be okay. I wish it didn't have to be this way, but maybe they'll still give me communication rights. I'll be able to call and check in on you both. That is if you want me to. A clean break might be better." His own voice choked on the last words, the despair of never being able to see or hear from his wife or daughter again almost breaking his resolve right there.

"Ben! Ben stop, you don't understand." Catherine finally managed to break in on his monologue, the grief still very apparent in her voice. "I was going to tell you tonight, right before…." She stopped to sob again as Ben held her closer.

"What is it Cat?"

"Ben, I'm. I'm pregnant again. I'm… We're going to have another baby."

The shock was almost audible in the room. Ben's arms reflexively clenched around his wife, his joy violently clashing with the horror of the moment. Another child. A son or daughter that he would never hold in his arms or kiss gently in love and benediction. Where moments before his only thoughts had been on the inevitable harvest, now fear caused rebellion to bloom. Thoughts spun madly in his mind, his own safety a distant thought when compared to ensuring the survival and well-being of his daughter and his wife who was carrying their unborn child.

"Listen to me, Cat." He shook her gently, bringing her focus back to him, instead of on the fear she was feeling. "We have to run. That's our only choice. The minute we try we are marked for death, so we can't make any mistakes. We have to get to my sister Trina. She knows some people who have been living off the grid, and should be able to help us get to them. Pack small things, things we can't do without. Tomorrow night, we'll wake Alexandra and put her in the car. She doesn't need to know why yet. We can tell her what's happening when we get to safety. We'll just tell her we're going to visit Aunt Trina." His mind spun with plans considered and rejected. His talented mind, previously put to research and science now raced along a rhythm of escape.

"We're going to have to stop soon, love. If we fill up, we should make it the rest of the way. Once we talk to Trina, we'll know where

we can go to hide. Start over, far from the Mi'go and their harvests."
Ben knew he was trying to convince himself but still he said the words.
The worry and fear was almost tangible inside the cab of the truck.
Blissfully ignorant of the danger, Alexandra lay sleeping in the back
seat her using her arm for a pillow. His mind continued to whirl
through possible plans, categorizing each scenario and trying to find
solutions. Escape, medical attention, and long-term safety. Every
moment, the seconds became more and more vital, but never as
important as escaping those hunting them already.

The truck stop was all but deserted, which suited them. They'd
finally had to stop to refuel, but this would be the last time before they
reached Trina's home. From there, they'd learn the route to take and
flee deep into the wilder places, where people could hide from the
insectoid aliens known as the Mi'go and their Harvest. Catherine had
used the restroom while Lexy continued to doze in the car. The
slamming of the truck door drowned out the sound of the shot, but it
could not disguise the shattering window glass. They hadn't shot to
kill. The sadistic bastards hunting them counted on a husband's desire
to save his wife to make him stop and find medical attention for her. It
would have worked, had Catherine not choked back the scream of pain
to yell for her husband to go. While she clutched her bleeding shoulder
and sobbed in agony, Ben violently pressed the pedal to the floor. The
tires screeched against the asphalt to the accompaniment of more
shots as the bounty hunter that had tracked them this far realized they
had no intention of stopping.

"Lexy, it will be okay. I promise. Mommy got hurt, but we'll fix it.

Everything is going to be fine. Why don't you get your tablet and watch some shows or play a game. We'll be there soon." Ben hoped she couldn't hear the lies in his voice, but it was all he had to give her. Despair had overgrown hope and fear was not far behind.

"Cat, put pressure on it. Hold tight. I know it hurts love, but we can't stop or he'll catch us."

"I know, just drive. I'll hold on." She tried to smile at her husband, but even she knew it was more a grimace than a comfort. She lied to him anyway, having spent enough time as the wife of a doctor to know that the bullet had passed through her shoulder, and the amount of blood leaking from it even still sentenced her to death, even if they headed straight to the nearest hospital.

Cat died less than ten minutes later. The blood loss eased her from consciousness into a sleep that turned final moments after. Ben had lied again, telling little Alexandra that Mommy was sleeping, while inside he could barely cope from mourning the loss of his wife and unborn child. Her death brought the reality home. There was no escape from the Mi'go and those who willing served their cause. It was up to him to protect his family, not place them in danger. If he continued on, it only ensured the death of his only remaining child and his sister. Reaching past the cooling corpse of his wife, he removed the gun he'd bought before the occupation for safety, and placed it on his lap as he pulled off to the side of the road.

The truck glided into the truck stop on fumes. Lexy had fallen into an exhausted sleep, which had given Ben enough time to get Cat out of the truck and wrapped into a blanket. He'd laid her in the bed of the pick-up and said his goodbye's before he leaned against the door, waiting for their arrival. As the first SUV pulled to a stop, he raised the gun to his own head and presented them with the only threat he had left before making his demands.

"You'll see my wife has a proper burial. I have a sister Katrina; she is spared. I want Alexandra to be with her family. She gets to talk to me whenever she asks. Do this, and I'll come in peace. Otherwise I'll blow my own brains out here and now."

It didn't take the bounty hunters long to make the decision. They knew the Mi'go would consider it a small price to pay. After agreeing on record, and after copies of the agreement were sent to his sister and a couple colleagues to ensure compliance, Ben gave himself up.

With the sensors and communication devices connected, it was another form of torture. Endless time to think and realize the imprisonment that would last for eternity. You could still interact with what they gave you, but beyond that you could only think, which is what they wanted you to do. Always be thinking on what they gave you and give them the answers when they made their check-ups. To fulfill his wishes, they'd given him sight and sound. The only thing he could see were the charts and papers they laid before his sensors and the small pink tube. It'd been there for a few hours before they came and hooked the sensors. That's when Ben learned true despair, as he realized his daughter too had been harvested, while the damned Mi'go had kept to the letter of his demands.

"Daddy? I can hear you, but why can't I see you?" the voice was robbed of Alexandra's lyrical tones by the mechanical speakers.

Even when you exist without a body, it's possible to cry.

# The Balm of Sperrgebiet is the Krokodil

by Steve Berman

*"Some of the evil of my tale may have been inherent in our circumstances. For years we lived anyhow with one another in the naked desert, under the indifferent heaven."*

—T.E. Lawrence

We had survived so long in the abandoned buildings of Kolmanskop because this was a forlorn desert, made so with constant gales carrying fog and grit. A paradox of nature sheltered five of us while the world beyond the Namib went mad.

Sand covered all things. The sand of the Namib retained the bite of gravel while never abandoning its mercurial nature. It forced open every door – every structure in stately Kolmanskop welcomed the desert. This had once been a mining town of German settlers where the wind revealed and hid the shells of humanity. I have walked through a ballroom without chandeliers, a doomed ice factory, and the remains of a hospital. I discovered the tracks I made the prior day gone, erased by the wind, which scratched plaster and color from walls erected more than a hundred years ago when diamonds had been discovered.

I read once that nowhere else on this Earth is wind this constant. It stole words from mouths and ears. It threatened to blind. We had to cover any water, any meals, or else the sand covered them like an inedible spice. I always had the taste of the desert in my mouth, a sensation not so much unpleasant – one became inured to any flavor, however first repellant, after a thousand swallows – but the texture was an irritant; the grit wore down my teeth, my palate, so that anything I chewed became bland. The desert weathered my face, my hands, and any exposed skin. Wrists and necklines were chafed 'til bloody, became scarred over, then debrided, in a perpetual cycle of scarring. We all stank, changed clothing only when needed, and became familiar with the odors of the others when downwind. I have not had a shower in nearly two years and my body's topography is no longer the same. Hygiene mattered only if it jeopardized our meager food and drink stores.

When the Internet died – and I still cannot comprehend how anything so rampant, so rife, could die... any more than imagining every bird across the globe becoming mute forever – and smart phones became lobotomized paper weights that would no longer even indicate time or date, I had thought some terrible war had happened. Blinding and deafening Africa south of the Sahara had been collateral damage.

*Torschlusspanik* made me decide that my life as a logistics clerk for African Development Bank in Windhoek was over.

I looted books from the public library. I walked in and took what I wanted. No one stopped me. Soldiers watched me with disinterest from the nearby Alte Feste, a monument to the colonial era pressed into service as a shelter.

South I went on roads that would lead me home. As an Afrikaner, a prodigal son of Bloemfontein and a coward. But the car quickly ran out of gas and I had to set out on foot. Trudging along worn asphalt roads, I could not avoid the other refugees. Some travelled in the same direction, some left South Africa. I heard that the City of Roses had fallen to some biological weapon that left buildings full of gall rot and molds. My parents were Calvinists and sure in their predestination, so I didn't mourn them. I turned back instead.

I entered the Namib Desert because of two German men and their dog. As a young man I read and reread Henno Martin's *Wenn es Krieg gibt, gehen wir in die Wüste.* My male peers preferred football, the females an undistinguished *plaasroman.* I knew that one could survive the desert, what could be eaten, and how to find refuge. I began my journey through Sperrgebiet National Park, the Forbidden Territory, believing it would be uninhabited. My fears of contamination left me, taken by the strong winds.

Others, though, had similar ideas. We arrived from different directions and lives. We met at Kolmanskop and stood and stared. Impasse or concession? Cook is Ovambo, a lapsed Lutheran, and brought a goat-drawn kitchen of pots, utensils, even bags of millet. His younger brother, Toivo, wore a corporal's uniform, shouldered a rifle, and squinted often. A White Namibian, Ludwigsone, claimed to be a journalist of late who had been covering prejudice at local hospitals.

He had stolen first aid supplies, including a great deal of codeine.

We made a pact. We suspected others would come: tribesmen, urban refugees. We admitted that any of us may not last long, that isolation might become an unmanageable burden. We looked long at the cleaver, the rifle, and the needles in Ludwigsone's bag. I shared the story of an older brother who had been an addict. I saw no need to tell them the truth. Enough years had passed that my perception of brother and lover had no depth.

And so Cook brewed krokodil. We stored it under the sand, above the floorboards of several buildings.

That was, by my estimate, fifteen months ago. I found purpose through everyday chores. With purpose came contentment. At night, I read. I hoped to memorize all of *Seven Pillars of Wisdom* and *Selbstbehauptung des Rechtsstaates* before I died. Both books were dear to me as apologetics for the role of strife in the world.

The fog flowed inland from the coast and brought us water, condensed on plastic tarps stretched taught like sails. Our diet, the occasional lizard, but mostly insects, beetles, and the termites that we found beneath the beautiful and short-lived fairy rings made in the coarse sand, left us with loose teeth and clothes. A treat was goat milk and porridge. We did not hunt game for fear of wasting bullets or wandering too far from Kolmanskop.

At dawn, Ludwigsone spotted four figures stumbling through the fog. The wind on occasion revealed the old rail line that led to Kolmanskop; they must have followed the cracked ties and burnished steel.

As we readied ourselves, I watched Cook use a handkerchief to cover fresh abscesses on his little brother's upper arm. Toivo would be abandoning us soon, though we may need to amputatee first.

We called out to the trespassers – that was what we named any who came upon us – in Oshiwambo, in Afrikaans, in good German, and in poor English. I waved to bring them closer. They carried nothing. I guessed them Bantu or the like. Their clothes were ragged; they had traveled farther than any of us. Two swayed from hefty stomachs – one man fat, one woman clearly pregnant – and were lead, hand-in-hand, by a pair so lean that the foursome's stagger up and down the dunes bordered on the comical.

The wind brought back their cries. A scattering of English amid other words that none of us understood.

Salt covered their lips. Why they had not licked the crystals loose I could not guess. Perhaps that would draw fresh blood.

Experience had taught us to keep our gestures and words welcoming. We guided them towards two particular buildings: I lightly pressed a hand on the woman's back and motioned to the left, while the others suggested that the men stay to the right. The gaunt man leading the woman did not want her to part ways. Cook and Toivo smiled and broke the man's grip on her hand and gestured again for the trespassers to separate. We offered them water. They saw Cook's cleave and Toivo's rifle. They had no choice.

I swept grit off the building's only furnishings, a single chair and table. I told her to rest and I would bring water.

I took a moment to look in at the others, to make sure that

nothing amiss had happened. I had worried that the heavy set trespasser might be difficult to handle, but now I saw how ill he was, bloated and hampered by his round stomach rather than possessing a bullish girth. The makeshift tray I brought had a jug of water, a chipped mug, and a capped syringe. The last I moved to my back pocket. We had seven thin syringes but lacked the bleach to clean them. None of us were really clean, inside or out.

"You traveled far," I said to her as I set the tray down.

She nodded. Her eyes watched me pour. Once you have been in the desert, you can never look away from running water. It became a living thing that seduced your every sense. The sight of it, the sound, you would hallucinate the taste, the smell, the sensation of it flowing down your throat.

"Why did you come to the Forgotten Territory?" I held the mug.

She mumbled. No food for days can lobotomize a person. I finally understood she was saying, "We are missionaries."

She wore no cross. Nearly all of Namibia was Christian and the desert beetle had no ear for Jesus' teachings.

I asked, "Is your heart full, drawn out in prayer unto Him continually for your welfare?" I had heard the Mormons say such nonsense.

She nodded. "I am full. Dof'mru has filled me." Her hands parted her tattered clothes to show the bare, distended skin of her abdomen. More bloody lines of salt whorled around her navel.

Was Dof'mru one of her companions? Perhaps it was some Bantu name.

153

"Do you know Ahtu?" I had to ask her twice before she shook her head. I handed her the mug.

We, the gestalt, had agreed to no women at Kolmanskop. We worried they would bring jealousy and discord between us. I had as much use for a woman as my icon Lawrence. I had guessed that the others were suspicions of my tastes and were thankful that I always volunteered to suffer the female trespassers.

I walked behind her as she drank. Thirst had caused the veins in her bared neck to rise to the surface. I did not hesitate – I had never before hesitated whenever I was needed to plunge the hypodermic.

She cried out, but the krokodil worked fast. Faster and more potent than morphine. Her limbs twitched, giving the illusion of a struggle, but it was really easy to lower her body to the sand.

As I went to work – stuffing a dirty rag into her mouth, which caused her caked lips to bleed; shutting her jaw and pinching her nose shut – I distracted myself with reciting a favorite passage from *Der Vater eines Mörders*: *"Mit seinen braunen, festen Händen hatte er auch zog einmal die Brücke auf Franz 'Instrument um einen Bruchteil eines Millimeters, so dass für eine Weile die Geige war schöner als zuvor klang."* German was an unrivalled language. I wished I could have seen the Rhineland, but I doubted what I would find now would be anything like I wanted it to be.

The very first time I had to dispatch a refugee, I fumbled around until I broke her neck. Nearly pulled a muscle in my back. Suffocation was simpler, though more time-consuming.

I felt a spasm travel through her body. Unexpected, unwarranted. I looked to her face. Her eyes were still, glazed, I am sure they remained unseeing. But her belly and chest roiled. Despite my grip on her mouth, her jaws were being forced open. A tip of a tongue pushed aside the rag.

A tongue colored not pink but a shade of red so deep as to first appear black until it met the air. It slipped farther and farther past her slack jaws. My own mouth must have hung open in shock. It was no tongue.

Sand slid through my fingers, flew up as my boots kicked, and I retreated a few feet to watch the segmented body escaped the dead woman. Her bloated stomach collapsed. The thing, which was larger than my entire arm, resembled a caterpillar in shape, except it had no tiny legs in the fore, no eyes of any kind, just a lamprey mouth to indicate the head. The rear did have the false feet of butterfly larvae. Above a gaping anus, two branches that ended in something akin to pipe organs wheezed.

That awful sound broke the stupor brought on by shock. I struck the thing first with the water jug, then smashed the mug and stabbed at it with the largest shard. Its blood burned my skin; the pain was not from heat, but the bite of salt poured on an open wound.

I didn't stop until I had nearly torn it in half. Both my hands and forearms would need to be bandaged. Lost to anger, I kicked the dead trespasser, the thing's host, before running off to warn the others.

The other three trespassers had been drugged and chained to a wall for interrogation. Ludwigsone slapped the gaunt one and asked about Ahtu, an unfamiliar name several who had wandered across

Kolmanskop uttered like a mantra — we had once thought it might be a warlord or a new disease like Ebola, but were still unsure.

I told them about the woman and the parasite. We began to pass words of concern between us while staring at the fat man's belly.

"They said they came to preach from Natron, which is a lake. I think in Tanzania," Ludwigsone said. "It was so alkaline people think it petrifies animals, but it just coats them with salt. And it's blood red from small organisms that live in the lake—"

I grimaced. "This was not small!"

He shrugged. "I don't know what you saw. I don't like the sound of it, but the lake's a fuckin' flamingo preserve."

Cook ripped the shirt from the fat man, whose head rolled, his mouth so dry that it hung open without any spittle dripping down to the sand. We could see the skin of his stomach filthy with raw and ruddy patches of salt.

"That ain't good," said Cook. "Ain't right, and I ain't having it here."

Toivo shrugged. "Then we kill."

We were all in agreement. Then the others saw what slithered out of the fat man. Cook swore. Ludwigsone wiped his glasses clean. Toivo took a syringe of the krokodil and walked away.

We would never consume the bodies of trespassers. We were afraid of contamination. But we did drag the corpses to a site and let winds carry the scent to scavengers, like we did with our feces. When you are hungry, what does it matter if you eat a jackal or a dung beetle washed clean?

But none of the scavengers went near the bodies. The must have known it was tainted meat.

Ludwigsone began bothering the rest of us with questions, new ones, about what might have happened to Africa, to the world. He muttered "Ahtu" to himself like a trespasser might. I have also heard him speak of Dof'mru but do not remember telling him anything that the woman spoke.

The trespassers have tainted Kolmanskop.

Cook told me that Ludwigsone had asked if they could travel north together, to the edge of the desert, that answers were needed. He did not ask me because I am White also; he needed someone dark-skinned to accompany him so he could convince folk he was born in Namibia and not a foreigner. Cook had refused. He would not abandon his brother, not while he still breathed.

Of course, Ludwigsone might quicken Toivo's parting with more krokodil. *Torschlusspanik* made men do awful things. Cook was smart and warned Toivo not to tell Ludwigsone where he was sleeping off the drug. But he did tell me.

We held the funeral the following morning. Cook recited what little of the Bible he knew. Ludwigsone remained quiet. I read Lawrence's dedication from his opus, but I could not bring myself to say aloud the line "And the blind / Worms grew fat upon / Your substance" because the memory of the parasite haunted each of us.

I expected the next evening would find me all alone in Kolmanskop. The others wouldn't return from their quest with answers. I did not want to know what they might find. Rather, I would busy myself with the chores life demanded: harvesting the water, gathering the food, and reading until the pages fall from the books. I might tire and take the needle myself before more trespassers find me. I am Afrikaans and have become cruel, but I am like no monster I have ever seen.

# Of the Fittest

by Evan Dicken

There was no one waiting to welcome us home when we stepped from the portal. I wasn't surprised; the Unspeakable One wasn't big on calling ahead. New Brighton looked about the same. More of the McNaughton Avenue businesses were boarded up, but there were a few cars outside Pike's Market, and the front window of Ready Hardware still glittered with strings of Christmas lights. In the distance, smoke from the munitions factory stained the horizon a dusty gray. There were Yellow Signs scrawled across doors and brick facades, but they didn't grate on me the way they used to. It's surprising what people can learn to accept when they've got no choice.

Although none of the Yellow Guard shifted from parade rest, the relief was palpable. The Unspeakable One demands five years from his conscripts, but he doesn't necessarily stipulate *where* they'll serve. We'd all heard stories of soldiers losing decades, even centuries, to tours in the Dreamlands. Fortunately, most of our fighting had been along what used to be the New England Coast, and while thinking of what crawled from the night dark waters of the Atlantic still gave me sweats, at least a day was a day out there.

We'd had it better than most, actually. Hastur disliked humanity, but he *hated* the other Great Old Ones, and hate was something we could work with. It had been bad at first, trying to resist the inevitable, but if you can say one thing about humans, it's that we're survivors. Somehow, we'd found a toehold amidst the alien geography of the Old Ones' enmity. They might be immortal, but their servants weren't – deep ones, dholes, star spawn, even shoggoths died once you sunk enough ordnance into them. Once we'd proven humanity was more useful alive then dead, the rest was just details.

A rattling gasp from front and center broke me from my ruminations and snapped the company to attention. Our tour was technically over, but hard experience had taught us to obey the Lieutenant in all things.

Five years ago, he'd been Curt Brykalski, nervous and soft-spoken, part of the yearbook committee. I hadn't known him well enough to guess why he ran from the Byakhee. It might have been lingering nationalism or maybe a misplaced conscience, but my best guess was plain, old cowardice. In any case, The King made an example of him, which was fine by me. There's no room for cowards in the Yellow Guard.

Like most of Hastur's servants, the Lieutenant affected a ratty mustard-colored robe, frayed along the hems and splattered with dirt and blood. What little flesh was visible looked like it'd been skinned and left to dry over the winter – all but the eyes, which rolled in their sockets, horrified and pleading.

"Sergeant Long." The Lieutenant spoke in an agonized scream, as if each word were a razor drawn across his flesh.

I made the mistake of meeting his gaze. His eyes went wide in wordless entreaty, begging for release even as a smile stretched his cracked and bleeding lips.

"We release you from service."

I don't know what I expected – fireworks, euphoria, even a sense of relief. There was none of that. If anything, I felt more on edge.

I turned back to the company, seeing my apprehension reflected by the few score of us who'd survived the tour of duty.

"Well, you—" My voice broke like a teenager's. I cleared my throat and continued in a hoarse rasp. "You heard the Lieutenant."

For over a minute, no one moved. Finally Jeffries, a corporal from second squad, took off running. She headed away from town, to the woods, stripping off her uniform as she went. I caught a flash of her naked back, fish belly white against the forest shadows; then she was gone.

Soldiers began drifting off in ones and twos, following Jeffries into the trees. Soon, uniforms littered the clearing like cast off snakeskins.

The forest pulled at my gaze. Leaves hissed in the warm summer breeze, whispers rising like an ocean tide to swamp the furious buzz of my thoughts. It was mid-afternoon, but somehow I could see the stars. The others waited for me beneath the spreading boughs – free to run, to etch sacred signs into our flesh as we writhed together in howling ecstasy.

We'd given Hastur our service when all he really wanted was our love.

I took a step towards the woods, fumbling at the buttons of my shirt, but a hand settled on my shoulder. Twisted, arthritic fingers clutched at my epaulets, holding me back.

"Not yet." The Lieutenant made a wet choking noise. He nodded towards New Brighton, but his eyes screamed at me to *run*.

Realization parted the sea of madness that flooded my thoughts. I had a wife, a baby – what the hell had I almost done? I clasped my hands to stop them from shaking.

Alone, I made my way down McNaughton, past hollow buildings and empty storefronts, resplendent echoes of rust belt finery. A woman stepped out onto the street. I smiled. She went back inside.

The madness was finally over.

I'd come home.

Shelly was cooking when I crept into the kitchen, knife in hand. I'd thought about knocking, but pounding on the door to my own home didn't seem right. My wife had set out a feast – spray cheese with little butter crackers, deviled eggs, pickles, salami, and a few cloudy glass bottles of the local corn whiskey.

"Hey, Punch." I said, soft as I could. It was my pet name for her, a reference to our senior prom where she'd gotten drunk on spiked cranberry cocktail and picked a fight with Pamela Jeffries over who would give the graduation speech.

She turned, slow and jerky like the second hand of a clock.

"I brought you something." I raised the knife, turning it to let the light play off the jewels set into its handle and crossbar. I'd snatched it from a ziggurat we'd stormed just south of Innsmouth. It had been rough, seeing what the Deep Ones had done to those women – made me grateful Hastur spent all his time in Carcosa.

"Am I dreaming?" She asked.

I shook my head.

"Are you?"

I didn't have an answer for that, so I just reversed the knife and held it out to her. She took it, her expression unreadable. I stepped forward, arms wide, but stopped as the blade pricked my chest.

"Sorry. It's very nice." She regarded the knife for a moment, then turned to slip it into a drawer before hugging me back.

I breathed in the fruity, slightly spicy smell of her hair, then turned my head for a kiss.

Shelly drew back, gripping my arms as if I might drift away.

I glanced at the food, embarrassed by the focused intensity in her eyes. "Looks delicious, how'd you know I was coming?"

She gave a little flick of her head. "I—"

"Uncle Brian!" Ronny came pelting into the kitchen, then skidded to a halt as I turned. When I'd left New Brighton, he'd been little more than bundle of blankets, red-faced and hungry. Somehow, the years had transformed him from a shitting, squalling animal into something approaching human. That, more than anything, hammered home how long I'd been away.

Ronny edged around me to hide behind Shelly.

"It's your daddy." She tried to push him toward me, but he clung to her leg, making nervous panting noises that prickled the hair on my arms.

"Who's Uncle Brian?" I tried for a casual tone, but the question came out menacing. It was every soldier's nightmare, well, one of them coming home to find your spouse or lover with someone else.

"Brian Klosowski." Shelly said with a wry tilt of her head. "And it's not what you think."

"How do you know what I think?" I knew Brian. He'd been three years ahead of me in school, graduated just ahead of Armageddon and went off to Ohio State to study German – one of the many majors that became irrelevant when one or another of the Old Ones had scraped Europe off the face of the Earth in a fit of pique. Brian and Shelly had been on the cheerleading squad, and I'd been pretty sure that they both had a thing for me, which was flattering as hell.

"He and a couple other friends are coming," Shelly said. "I – we didn't know you were back, but it's good you're here. This involves all of us."

"What do you mean?"

"C'mon, I'll fix you both a plate." She pulled out a chair and set Ronny down on it. "Daddy missed you."

My son fidgeted as I sat down next to him. I fished around in my rucksack and laid out a dozen or so figurines.

"They're soldiers, like daddy." Carved from bone and inlaid with obsidian and pearl, they were from a chess set I'd found during the siege of Boston. Half the pieces had been missing, and the board burnt and bloodstained, but Ronny didn't need to know that.

"Have they killed anyone?" He picked up a pawn, holding it with both hands, fingers interlaced almost like he was praying.

"They're just toys, Ronny."

"Have you killed anyone?"

"Those will look nice in your Lego castle." Shelly set a plate in front of me and handed Ronny a cracker with some salami. "Why don't you go upstairs and see?"

There was a knock at the door. I was thankful for that – I don't know what I would've done if Brian had just walked in.

"Uncle Brian!" Ronny went running.

"He'll warm up to you." Shelly rested her hand on my back. It was all I could do not to cringe at the unexpected touch.

Brian scooped Ronny up, smiling as he slipped a piece of hard candy into my son's hand.

Candy, damn, I should've thought of that. With most of what had been the Southern U.S. under water, sugar was hard to come by.

Brian stepped into the kitchen, leaning down to give Shelly a quick peck on the cheek with an ease I couldn't help but envy. The other guests who arrived were more furtive, closing blinds and checking windows.

I'd known them all a lifetime ago – Deacon Lasko, who I'd shared my first cigarette with crouched behind the dumpster out back of Pike's; Beth Antonelli, who'd broken her leg when she tried to jump her bike across Raccoon Creek and spent half of fifth grade in a cast; Rosa and Carlos Martinez from the soccer team, Jackson, Hawser, Lee. I could see them all, like my memory had been filmy glass, now wiped clean.

Brian turned as I pushed back from the table.

"Holy shit." He glanced at Ronny, blushed, then set the boy down. "Sorry, Shelly."

"S'okay." She smiled, taking Ronny from him.

He was across the kitchen in two steps, arms wrapped around me. "You made it, Long, you fucking *made* it."

Then they were all around, laughing as they pawed at my shoulders and hands. It took a while to fight clear of the press. The next few hours filled up with corn whiskey and reminiscences. Brian told the story of how we'd smuggled a baby goat into Rosa Martinez's piano recital, which meant Rosa had to tell the story of how she and Beth had lured us into skinny dipping in Raccoon Creek then stolen our clothes. After Ronny went to bed, we worked our way through the rest of the whiskey, the familiar rhythms of shared lives obscuring the strange distance the years had set between us. Shelly slipped her arm around my waist. I'd had quite a few drinks by then, so it was nice to hold her close.

For a moment, it was like I'd never left, but only for a moment.

"Is Pam back, too?" Brian asked after we'd laughed about Shelly and Pamela's drunken prom brawl.

"No," I swallowed at the thought of the forest, almost able to feel the caress of branches on my face. "I mean, not really."

Brian's smile slipped. "And the others?"

"Just me."

"Damn. What about Brykalski?"

It took me a second to realize he was talking about the Lieutenant.

"He's here. Why?" I looked around the table at expressions gone guarded and wary.

"Can we trust you?" Beth Antonelli leaned across the table. Her cheeks had that flushed look she got when she was more than a little drunk.

"C'mon, it's *Long*." Brian slapped me on the shoulder. "He's got as much reason to hate the Old Ones as we do."

They watched me.

"I hate them." And in that moment, I did.

It might have been the raw anger in my voice, it might have been that they wanted so badly to believe, or it might have been the three bottles of hard liquor, but my pronouncement seemed to cut the tension in the air.

"We were going to hit the factory," Shelly said, her voice barely above a whisper. "But Brykalski is better."

"He's an emissary, you see." Brian spread his hands, grown expansive in drunkenness. "The King in Yellow, writ small. The Unspeakable One can't come to our world, yet. It still works through avatars."

"Whatever you're planning, it won't work." I said. "You haven't seen—"

"But it already *has*," Brian said. "The Toledo Militia grabbed an emissary three months ago. They were able to banish the thing, hurt Hast—"

"Don't say its name," I said, fear cutting through the warm buzz of the whiskey.

"We're not alone," Shelly said. "Remnants of the old U.S. Army went north of the border. They've fortified Toronto and are looking to strike back."

I frowned. We'd all heard the rumors, but that's all they were. If there'd been any resistance left, The King would've turned out the Yellow Guard to grind them to dust.

"It's true." Brian refilled my glass. "I've been talking to them. They can get us out, but we need to prove we can be trusted."

"You'll be killed, or worse." The room was too hot. I pulled at my collar, the liquor making my head swim.

"We're *already* being killed," Shelly said.

"Death by inches," Brian added. "They call it conscription, but taking ten percent of us every five years – Long, they're *decimating* us."

I wiped a sweaty hand across my forehead. Decimating – trust Brian to whip out ten-cent words to make his point.

"The King made a slave of you, of all of us," Beth said.

"The Byakhee will be here soon," Brian said. "We need your help."

I glanced to Shelly for support, but she was watching Brian, they all were.

"I need time to think."

"We've got a day, maybe," Brian said, hand on my shoulder. "I'm sorry, Long, I really am, but this is the only way clear of this mess."

It felt like a dream. My friends and family – would-be rebels with no idea what they were up against. I could see there was no stopping them, not that I would've tried.

"A day, then." It was less than I'd hoped for, but it would have to be enough. There were nods around the table, some hopeful, some skeptical, but no one disagreed. Just like me, just like everyone, they had no choice.

Wind stirred the meadow below Parson's hill, breakers of shadow rippling the tall grass into symbols of imminent doom. I helped Shelly spread a ratty checkered blanket by the crabapple tree where we'd shared our first kiss. Remembering the night made me smile – the smell of her hair, not quite knowing where to put my hands. Necking beneath the tree had been something of a rite of passage for New Brighton teens, and its scabby bark was etched with a tapestry of awkward declarations of love.

Strange, how long I'd looked forward to coming home, but after one night, the walls had already started to crowd around me. I'd tried to go for a walk, but the forest kept whispering. Thankfully, the apple tree was quiet.

I set the picnic basket down to search the tangle of scars for where I'd carved an equation of Shelly and my names. Something had left long claw marks on the trunk, abrading scores of lopsided hearts and ragged "4evers," ours included. I unfolded my penknife, intending to rectify the loss, but a soft moan from Ronny stopped me. He watched the tiny blade, lips twisted into an expression partway between a sneer and a snarl.

"Give it here." Ronny's reedy voice belied the intensity of the command.

"Put that away." Shelly stepped between us, then knelt to press her hands to Ronny's cheeks. "Look at me. *Look at me*."

He gave a little whine, but Shelly held his face, forcing him to meet her eyes.

"It's okay, honey. Go play while Daddy and I get lunch ready."

"But, the Splinter Man—"

"Go play." She gave Ronny a little push. He ran a few steps before glancing back, watching until I folded the knife and slipped it into my pocket. This seemed to break whatever spell held Ronny, and he took off down the hill with a burst of singsong nonsense.

"What was that?" I asked.

Shelly ran a hand through her hair. "He has dreams—some man tells him to do things. Mostly it's okay, but I had to lock the knife drawer in the kitchen and put all the scissors up. Sorry I forgot to tell you, but—"

"It's fine." I reached for her hand. "Five years is a lot to unpack."

Her fingers were cold and stiff in mine, but she gave a little smile.

Down in the field Ronny tromped through the grass, scattering flights of crickets and mayflies. Their tiny, terrified screams reminded me of the calls of hunting horrors, and for a moment it was all I could do not to scuttle into the gnarled shadow of the apple tree.

Shelly gave a low hiss.

I realized I'd been crushing her hand, and let go. "Sorry, I—"

"S'okay." She massaged the blood back into her fingers. "Five years is a lot to unpack."

There was chicken salad in the basket, along with a thermos full of fresh sweet tea, oatmeal cookies, and fried bologna sandwiches in little plastic baggies. We laid it all out, then laid ourselves out, sipping tea while the afternoon sun seeped into our bones.

"I haven't been here for years." Shelly brushed an errant leaf from the blanket.

"I hope not," I glanced at the tree. "I'd hate to have to thrash any of the other boys for getting fresh with my wife."

"I've only had time for one boy," Shelly snorted, a bit of the girl I remembered peeking through. "And he says he's getting too old for kisses."

"More for me, then." It was a lame line, but when I leaned over she didn't pull away. The kiss was just like the first time, tentative and awkward, but I still got that little tingle down my neck at the smell of her hair, and I still had no idea where to put my hands.

"I used to think about this all the time," I said when we came up for air.

"What?"

"How it would be when I got back."

"Is it all you hoped?" Her question came rimed with wary caution.

"Dunno." I said just before the silence became uncomfortable. "It still doesn't feel quite real."

She slipped an arm around my shoulder. "Well, it is. You're back, and—"

Overhead, a flight of Byakhee broke through the clouds. Ungainly outside of the void of space, they tumbled through the air in a riot of membranous wings. We watched as they circled the hill, gargling and hooting to one another in playful tones.

I took another sip of tea, feeling the anxiety drain from me. "Ready for lunch?"

"I *hate* them," Shelly said.

"What, the Byakhee?" I turned, surprised by the anger in her voice. "They're the good guys."

She stared at me, a strange expression on her face.

"I mean, they're not *good*, but they keep Mi-Go and Nightgaunts away. I can't tell you how many times those ugly bastards saved my life."

Shelly stood and cupped her hands around her mouth. "Ronny! Get back here!"

"Calm down, it's fine." I reached for her, but she hurried off down the hill, dividing anxious looks between the sky and where Ronny was just coming out of the grass.

The Byakhee wheeled once, then flapped off toward town.

"See, nothing to worry about." I jogged up to her. "I know back home it's easy to forget about—"

"I haven't forgotten. I *can't* forget."

"That's not what I meant."

"I can't pretend everything is okay. Ronny, the dreams, those *things*, you have no idea how hard—"

"No idea?" It was my turn to stare. I used to shake when I got angry, but now the fury came cold, coiling tighter and tighter inside my chest until I thought my heart would burst from the pressure.

"I'm sorry." She wilted under my glare.

I flicked a hand at the Byakhee, now no more than distant blotches on the horizon. "A few bad dreams, the occasional flyover – New Brighton has it easy. Let me tell you about Boston: the Deep Ones *took* the men and women. They've got a use for us. The children though, we had to go house to house with flamethrowers. Once the damp took hold it was *kinder* to burn them. There was this shelter in Hyde Park, must've been a few thousand kids inside. Luckily, someone thought to seal the doors or they'd have torn into us like—"

"Stop."

I noticed her hands had curled into fists. Good. She was getting the point.

"Humans aren't in charge anymore." I forced myself to breath, long and slow. "It's their world, now."

She shook her head. "Is this what you want?"

"What I want doesn't figure into it. It's about survival, Shelly."

"Things are falling apart. *We're* falling apart. What's the use of surviving if we're not human anymore?"

I didn't have an answer for that.

"They *took* you." She knuckled an eye with a scowl – crying always made Shelly mad, it was one of the things I loved about her.

"I came back."

"What about when they come for Ronny?"

"They won't—"

"Yeah, I know. They've got no use for children, right?"

I rubbed a hand across the stubble on my chin. She was right, but it didn't matter.

Ronny came running up, cheeks flushed with excitement, hands clasped around something.

"Mom, Dad, look!"

I knelt to inspect Ronny's prize, feeling a swell of relief when he didn't shy away. He opened his hands to reveal a beetle with a tiny human face.

Shelly made a disgusted noise in the back of her throat. "Kill it."

Ronny took a step back.

"It's okay, honey." I held out my hand. "I won't hurt it."

Ronny looked to Shelly, who gave a tight-lipped nod.

I took the beetle from him, then let it scuttle off. It glanced back just before disappearing into the brush, and I grimaced, mouth unaccountably dry.

We walked back to the apple tree in silence.

"Can I have a sammich?" Ronny asked.

"When we get home." Shelly started packing up the basket.

I regarded my wife and son, wondering what it would be like to watch them die. The world was changing, logic and meaning stretched tight as a drumhead across the warped skeleton of reality. We'd already fought and lost, spectacularly. The Old Ones did as they pleased while we crouched in the margins, telling ourselves it wasn't too late.

It's surprising what people will believe when they've got no choice.

"I'll do it," I said.

"I'm almost finished." Shelly didn't look up.

"No, the Lieutenant. Tell Brian I'm in."

She let out a long, slow breath, eyes closed, then stood to face me. The relief on her face was palpable. For the first time, I noticed the dark smudges under her eyes, the hollowness of her cheeks, the worry lines bunching the corners of her lips – all the things I'd overlooked as a matter of habit.

Shelly stepped in, threading her arms through mine. "I love you."

I looked at Ronny, laughing as he kicked crabapples down the hill, seemingly unconcerned by Byakhee or human-faced beetles. And why should he be? He'd never known a time before the Old Ones. This was normal for him.

"I love you, too," I said. "Both of you."

Strangely enough, I was surprised to find I did.

The Lieutenant stood at the edge of the forest, head tilted, his lips peeled back from teeth the color of wet concrete. I could feel the others behind him, flashes of bloody skin against the muted green, murmurs slipping into the cracks between my thoughts. I ignored the calls – they weren't my responsibility anymore.

"Sergeant Long." He straightened as I approached, dried skin stretching with a sound like overtaxed rope. "Come to re-enlist?"

"No." I avoided the Lieutenant's eyes, knowing I wouldn't be able to go through with it under the hopeless agony of his gaze. "Are the

Byakhee here?"

"They never left. Why do you ask?"

The plan was for me to lure the Lieutenant away from the Byakhee, into town where Brian and the others could capture him. There were Jeeps waiting, speckled with the riot of primary colors that would confused the senses of pursuer used to hunting in the featureless expanse of space. Then it was a mad dash to the lake and the dubious safety of Brian's northern contacts.

The Lieutenant cupped my chin in one of his leathery hands. I could smell the mildewed damp of his robes, the iron and blood of his breath, and below that the strange, almost smoky incense that infused his weathered flesh.

He raised my face. Tear tracks glittered on the cracked hardpan of his cheeks, but his eyes brimmed with accusation. I'd thought Brykalski had run from the Byakhee out of fear, but I realized now his cowardice had been a species of bravery, born of a desire to deny the inevitable, to rob the Old Ones of their due.

My resolve almost cracked. Brian, Deacon, Beth, all of them were my friends. How many times had I thought of them in the midst of battle, hissing prayers to a god I knew to be false, promising life, love, anything if he would just see me home. I imagined Shelly's eyes staring out from the Lieutenant's ravaged face, wild with hate and terror. No, I couldn't watch her die.

It's surprising what people will do when they have no choice.

It was over quickly, Byakhee slipping from the shadows behind Pike's Market to collect Brian and his would-be rebels. There was a burst of gunfire, then a single report as Beth Antonelli shot Rosa and Carlos, then turned her pistol on herself. Brave woman. The rest were dragged out of their hiding places, struggling in the Byakhees' rubbery grasp. There were a few hundred all told – more than enough to fill the tithe.

New Brighton would be safe for another five years.

The Lieutenant waved, and most of the Byakhee clawed their way into the sky, cradling their screaming charges with the tender care usually reserved for heirlooms or newborn babies.

Two remained.

"You bastard," Brian gritted out as the Byakhee holding him flopped forward.

Up close, I couldn't focus on the creature, my eyes watering as if I were looking at the sun. I met Brian's hateful gaze, surprised that I felt nothing.

"Did you plan it from the beginning?" he asked.

"No." It wasn't a lie – I hadn't planned anything. "There was just no other way."

He sagged in the creature's coils. I could've kept talking, could've rationalized my actions by explaining there was no Northern Resistance, but that wouldn't have helped either of us. I could see in his eyes that he'd always known. There was no future, no hope, nothing outside the malign indifference of the Great Old Ones. Not for us, at least. Our only choice was to forget the past, to become what we needed to be to survive. My son was proof of that.

"You promised." I turned to the Lieutenant as the Byakhee holding Brian took flight.

"All yours." He smiled at Shelly even though his eyes were squeezed shut, then did a crisp about-face and made his way back up McNaughton Avenue. The Byakhee set her down almost gingerly before skittering after the Lieutenant, leaving us alone in the deserted parking lot.

Shelly slapped my hand away, and spit in my face when I knelt. Her fingernails left ragged marks on my cheek as she pushed me away. She took a few steps, then turned back and tried to say something, all that came out was a garbled shout.

"I did it for you and Ronny," I said, knowing it would fester.

I hadn't seen Shelly this furious since prom. She took a step toward me, hands balled into fists, then with a disgusted groan, she turned and ran back toward the alley.

I didn't follow. There was no point. She would come back – there was nowhere to run. In time, we might even be a family again.

It's surprising what people can learn to accept, even love, when they've got no choice.

In the distance, the low hiss of wind through the leaves mingled with the shrieks of the rebels and ecstatic howls of my former comrades. For once, their calls were not for me. I'd had enough war, enough madness, but even if I'd wanted to return, they wouldn't have accepted me.

There was no room for cowards in the Yellow Guard.

# *Overcome*

by Jason Vanhee

They crept out just before dawn, when the light was brittle and the air was cold as the vastness of space. George's breath fogged up the air as he trailed behind his mother, her hand absently and loosely holding his. There were nine of them, all gathered at Mama's house to go out to church.

"You need to be very quiet, George," his mother had said. "Just keep yourself hushed up, and it'll all be fine."

He knew that wasn't true, though. He was eleven, not a little kid any more, and he knew they couldn't just go out to church if they wanted to. Every time they'd had services, they had gone in the middle of the night, and to a quiet, empty old church way off in the ruins, where there was sometimes an old man who had been a preacher to talk about God to them. But this time, they were headed to their old church—not George's church, though he'd seen it plenty. His mother's church. And that wouldn't work at all.

First, the church was closed, and second, there wasn't a reverend, and third, the masters would be mad. So he'd told Mama that he didn't want to go because he didn't want to get in trouble. It was almost worth it just to go outside, because he wasn't let out very often; the masters liked young children, they said.

180

"Oh, you don't want to go? You want to go to hell, maybe?"

"I think maybe we're already in hell, Lou," Uncle Jimmy said to Mama. He was younger than Mama by about ten years, and he had been only a little older than George was now when it happened. When *they* came out the sky. People said he hadn't been quite right ever since. George liked him well enough: he played with models of old things, cars and trains and stuff, and could get them to work sometimes.

"Even if I was in hell, I'd pray to Jesus all the same," Mama said, and she snapped at George to get on his coat and hat and don't forget his gloves, and that was the end of him staying home.

The city was quiet. Mostly it was quiet all the time, since there weren't too many souls left in the place to make noise. Half the buildings were falling right down, and another quarter were well on their way. Here and there, you could tell someone still lived in a place, or worked in it, if you could say anyone worked much anymore. And from one or two of those buildings, down front stairs that creaked and thumped, and with their faces hidden behind scarves, came more folks to join Mama's little group.

Sunday morning, and they were off to church.

"Why we got to go to church at all?" George asked.

"Because the Lord above says we ought to," his Mama hissed back at him.

"There's not a Lord above anymore, is there, not unless you mean—" Before he could say the name, Mama had whipped about and slapped her hand over his mouth.

"Don't you say that name, George, not out in the street, not when we're trying to be quiet and not call any attention at all. You understand, boy?"

He nodded behind her mittened hand, staring up at her eyes, which were narrowed in her soft face. Her skin was starting to look a little ashy, he thought, but it was still smoother than most ladies' her age. She was a pretty lady, his Mama, and he was proud of that. But she could look really angry when she wanted to, and right then she did, so when she pulled her hand away, he didn't say anything else.

"I'm speaking of the Lord God, Jesus himself, who saves us all with his sacrifice, and not any old foolishness like they get to talking to in the streets these days. And my God wants me to go to church, and for you to come along too, you hear me?"

He just nodded again dumbly and let her lead him on again, catching up with the straggling group ahead of them.

They were two blocks away from the church when the first trouble came. A tall old man, his hair gone mostly white and heading way back on his head, stood on his porch in a bathrobe with a steaming cup of coffee in his hand. "You all should be in bed," he shouted out at them. "What you doing up? You think you're going to church?"

There were nearly thirty of them now, hurrying along the street, and they didn't respond to the man on his porch, only murmured to each other things like *Don't pay him any mind*, and *Everyone just keep walking*.

"You think they don't know you're out? You think you're sneaky? I see you, Miss Lou, and your brother James. I see you, Martin Washington. I know your names."

"God bless you," Mama called out.

"God? You think God cares? You think that one they got up to the mountain, that He didn't eat God up for breakfast a long time ago?" But they were past the old man's house, and he was falling behind them. "When the masters come, you'll forget all about this foolishness, but not in time." The man's deep voice resounded down the street like some kind of prophet, but that was the last of him.

George lifted up his eyes from the worn tips of his shoes where they'd been resting. He wondered about the boy who'd owned the shoes before; probably he'd been dead for fifteen years or more, George guessed. Dead since the masters came down from the sky. He wondered if the boy had been dragged out to church by his mother when it wasn't even daylight yet, not really. He bet, back in those days, boys didn't have to go to church unless they wanted to.

"Don't let him scare any of you. If they really knew we were up and about, we'd none of us be here. You think the Mayor's just going to let us go to church and all, if she knew we were going?" Mama's voice was barely louder than a whisper, but in the quiet of the morning, just shoes slapping down on the broken pavement and the faint puff of breath and the wicking of fabric against fabric, her words carried to everyone, and they nodded and said it was true, and a few of them thanked God and blessed Miss Lou.

They turned the last corner. The church still stood, and George had always wondered why the Mayor hadn't just torn it down, or why the masters hadn't got rid of it a long time ago. They knocked down buildings whenever it suited them, and surely it would suit them to

183

have the church gone, as much as they didn't like it. This was the first time George and his folk had been to church in this building, but other people used it: they heard the stories. It wasn't the first time the old Congregational Church had been put to good purposes, or even the tenth. George half suspected his Mama had been to services there a time or two, and finally got up the nerve to put one together herself.

"Lord have mercy, they know." That from Uncle Jimmy, who was shaking and not just from the cold. "We're in for it now."

On the steps of the church were six people. George didn't know them all, but he knew two of them: big, heavy Lawrence White, who was the Police Chief and used to be a soldier when there were soldiers still; and beside him, in a fancy fur coat and with her hair straightened and pulled back, and looking even smoother and prettier than Mama, the Mayor. Everyone just called her that: Mayor; but she had a name, and it was Martha Washington, and Mama said she was Martin Washington's sister. She had her gloved hands clasped in front of her, and she was staring right at George, it seemed like. He shuddered from his tip to his toes from the dark eyed stare. The other four had billy clubs and masks on their faces, wood masks carved to look a little like the masters: curves and feelers and tentacles, like something from up out of the sea. Everyone said they came from the sky, from the stars, but maybe there was water up there, too.

The Mayor lifted a bullhorn to her mouth and her voice echoed out to them. "You all need to go home, right now, or there will be trouble."

Hands reached out and touched, grasped. The group of thirty

anchored each other, and held. George was in the middle, behind his mother, looking between her and Mister Washington to the church's boarded-up front not fifty feet away. His free hand had been taken up by Monica, a girl three years younger than him who clutched desperately and leaned into the older boy. "It'll be all right," he whispered down to her, though he didn't really think it would be. He just wanted to go home.

"We're going to church, Martha," Mister Washington shouted. "It's Sunday."

"No one's going to church, and it's not Sunday. We don't have that day anymore. You go on home, Martin, and maybe we can pretend none of this happened."

"It is Sunday, whatever you want to call it instead, Martha. Now get out of the way. God is calling us to our real home." Martin took a step forward, the whole group shifting a little as he did.

The Mayor passed the bullhorn back to White and drew off her gloves one after the other, revealing her dark hands with one gold ring on each. Those twisted bands of metal seemed to curve in ways George's eyes couldn't follow, clearly visible even from this distance.

"We don't have to be afraid of her. The Lord is with us," Mama said.

"Yes, Lou, Jesus is with us." Uncle Jimmy, his voice shaking. "Oh, help me believe it, Lou. Help me."

"Let's sing," Mama said, and then she raised her voice, just one voice for a moment and then they all started in, singing *We Shall Overcome*. George swallowed as they started, but he chimed in on the

185

third line, "We shall overcome, some day."

They started forward, Martin Washington again taking the first step and then rest of them pulled along by their shared hands. The song was echoing over the empty streets now.

The Mayor clasped her hands and bowed her head, as if in prayer. The four policemen stepped down and drew back their clubs, but didn't come any closer than the lowest stair. And then the Mayor lifted up her head, frowning. She looked so sad, George thought.

A faint thrumming inserted itself into the music, a low bass kind of noise that disjointed everything. A few singers fell out, uncertain, and the chorus stumbled. Only Mama's voice kept on full strength, an anchor for people to find their way to. They started back to the verse, coming together, drawing closer...

The air shimmered in front of the Mayor, on the sidewalk below the steps of the church, and then... something was there, something that caused the song to turn to shrieks and gasps, but only for an instant. One of the masters had come, and it was just like the old man said: they forgot. Time ceased to exist, their minds went away and hid. A cloud of darkness and confusion passed over George's mind, but he thought, somewhere far off, he heard screaming and that something was hurting his hand.

George came to himself still standing, his lips still moving silently in the words of the song: *deep in my heart, I do believe we shall overcome.* There was silence about him for a moment as he opened his eyes, saw the clubs coming down on some of the marchers, and wood biting into flesh without making a sound. His hands were empty. His mother was down on the ground before him, blood on her cheek and her lips, writhing, but still singing, he thought. His other hand ached but—the girl, Monica, she was just gone. They had taken her, he knew. They liked little kids, the masters, everyone knew that.

Sound rolled back in, the crack of clubs on weak bodies, the screaming of humans battered and broken, and the song, still resounding on the street in fragments and pieces, in whispers and gasps.

George looked at the Mayor, drawing on her gloves with that look of deep sadness still in her eyes, and something else, something like fear, maybe. Her lips moved, and though she was ten yards off and he shouldn't have been able to tell what she was saying, it was clear as day.

*Go home, George.*

He thought of Monica vanished, and of Mama down on the cracked pavement, on the frost, writhing and still singing. He dropped to his knees beside her, and took up her hand, and he opened his mouth to call out the words of the song with his mother.

"We are not afraid, we are not afraid."

The Mayor shook her head, and George smiled around the words he sang, and then a club cracked into his head.

# Paradise 2.0

by Glynn Owen Barrass

They kept moving, the vagrant lifestyle proving the best way to survive in the Human Race's twilight years. It was difficult to hide from the enemy, those things that filled the sky and stampeded through the deserted, broken canyons of the old cities. They worried at minds and sniffed out human flesh with snouts designed by no sane evolution. Travelling away from once-populated areas, through the overgrown countryside, had kept them safe so far. Archer was their leader, and had been since the group broke off from the corrupted, dying settlement they'd been a part of some months earlier. She kept them safe, had made good decisions when it came to surviving, and kept them moving, always moving.

The dissent began shortly after they found the farm.

It was meant to be a short stop: a search for food, water, and some new clothing. A day later, Archer sat in the dining room facing four stubborn group members who wanted a compromise, a big one, in their regular way of life.

The dining table, a large, dark wooden rectangle covered in a fine layer of dust, had been set with vases of wildflowers from outside. Archer stared at the flowers as those around her talked.

"For one, there's a well here, a bonafide, working well with fresh water," said Andy. Tall, thin, with long black hair balding at the top, he had a habit of working his lantern jaw even when he wasn't speaking.

Archer nodded, looked at the water filling the glass vases before her.

"There are chickens, cows, an orchard…" said Sarah. She was short and dumpy looking, with wiry brown hair and breasts that sagged down to her navel. "I think we could really make a go of things here. We've already eaten the eggs."

"And next we'll be milking the cows," Baker said. No one knew the man's Christian name, he just went by 'Baker.' Tall, taller than Andy even, he was wide too, and red-haired. He had a chubby, friendly face, and of the three who'd spoken, he was the one Archer liked the most.

The other two made noises of agreement. The only person who wasn't speaking sat at the opposite end of the table. Archer looked up, met her gaze. Rhian, face between the flowers: small, petite, and with big brown eyes. Her brown, shoulder length hair was still damp, recently washed with water from the well. The girl had been Archer's closest friend and companion since they left the Templedog settlement, so the fact that Rhian had joined this little group of… usurpers, upset Archer a little, and riled her a lot.

A hint of a smile crossed Rhian's face, and Archer's anger melted some. She pulled her arms from under the table and pressed her palms against the dusty tabletop.

"Guys…" Archer looked at the other faces before returning her gaze to the table. Avoiding Rhian's eyes, she stared at the flowers. "We've gotten by this long by being on the move, with only a few brief stop-offs to rest. It's survival, plain and simple. And you want to change that over a couple of farm animals gone wild and a well that could run dry anytime?"

"The animals are fine, getting used to us already," Sarah said.

Archer looked to her, finding the woman had folded her arms over her ample bosom.

*Stubborn defiance there,* Archer thought.

"We could always just put it to a vote," Baker said, and this surprised Archer so much she found her cheeks reddening. She'd been sure Baker would be the first one to relent, next to Rhian.

"A democratic vote, yes," Sarah said, and Archer felt the urge to punch the smile right off her face.

Baker had folded his arms too now. Archer bit her lip and tapped her fingers on the table. She looked to Rhian again, and found the girl's eyes lowered.

"Well if democracy is what you want…" She paused her speech, but not her thoughts, considering her next words carefully. "Let's go outside, get everyone together and make a vote." Archer went to wipe her brow, which was beginning to perspire, but instead wiped the dust off her jeans, tucking her hands in the pockets so no one saw an action that might betray weakness. *Things will go downhill from here, I just know it.* The varicolored flowers, Archer just wanted to reach over and crush them.

By a show of hands, there were nine people for staying, four for moving on (including Archer's vote), and three that simply couldn't decide. The vote took place at the front of the farmhouse, and three hours later, Archer sat on the porch and rued what she knew was an obvious mistake.

*This place has seduced her people, and with what?*

The farm had probably been something in its heyday, but now, abandonment and Mother Nature's ministrations had taken their toll. The house behind her, a wide, two-story structure with whitewashed walls and a grey slate gambrel roof, had survived fairly well. There were a few broken windows on the first floor, with water damage and mold within those connected rooms. It had eight bedrooms that had pretty much been cleaned out of personal belongings. Archer guessed the people had left in a hurry, however, considering the odd book or memento lying around, or maybe they had just run out of room to take everything. It was good they hadn't killed the animals before leaving, or not so good, considering this was one of the main reasons she was being forced to stay.

Two cars were parked up in the lot in front of the house: a large Black Cherokee SUV and a compact red Buick. Both were covered in dirt and bird shit, but one of her people had cleaned the windshields since they'd arrived.

She stood, cracked her neck, and began a slow walk, turning left to pass the corner of the house a minute later.

Behind the house lay a small orchard bearing two rows of apple trees with green fruit on their boughs. The ground around the trees was overgrown; the grass and wild weeds already above knee length. This continued past the orchard to the hen enclosure—well, enclosed no more, as when the original owners had left, they'd pulled down the wire fences and left the hens to run free around the farm. They still nested in the little wooden hen houses though, and from what Archer had seen, spent their days pecking around the orchard for whatever bugs lived in the overgrown grass. She saw some as she neared the orchard, one of the birds striding towards her as she walked.

To the southeast of the house, beside the orchard, stood a large rectangular dairy barn with terracotta paneled walls and a white, barrel-arched roof. There was a small square milking parlor at its rear which adjoined a tall grain silo the same terracotta as the parlor and the dairy barn. One of her group, Simon, said it was still half full. The cows, all ten of them, strolled around the farm, and where the fences to the surrounding fields were down, they wandered there too, living off grass and shitting everywhere they went, a little skinny but still alive and fairly well.

She paused just before the orchard, looking around at the remainder of their domain.

The rest of the farm, squared off in a whitewashed fence, contained overgrown grass, machinery gone to rust, that well, and an ever-present cow shit stink. Still, being the leader, she'd set a couple of her group to shoveling up the shit, mainly because she hated the smell, and secondly because it was a farm (and didn't they need manure?).

192

Thirdly, and this was only partly due to revenge, or so she told herself, Baker and Andy had wanted this farm, so there they were, cleaning it up by shoveling the shit.

Archer saw Baker appear beyond the orchard, walking around with a black sack in one hand and a shovel held up on his shoulder, and she wondered whether she should extend that duty to the fields surrounding the farm. Those fields, overgrown like the farm, flanked it on all sides except for the mostly wooded area to the east. It was nature's realm now, she told herself, and they had no right being here. Archer turned back towards the house, avoiding the unwanted attention of the curious hen as she walked, when a holler appeared from the woods behind her.

She looked, squinted, and saw a shape gesticulating from the edge of the woods. Judging by the tan leather jacket, black jeans, and long grey hair, it was Reggie. Curious as to what he'd found, Archer rushed towards the fence, clambered over it, and began jogging across the overgrown field towards his position. As she approached, Archer saw some others who'd been wandering the fields also heeding his call, but she arrived there first.

"Reggie, what's up?" she said, panting from the exertion.

The man had a piece of straw in his mouth, chewed it nervously as he stared at her, wide-eyed.

"You won't believe this, no way you won't," he replied, and turned, rushing back into the woods.

Archer frowned and followed him inside, stepping across brown undergrowth and between the greyish swollen boughs into the shadows of the woods. After a few minutes of walking, she reached a clearing. Reggie stood there, plus Annie, a small, pretty Hispanic girl in a sleeveless, dirt-stained white blouse and cut off denim shorts. Behind them was a large, roughly circular ditch, dug fairly recently by the fresh look of the soil surrounding it.

"You wanna brace yourself Archer," Annie said. Her eyes were wide, like a deer caught in headlamps. As Archer passed her, she patted the girl on the shoulder.

The contents of the ditch made her freeze mid-step.

She swallowed hard, and said, "What the fuck?"

Filled with black and brown matter, charred bones and skulls of human origin spotted the bottom of the ditch in grisly abandon. Skulls with gaping mouths, skulls where the tops were only visible in the muck, all had been smashed in. Ribs, hands… the skeletons looked like they had been torn apart. Before or after the bodies' decomposition, Archer couldn't hazard a guess. The smell hit her nostrils, a sour odor of smoke and ash, and she blinked away tears. There were a couple of blackened petrol cans in the ditch and tiny, charred remnants of clothing. The petrol cans matched the ones lying about the farm, and Archer thought of the hurriedly emptied house behind her.

"Ahem… what do you think?" Reggie said.

Archer shook her head and thought: *Trouble comes to paradise.*

Footsteps appeared behind her, no doubt those from the field catching up. This was good; she wanted everyone to see this.

"Tell the rest," she said to Reggie and Annie, "and make sure everyone has a look." Archer turned, avoided eye contact with the two just entering the clearing, and headed back towards the farm.

Alone in the dining room, the white walled area, usually bright from the windows lining the east wall, had turned shadowy after she'd pulled the curtains closed. After what had been discovered earlier, the last thing Archer wanted to see was the farm outside.

A knock on the door made her pause her current pacing. Standing at the other side of the room, she approached the table and sat before saying, "Come in."

The door opened, admitting Rhian, followed by Annie. The girls had formed a friendship. Sometimes, they seemed to get along better than Archer did with Rhian, but they were of closer ages, after all.

Rhian smiled, though it was a forlorn one. Annie closed the door behind them and they stood side by side. It appeared by their fidgeting that they were anxious to talk, but somehow reticent.

Annie broke the silence. "Everyone's seen it. And, uh… Aaron stuck on some protective gear, fishing galoshes and gloves, and went inside the pit to explore."

*A great way to catch diseases*, she thought, and said, "So what did he find?"

"Eight skulls," Rhian said. She stepped towards the table and pressed her hands against its surface.

There was silence for a few moments, then Archer said, "Eight skulls, and we have eight bedrooms in this house." She would have smiled if the ugliness of the situation hadn't been so great. *Those smashed in skulls. The people living here were executed.*

Annie stepped forward to stand beside Rhian. "We're scared, Archer." At her words, Rhian nodded eagerly. "And we want out," Annie continued.

Vindication, finally, and still Archer didn't allow herself a smile.

People began entering the dining room not long after the girls. Soon it was crowded, and the arguments began. This time, Archer took a back seat to it all as words of anger, confusion, and fear bounced around the room.

"Whatever happened, it's all over with now, isn't it?" said Sarah, obviously refusing to accept that being here was anything but a good idea.

"Is it, though?" Ted said. Normally composed, his dark-skinned face was red with anger. Dressed in a faded denim shirt and jeans, the thin, shaven-headed man stood near the door and looked ready to bolt.

He had been one of the ones to abstain from the earlier vote, Archer noted.

"We should just pack up, leave already," said Annie. She and Rhian had taken up positions flanking Archer at the end of the table.

"We don't know what happened though, do we?" Aaron said. Standing at the other side of the room near Ted, he still wore the green galoshes and yellow rubber elbow gloves he'd worn for his excavation. Aaron's face was pale and pinched looking, his normally shaggy blonde hair pulled back in a ponytail. His arms and legs were black with dirt.

Baker laughed, shifting his big bulk in his seat at the table. "You

196

saw it the closest. Those were the people that lived on this farm, executed like animals to the slaughter."

"No, that's just speculation," Sarah said. Seated directly across from Baker, she was growing red-faced too.

"No. What you're saying is bullshit," Rhian retorted, and Archer smiled. A few people clapped and heads turned her way.

Baker looked to Archer and said, almost apologetically, "If you want to do that vote again, I'm on your side."

"Me too," said Ted, followed by other voices of affirmation.

Archer rose from her seat, clearing her throat as she did. *Now's the time to take charge again*, she thought. She was about to speak when the door to the dining room burst open.

It was Magee, panting and flustered. The small, grey haired woman had a checkered bandana around her head, wore baggy black trousers, the pits of her white blouse dark with sweat. She quickly glanced around the room and found Archer.

"Someone new just walked into the farm. You'd better come see." And with that she was off again, leaving the people in the room to mutter collectively.

Magee's statement left Archer struck dumb. A gentle pressure on her shoulder made her turn her head, and her eyes met Rhian's.

"Let's go then," she said, addressing Rhian and the rest of the room. She felt a measure of satisfaction when everyone waited while she and Rhian approached the door. Hearing Magee leave through the front door, she turned left onto a short corridor and left again at the stairs. Other footsteps followed hers and Rhian's as she approached the door. Speeding her gait, she was through it a few moments later.

Cold air tinged with the smell of dung hit her when she stepped onto the porch. A dozen feet away, she found Magee, Andy, a few of the others, and a white haired stranger.

Archer paused to examine him. He wasn't old; rather, his white, shoulder length hair and deathly pale skin looked like its cause was albinism. Beneath his tattered desert camouflage jacket, the man wore black bikers' leathers, reinforced with protective plates scuffed and spotted with dents. He wore black webbing under the jacket with a scratched black machine pistol tucked in one of the pouches. It was a warrior's getup, not a traveler's, though there was a large green rucksack at his booted feet.

"Wait here a minute," she said to Rhian, and as she approached the stranger, she kept her eyes on the machine pistol. She glanced up when she saw him scrutinizing her back. His eyes were bright blue, too blue, and Archer surmised they were contact lenses. He had handsome features, skin so smooth he might never have shaved in his life, but there was an ugly, round scar to the left of his Adam's apple.

He raised his hand as she paused before him, white fingers spread for a greeting.

She ignored it and nodded at his chest. "The gun, hand it over."

The stranger lowered his hand and smiled with the left side of his mouth. "Not very trusting, are you?" His voice had a coarse, strained quality.

"Who are you? How did you get by out there?" Archer said, ignoring his reply. Behind her, she heard people coming out onto the porch.

The stranger briefly examined those behind her and said. "The name's Piece, formerly of the Tigeraspect Colony. Some roving band of former military hit it hard, dispersed everybody."

"I've heard of Tigeraspect," said Magee. Archer nodded, pointed at the gun.

"Alright, you've got it," he said.

"Slowly," said a male voice behind her, and Archer heard a pistol cock.

*Who took a pistol out of storage?* she wondered. All the guns were tucked away in the oven, an unlikely hiding place that Archer liked.

The stranger raised his hand, gently removing the gun from the webbing by the muzzle. He held it out, and Archer accepted.

"I guess you might be able to join us," Archer said. "Come inside."

The stranger's presence waylaid the immediate plans for a new vote. Introductions were made, and Piece was forced to endure all the attention a new group member suffered. Some talk at supper, less stressed than earlier, had the group deciding, with barely any dissenters, to leave the next morning. It was a fine ending to a stressful day, Archer thought, and she took to the bed she shared with Rhian feeling content that the farm would soon be behind them.

Sleep came quickly, more so because of her companion's warming form, but it didn't last. A short time after dropping off Archer awoke suddenly, her body spasming as with the end result of a falling dream, but no dream lingered in her suddenly awake, alert mind. Her body was soaked in sweat, the mattress beneath her damp. She turned to Rhian and found her awake, laid on her back with her eyes wide open.

"Rhian," she said, "couldn't sleep too, huh?"

Her friend's jaw fell open, a stream of drool pouring from her mouth. Archer's body turned cold despite the clammy warmth around her. She reached for Rhian and shook her, gently at first, then much more firmly when no response was forthcoming. Her panic solidifying, she ripped the quilt away, got to her knees, then leant over to check if Rhian was breathing. An ear to mouth examination gave signs of life, but the breathing was shallow.

*What the hell is wrong with you?* She'd never learned how to take a pulse, so that was out. *What do paramedics do? They check the eyes, don't they? So I light up the storm lamps, dig out a torch... Oh wait, Ted has some medical training.*

She climbed from the bed, slipped out of her damp shorts and t-shirt, and – while keeping her eyes on Rhian's shadowy form – got dressed in her jeans and a white shirt. She did up most of the buttons then put her feet into her boots but didn't bother fastening them.

"I'll help you, I swear," she said to Rhian, heading past the bed towards the door while trying to waylay the panic the girl's condition instilled. She gave Rhian a final, worried look as she reached the door. Turning back to it, she froze as a dark shape moved quickly past.

*Who?* Taking measured steps, Archer crept to the door and looked right, seeing the dark shape enter the room next to hers.

She crouched, removed the small knife she had tucked into her left boot, and crept towards the door. *What is this, some secret nighttime liaison?* No, Archer suspected something else, something more insidious. She reached the door in nervous seconds, found it ajar, and looked through the gap into the bedroom. This room housed Reggie and Annie, and she saw the two shadowy beds to either side of the window. Enough moonlight entered between the curtains for Archer to see the dark shapes of her companions, and the bed on the right - that held an extra form.

She swallowed a gasp. It was Piece; Archer could tell that by his hair and the paleness of his skin. His jacket and the leather one beneath were gone, his topless white body shining in the meager light. He was straddling Annie's sleeping form, and in his left hand... *was that a syringe?* Yes, a syringe, already being retracted from her neck. Archer held back another gasp, but her boot heel found a loose floorboard. It creaked quietly, but was noise enough to alert Piece to her presence.

He spun around on the bed, fast, and she saw the Devil's eyes in his pallid countenance. A moment later and Piece was charging her. She saw the flash of movement of his hands reaching for her throat, wondered absently where the syringe was, and thrust forward with her knife.

His face was inches from hers, teeth bared and his eyes still blazing, but the light there dwindled as she twisted deeper into his gut. Piece's hands fluttered at her throat, then dropped to his sides.

"You shouldn't..." Piece's words ended in a croak and he

collapsed, his body escaping the blade with a wet squelch.

Numbness replaced the fear and adrenaline of the recent seconds of action, and looking down, Archer stared at a blade not stained with blood, but dripping a white, watery fluid. Beyond the blade, sprawled on the floor, lay the man, the thing, clutching a chest that continued pumping the unnatural gore. A quick examination revealed numerous crescent shaped scars on his chest, plus a barcode tattooed under his left pectoral.

Archer stepped over his prone form and rushed towards Annie. She found the girl in the same condition as Rhian: unresponsive with her eyes glazed. Reggie looked the same. The syringe Piece had used lay to the left of Annie's head and contained a dark, cloudy fluid. Hearing Piece moan behind her, she picked it up.

She turned and approached him, preparing to jab him in the neck. On his knees now, Piece glared at her. "Won't work on me," he said. "Benzodiazepine only works on humans."

Archer paused before him and looked at the syringe in her palm. She then kicked him squarely in the face.

Piece went down sideways and Archer moved after him, jabbing the needle in his arm.

"Fucker!" she said, then shouted, "Anyone awake? I need help here!"

Nothing was forthcoming but the silence of the house, then Piece laughed hoarsely. She'd broken his nose with the kick. White fluid dripped from it onto the floor.

"Fuck, fuck, fuck!" she said, and standing, she rushed back to her room. *I'll get us out of here, don't worry.* Her panic over what Piece had done, his seeming invulnerability to serious harm, and the possibility that he wasn't alone, gave her one single option: to get out of there with Rhian. With this in mind she knelt on the bed and clumsily picked up the girl in a fireman's lift.

A bit unsteady on her legs at first, she carried Rhian to the door, then the lobby, and then turned left to descend the stairs. She avoided looking at Piece, but heard his laughter as she made her precarious way down the steps.

A right turn on the downstairs lobby took her down the corridor towards the front door. Behind and above her, she heard a grunt and a clatter; hopefully, Piece was suffering the effects of the tranquillizer despite what he'd said. "It's alright Rhian, I'm getting us out, getting us out." She repeated this mantra as she paused at the door. With her free hand, she turned the latch and pulled it open. The cool night air hit her in a rush, clearing her head somewhat and focusing her for what would come.

Of the two cars parked before the house, she chose the black Cherokee over the Buick. It was closer, and she knew it worked after seeing Baker start it earlier.

She left the porch and the front door slammed closed behind her; a quick, unsteady turn showed there was no one there. Seconds later, she reached the car. Opening one of the passenger doors, she dropped Rhian inside and ran around the car to the driver's side.

Archer locked herself inside and paused. It had been a long time since she'd driven a car, but despite her panic, it quickly came back.

The key was already in the ignition, so she pushed down on the clutch, turned the key, and the engine emitted a coughing whine. A second try, and it started with a roar.

*Thank God.* She put the gear stick into first and pressed the gas pedal. *Shit, the handbrake.* She released it, slowly released some pressure from the clutch, found the biting point, and was off. Releasing the clutch fully, she pressed harder on the gas as the car took her down the weed-covered path.

As she drove, she thanked heaven the locked gate was such a rotten mess. Raising the gear, she steered towards it. She avoided the rear mirror for fear of seeing the worst behind her, and with twenty feet or so left till the gate, she felt a sensation of relief.

Then the cow appeared, the slow lumbering beast walking right into the car's path. Archer went to stamp on the brake, too slow as the car irrepressibly closed in on the mobile barricade. She gritted her teeth and flinched in her seat awaiting the impact. The car slammed into the cow's legs, its hefty torso hit the bonnet, and Archer's mouth opened into a scream as the cow exploded.

The tires screeched as the car lurched to a halt as pink gore spattered the windscreen and the cow transformed into a thrashing mass of green and black tentacles. The impact had barely fazed her, but the aftermath? Screaming as uncontrollably as her body was shaking, Archer leaned sideways and opened the car door.

She pretty much fell onto the path just as one of the tentacles hit the windscreen so hard that it cracked into a spiderweb of broken glass. The pink gore was everywhere, under her hands and butt and splashed across the dirt path. A constant rain of it fell from an animal that was now a mass of spastically flailing tentacles.

*Rhian!* This thought brought Archer to her feet in a hurry, but as she reached for the passenger side door, a noise behind her made her freeze mid-step. It was the sound of a man clearing his throat, and of course, Archer knew exactly who it was before she turned to face him.

Piece held his machine pistol two handed, aimed towards her chest.

Archer raised her hands. With the squirming horror behind her and the smiling albino pointing a gun, she had nowhere to run, nowhere to hide.

The wound to his chest already healed, Piece's demeanor was confident; arrogant, even. It compelled Archer to ask the one question she required from him.

"Why?"

The smile disappeared from Piece's face. "The Masters want you back of course. Good subjects are hard to come by."

The masters of Templedog, of course, those eldritch horrors that kept humans like sea monkeys, breeding and working and farming…

Archer scowled and, despite the gun, took a challenging step forward.

"Your creators set this up, didn't they? Pre-empting us all along, hoping we'd settle down here."

Piece nodded. "It beats vivisection, which I would've recommended."

A sound of squelching, heavy footsteps issued behind her. Archer glanced back to see the fake cow, the monster, flanking her rear.

"Come back to us, Archer," Piece said. "These people need a leader. They can awake back home with you to guide them."

"And the alternative?" Archer asked, knowing the answer already.

"Death," Piece said, and as if to emphasize his words, a tentacle brushed Archer's legs.

Archer sighed. Her arms dropping loosely, her whole body sagged in resignation.

"Let me carry Rhian back to the house," she said.

"We'll help you," Piece replied.

# The Divine Proportion

by Jeff C. Carter

The spider wriggled in my hand as I cooed to it.

"You'll thank me for this."

I plucked out one of its legs. It had scurried across the floor of my hospital room on seven legs. I don't know how it lost number eight, but it had to be fixed. I flicked the twitching, odd numbered leg away and admired the spider. An even number of legs and an even number of eyes. Perfect.

I let the poor creature flee.

*You broke it. You stupid bitch, you broke it. It's your fault. You broke it. You stupid bitch, you broke it.*

That runaway train has been circling inside my skull for three years.

I picked up my sticky, bloody tooth. I thought teeth were nice white squares, but they have ugly, twisted roots that snake deep into the bone. I ignored the pair of aching holes in my gums. The stupid dentist pulled the first one after it cracked. I explained how I needed to touch my tongue to each tooth before I went to sleep. There is a system.

He didn't understand or didn't care. He left me with a mouth full of odd numbers. I begged and pleaded with him to take out another. The odd number burned in my head like a hot coal, worse than the cracked tooth, worse than what I did next.

An orderly discovered me drooling blood in the janitor's closet. I had gouged out the odd tooth with a claw hammer. That's when they locked me in my room.

Screams ripped through the halls. There were always screams in the Arizona State Mental Hospital, but the last few days had been different. The routine clop-clop of orderlies and squeak-squeak of cart wheels were gone. The power had gone out and the trays of food had stopped arriving. The violent outbursts I heard on the other side of the door were no longer met with the bustle of guards. Now there were only the screams.

I didn't know what was going on, but I was sure I caused it.

*You broke it.*

I traced the thick purple scar that spiraled around my right arm, the self-inflicted injury that got me committed. It was beautiful, my eye in the storm of uneven, disordered chaos. A perfect spiral is built from right angles. It is called the Divine Proportion. That is what my father and the doctors and the dentists don't understand. When you get everything positioned at the proper angles, you fit into the perfect order of things.

A key scratched at the lock. My door swung open for the first time in days.

It was Tariq, one of the other patients. He was the only true sociopath at the hospital. His olive skin had fresh bloody scratches from the corner of one beady eye down to his jaw line. I pictured the finger nails of a petite woman, like me. The tracks were not quite parallel.

He grabbed me with one thick arm and hauled me out of bed.

The hallways were black except for the scattered green blurs of the fading battery-powered exit lights on the linoleum floor. The sharp sting of Clorox had been replaced with the cloying stench of rotting meat. Dead doctors and orderlies lined the corridor. I counted fourteen, including the dentist. I shut my eyes and tapped my tongue against my teeth.

A group of patients stood in the cafeteria, looking wet and haggard. Lizzy bit her lip and squirmed with manic energy. The blonde hair on the unshaven half of her head hung wet and limp across one bare shoulder. She stood next to a large steel tub.

Dan chewed a filthy fingernail and slouched with his eyes fixed on the floor. His clothes were stained with feces but his face and scraggly beard were clean for once. Maybe they were bathing in the tub?

I saw more bodies in a pile, not quite diagonal to the kitchen door. Tariq let me go and I ran to fix the bodies. How could they rest if they were not part of the perfect order?

I smoothed the cold wet hair and uniform of the cafeteria lady that had always been nice to me. She even used to count out my peas. Her face was blue and she smelled like the ocean.

Did I chew an odd number of times in my sleep? Had I tapped my thumb against my fingertips in the wrong order?

*It's your fault. You broke it. You stupid bitch, you broke it.*

I looked up to see a man in a gray robe. I knew everyone at the hospital and this person was a stranger. His robe wasn't a hospital gown; it was made of thick wool. His bald head was anchored by a steely beard in tight curls like a Greek statue. His skin was inscribed with thirty four scars. Each scar was a symbol, and they all looked self-inflicted.

His shale gray eyes searched my face and I knew he was like me. He understood the perfect order.

He spoke in a hoarse voice.

"Are you worthy of the great god Nodens, our once and future savior?"

I flicked my tongue against the small pits of my missing teeth and asked him in a small voice. "Who are you? What do you want?"

He peered at me from the crevices of his wizened, rune-scarred face.

"My name is Leith. I want you to help me save the world."

He nodded to Tariq.

Tariq rammed my face into the steel tub so hard my head bounced off the bottom. Salt water flooded my mouth, stinging the open gaps in my gums. I tried to buck him off but he was too strong.

I opened my eyes. Shimmering bubbles oozed out of my nose and tickled my cheek. One. Two. Three. Four. Five. Six.

The water grew darker. Was that my blood? The bubbles came slower. Twenty two. Twenty three. The salty water coursed into my lungs. I squeezed out one last breath for an even number. Twenty four.

My limp body hit the floor. My lungs kicked and a geyser of salty water jumped from my throat. I turned my head and wretched until my chest was clear.

Leith ran his hand through my dripping hair.

"Merciful Nodens has found you worthy. Welcome to the

Brotherhood."

Tariq slapped me on the back.

"No hard feelings?"

His face split into a toothy grin. His jaw never stopped moving, even when he smiled. It clenched and chewed like a burrowing insect. Veins throbbed at the corners of his jet black hair and his empty eyes drilled into mine.

I nodded and returned a weak smile. Whatever had knocked out the power must have given Tariq and the other criminally insane inmates their chance to take over the hospital. Dan and Lizzy and I would have to play along until we got a chance to escape.

Sickly pale light crept over the room. Outside the windows, a smudge of sunrise dissolved in green air. The husks of ruined buildings wavered in the distance. Black tumors of fungus clung to sign posts and sprouted from cars. A tangled carpet of rotting corpses clogged the streets.

An avalanche of guilt smashed over me. I let this happen. I didn't gouge out the odd tooth fast enough.

*It's your fault. You broke it. You stupid bitch, you broke it. It's your fault.*

Leith placed a hand upon my trembling shoulder.

"You have forgotten Nodens, but he remembers you. The Greeks called him Poseidon. The Romans knew him as Neptune. He is our father, and he has chosen you to serve him."

I knelt down and clutched his legs.

"Please…just tell me what to do."

"The natural order has fallen. Our world has been invaded by outside forces. We must enact the proper rituals so that Nodens and the old gods can drive them out."

Dan stammered without looking up.

"How can we be worthy? We were locked up and left to rot. Because we're garbage."

Leith shook his head.

"I recruited others, hiding in the rubble. Their untested minds shattered as soon as they set foot into the unmade world. You are visionaries and holy fools, touched by the gods. The outside forces shall not so easily unmake you. Come and see."

He led us through the blood-streaked hallways to the front door. I had not been outside the hospital since I was committed eight hundred and seventy six days ago.

Downtown Phoenix was smothered in a clammy fog that circled the buildings and congealed in the streets. The blazing sun I had grown up with was barely a lunar eclipse.

*You broke it. You stupid bitch, you broke it.*

Leith pointed to the spires of an old stone church that jutted through the fog.

"That church is where the degenerates betrayed mankind and opened the gateway to the invaders."

Lizzy perked up.

"And we're going to close it!"

"Only mighty Nodens has that power. Our task is to find the cult and stop them from strengthening their masters with sacrifice."

He led us to a station wagon with four flat tires crashed on the hospital steps. He pulled out a duffle bag bulging with weapons. Tariq shoved us aside and rummaged until he found a tree pruning saw with a long, curved blade. Lizzy dove for a chunky shotgun. Dan hung a pair of binoculars around his neck.

I stared at the clots of old books that spilled from the station wagon. Bibles, scrolls, and stacks of crumpled religious tracts littered the ground. Leith grabbed a handful for each of us.

"These are your sacred traditions. Remember what we are fighting for when you encounter the blasphemies of the new order."

My book was written in tightly packed Chinese symbols. The precise columns of evenly spaced characters soothed my jangled nerves.

We stayed low and hurried through the gloom towards the church. I had to step over charred bodies filled with yellow, corroded bones. I counted thirty eight of them. Seven sky scrapers had been split open to reveal steel bones draped in curtains of glowing moss.

A tremulous whistle rang through the iron gray sky. We crouched under a school bus and waited for a bomb to drop on our heads. Something that was not a plane shrieked through the clouds on its way over the city. Dan raised his binoculars to follow it. Leith covered the lenses with his hands and made us hurry on our way.

We stopped outside the church parking lot. The jagged shadow of the church roof loomed over a row of dead brown hedges and a long ornate railing. We saw no movement inside.

We moved towards an alcove with our weapons out. I scanned the sidewalk for cracks and counted cars. The shadows were all wrong.

They didn't fit the contours of the church. They were superimposed over the world, like mine shafts snaking in impossible directions.

I froze in place and dug my tongue into the holes in my gums. Everything was wrong.

*It's your fault. You broke it.*

I spread out my arms to stop the group. Dan shuffled around me and yelped. He lurched and fell, but not forward on his face. He flailed and spun sideways down the mine shaft. No one could believe their eyes, but we all heard his high pitched scream reverberate and fade as he dwindled into the unknown void.

Tariq flinched away from the shadow and bolted to the church door. Lizzy followed with her shotgun swinging in her small hands.

Leith took me by the arm.

"You saw it before we did."

I whimpered and hid behind him. As I moved my head the mine shaft folded into itself and vanished. I dragged my fingers across the spiral scar on my right arm until the world stopped spinning.

"You perceive the perfect order of things. You understand that only ritual can restore it. Come."

He drew a long dagger from his robe and handed it to me. It was straight, with a small perpendicular bar between the blade and handle. There were eighteen lines circling the grip.

We entered to the roar of Tariq's laughter. People were screaming. A shotgun barked twice. Leith ushered me towards a flight of curving stairs and then shouted, "Stop the sacrifice at all costs!"

The dagger quivered in my hands as I counted steps. They spun at well placed angles around a central pillar. I froze on the second to last step, number fifty six. I couldn't skip the last step and I couldn't end on an odd number. The orderlies used to drag me screaming up stairs like this. Now I was free. I could escape the church and go anywhere I wanted.

I tip toed back down. Tariq was holding a shredded green robe drenched with blood and arguing with Leith.

"You wanted the robes, didn't you?"

I snuck outside. The shadow with the broken angles was waiting. I searched for another route, but it was the same everywhere. Wrong angles simmered everywhere beneath the oily fog. The horizon skewed and shattered like a compound fracture and the vertex of certain angles opened like hungry mouths. Like the one that ate Dan.

Shame churned through my guts.

*You broke it. You stupid bitch, you broke it. It's your fault. You broke it.*

I had to set things right. I went back and climbed the stairs. I rubbed the spiral scar until it was red. I dug my nails into my palms, squeezed my eyes shut and dragged my feet across number fifty seven.

The light that seeped through the old wooden shutters struggled against the tar black air of the steeple. Eddies of dust swirled in chaotic patterns, as if stirred by the beating of invisible wings.

A tarnished metal box squatted on a table in the center of the room. The box sent chills through my clammy hands and I nearly dropped it. I wiped my hands ten times and then opened the lid.

A polished stone sphere the size of a golf ball rested on a pronged setting. The dim light struck the rock to reveal thousands of shimmering facets. I seized the stone and scraped its surface with my thumb nail. I turned it over and over, desperate to count the number of angles and faces. There were too many. I stared into the maddening thing and felt its alien geometry swallow my mind.

My consciousness hurtled into space like a meteor. The only solid thought my mind could grasp was that I was not alone. Grotesque, three-lobed eyes burned behind every star and gazed through the cold dead space between.

The eyes reflected an infinite universe fractured into chaos. To think that I could impose order onto anything with my feeble rituals was the true insanity.

The box teetered in my hands as I swooned. I grasped for the shining stone but it hit the floor first. It passed through the wooden floorboards as if the world itself was shadow. A flutter of wings stirred the air and then there was nothing.

I woke up to the glare of a flashlight in my face.

"Wake up, sleepy head!"

Lizzy did a spastic, hopping dance around me with her flashlight.

Leith leaned down and spoke slowly.

"The infidels are gone, no doubt preparing another sacrifice. I know where they'll be. Help us search for robes. We will infiltrate their rites and then administer Noden's justice."

Liz slid the light across the room to reveal a rack of green robes.

"I found them! Let's go! Let's go! Let's go!"

Leith helped me to my feet. His face puckered as he inspected me. I couldn't tell if he was concerned or suspicious. I looked down to the spot where the shining stone had slipped through reality.

We took a van from the parking lot and headed out to the big sacrifice. Leith said it was being held at the Hoover Dam. I'd always wanted to visit someday.

Tariq drove while Leith preached about the gods of earth. I tuned him out and watched the broken world roll by.

We arrived several hours later at the Arizona side of the dam. From a distance, it looked like a castle wall protecting a drowned kingdom. When we got close enough to park, it loomed impossibly high.

A roaring bonfire at the center of the massive structure backlit a throng of people in green robes. Bound captives wriggled along the wall that overlooked the nauseating drop to the Colorado River. Their muffled screams could barely be heard over the howling wind.

*You stupid bitch. It's your fault. You broke it.*

We changed into the green robes and approached on foot. We crossed without resistance and tucked ourselves inside the mass of worshippers. Leith had a plan, but Tariq could not contain his bloodlust. He pulled the pruning saw from his robe and ripped into the crowd.

The knives of the cultists were no match for buckshot. Screams and gunfire bounced off the concrete until the top of the dam was stained red.

I dropped my dagger and backed away from the massacre.

*It's your fault.*

The last of the cultists died with a piteous moan. Leith pointed to the captives.

"Now, attend to the victims!"

Lizzy pulled the gag off a tall bearded man. He gasped and shook with relief.

"Please help my son, I think he's over--"

Leith drowned him out with a thunderous command.

"Glorify our gods as I have taught you!"

Lizzy pounced onto the bearded man and punched the steel point of a knife through his ribcage like a jackhammer. His face froze in a silent mask of surprise.

She reached into the steaming red cavity and excavated a fist sized clump of pulpy tissue. She held it aloft and howled.

"Kukulkan!"

Leith smiled and swept his blade cleanly through the neck of a woman. He bowed his head and intoned, "Io! Saturnalia!"

Tariq exploded into giddy laughter and snatched up a boy in red racing car pajamas. He hefted him towards the crackling bonfire, spraying drool as he screamed.

"Moloch! Moloch! Hail Moloch!"

*It's your fault it's your fault it's your fault it's your fault...*

A teenaged girl with pink hair craned her neck up and implored me with tear filled eyes.

I continued to back pedal until I hit the edge of the side of the dam. I spun around and looked down its colossal face. The river frothed with a whirlpool of massive tree trunks. I wiped the tears from my face and looked closer. The trees emerged from the water, lifting an immense bulk from the muddy rapids. Ebony whale skin stretched taut over spiny segments like a lobster shell.

*You broke it you broke it you broke it you broke it...*

The Hoover dam towered over the obscene thing but also imparted a terrifying sense of its scale. Thousands of pearlescent eyes breached the surface, reflecting the night sky as fractured galaxies.

Leith grabbed me from behind and hissed in my ear.

"That is what the blasphemers would feed with their sacrifices. Let that mongrel starve while the true gods feast. Join us and honor the ancient host. That is the sacred order of this world."

*You stupid bitch you stupid bitch you stupid bitch...*

The Colorado River thundered as it plunged into the nightmarish spider's open maw. I gazed into the abyss and was sure. This was an odd numbered universe.

I pulled Leith over the edge of the dam. If there was no perfect order, it could not be broken. If I didn't matter, nothing was my fault. The runaway train of thoughts in my head fell silent as we tumbled past endless rows of odd numbered teeth.

# The Resistance and the Damned

by Gustavo Bondoni

Paulo looked at me and smiled happily. Then he turned, ran for a few steps, skipped for another few steps, and raced headlong off the edge of the cliff. He didn't scream as he fell.

I wondered if any of us were going to reach the temple alive. We were losing two or three people every hour. Battle-hardened veterans were dropping just as quickly as everyone else – and all of them had been screened by our psych people to be resistant to mental assault. Those too weak to resist were already gone, and had long since become part of the horde we were up against.

The problem was that if we kept losing people at the same rate, there wouldn't be anyone left when we got there. "Everyone come here!"

There were eight of us, probably the most pathetic excuse for a fighting force ever seen on the face of the planet — three former soldiers, a couple of Sem Terras, some civilians that had drifted in, and me. Some of my troops probably still believed that I was glad the madness had arrived in Sao Paulo.

"Concentrate on the plan. Go over every detail of the mission in your head, over and over again. Concentrate! It's the only way to keep the buzzing out, the only way to hold the voices at bay."

They nodded. "Whatever you say, Maria. We're with you till the end," one of them said. I thought it might have been Felipe, but it sounded a little hollow, a little forced – as if he was more than convinced that there was no way ahead, and no way back.

"Will the Americanos come help us?"

That was Flavia. Her voice was strong and steady, but if she was pinning her hopes on rescue by a major power, she was headed towards bitter disappointment. "Of course they will. They always help people in trouble. They know how to deal with these outbreaks."

Sometimes I hated myself, but it wasn't my job to tell them the truth – my job was to get them into the compound and plant the bombs. If that meant lying to a country girl who believed that the Americans would be dumb enough to send men and material into a madness zone, then I would lie to her.

"We also have to help ourselves. Once we get inside, we'll have a much better chance of getting help." If we made it inside, and if the horde of mad people wasn't waiting to tear us apart once we did. But I didn't say that. I just looked them all in the eye, one by one. "Do you have your explosives?"

They checked, and nodded – some firm, others doubtful. It would have appalled any military strategist to see that every one of my soldiers had a large explosive device in his or her pack. He would have thought it inefficient and unsound. But there were reasons: we didn't know which one of the soldiers would be strong enough to make it. And we also had more bombs than people.

Our objective was less than five kilometers away, but I was certain that almost none of us would see it. As we started walking again, the buzzing of a million insects began to sound in my ears. It alternated with the whispers of a million corpses telling me that madness would be a welcome relief.

I put one foot in front of the other, trying to concentrate on the plan.

It was called the compound, but it was really not much more than a large house in a small valley. The central structure was surrounded by walls, but they were meant to keep Brazil's formerly enterprising criminal classes from gaining easy entry, and were only about ten feet high. The current occupants had no need for such things. Criminals would never be a problem for them… for him. The defenses had been abandoned, and the jungle had grown all over the walls.

It's much too soon for this, I thought, looking at the overgrown masonry. Less than two months ago, that very wall had been lovingly tended by a battalion of care-takers and maintenance men. There shouldn't be anything growing in them yet. The jungle should still be miles away. It wasn't natural.

But in natural times, there would have been cars running along the road – now completely covered by dense undergrowth – which we were standing on. In natural times, I wouldn't hear the sound of a million hungry souls tearing each other to shreds in the crawling chaos. In natural times, more than three of us would have survived a walk of a few kilometers across a deserted meadow.

Bettina crouched on the opposite side of the open gate. If I'd been giving odds, I would have pegged her as the first to succumb to the madness. She looked ragged, her hands were shaking, and her blonde hair covered most of her face, but she was still there when so many others had gone.

Felipe was right behind me, large and reassuring, but still behind me, letting me enter first. Well, I had wanted to lead the team personally.

One deep breath was all I allowed myself before plunging through the opening. I half expected to be cut down as soon as I cleared the gap in the wall, but nothing happened. I ran halfway across what had once been the lawn before realizing that Bettina and Felipe weren't near me – or even a few yards behind. I turned to look.

The sight I saw would have haunted me forever, had I not already borne witness to too much horror over the past few weeks.

Felipe, an expression of rapturous delight on his face, had driven his fingers into Bettina's neck, right under her chin. He was slowly, methodically and happily pulling her head off, ignoring the woman's feeble attempts to dislodge him. I could do nothing but watch, rooted to the spot, as blood gushed onto the knee-height emerald grass until, with a loud pop, something in Bettina's vertebrae gave way.

Felipe lost interest and wandered back towards the gate, singing an old football song at the top of his lungs.

Now alone, I turned back to the house, thinking I might be able to do it. But then it hit me. The wailing of the millions, the anguish of lonely souls and, in my mind, the death throes of a million maggots gorging on their abandoned corpses.

Within the mental onslaught, there was one single moment of clarity when everything I'd been seeing and hearing, the essence of madness and horror, coalesced into a single clear and ringing sound.

Something enormous, ancient and incredibly evil laughed at my sheer inconsequentiality.

Then all was dark.

Birds were singing. They sang tunes of joy and tunes of sorrow. Of carefree times and of abject terror. They sang of life. And I realized that, somehow, I'd woken sane. I remembered the horror clearly, but the sound seemed to have vanished.

I hadn't heard birds for weeks – perhaps not since the madness had come to Brazil. Perhaps even since before that, since it wasn't something I normally would have noticed in my day-to day existence. I sat up and looked around, scanning the trees, trying to locate the bird.

There were no birds in the trees. There were no leaves in the trees – in fact, the trees themselves looked like the skeletal apparitions that I used to see on my trips to New York in the winter, back when that was an option. But what remained weren't the thin twigs of northern climes, but the plump branches of the tropics. Seeing them bared to the elements was grotesque, an insult to the natural order.

Worse still was the figure from which the birdsong emanated. Dressed like a carnival sideshow, a dark, sinister-looking man leered in my direction. I got off the ground, came unsteadily to my feet and walked towards the man, all the while convinced that I didn't want to do it. My feet moved of their own accord and, despite the screaming of my consciousness, brought me face to face with the singing man.

A glance at his visage would have weakened my knees had they been under my own control – but in this tropical winter, that certainly didn't seem to be the case. Deep lines cleaved into the brown skin, thin and packed, but seemingly bottomless, becoming even more pronounced around his lips.

And they became even deeper when his mouth closed.

Suddenly, the singing stopped, and I forgot about his mouth and remembered my body. I could feel the adrenaline coursing through it, the thumping of my heart as it attempted to escape my chest.

The man chuckled and I had to fight to control my bladder.

"It seems you arrived just in time, doesn't it?" he said. His voice was like the rustle of dying locusts as they fell from the sky.

I couldn't find my voice, but he didn't seem to notice as he went on.

"The land you knew is gone forever. I can feel your disbelief, but trust me." The old thing smiled and shook its head. "This land, with its ancient traditions lost deep in the jungle will return to what it once was: a land without the interference of you pale modern interlopers. Yes, a land in touch with its old gods, and one that I will enjoy visiting every so often."

I tried to get up, to scream, to run, but was rooted to the ground.

"So, you wish to go elsewhere? Perhaps you might prefer to return to a more civilized land?" He paused. "Very well, if that is what you wish…"

The landscape, the barren trees, the wasted ground, disappeared, and I was in London. I recognized it immediately because of the slight wisps of fog on the ground and the large bullet-shaped building to my right. I'd been in London before, and knew the building well, having walked past it about a hundred times when doing the obligatory touristy things. I found myself leaning on a pole beneath one of the city's ubiquitous security cameras. I wondered what the camera operators would have thought of my torn, tattered shorts and stained shirt. They were probably mobilizing some kind of response team even as I stood there.

It seemed to be early morning, and a small girl walked towards me, tears flowing from her eyes. She was dressed in a dark blue school uniform, and must have been about seven or eight.

"Excuse me, miss," she stammered through the tears. "Have you seen my mother?"

I opened my mouth to answer, but my mouth wouldn't open. Instead, my hand shot out of its own accord, and a sharp blade that I hadn't realized I was still carrying sliced through her throat like lightning.

Blood spurted onto my hand, but the little girl didn't scream or thrash or make any sort of commotion. Her gaze simply held my own for a second, then two, and she crumpled to the sidewalk in a heap.

The body I inhabited moved its gaze from the girl on the ground and stared straight into the lens of one of the cameras as London dissolved around me.

"Did you enjoy your trip?" the creature asked me. Its aspect had changed, and somehow it seemed thinner, less substantial – although younger. "Your actions leave you with little choice, I think. If you stay here, the new masters of your old country will probably have very graphic ways of reasserting their dominance over you. And if you leave, if you run back to what you so laughingly call civilization, I suppose you're strong enough to survive in prison. Although most people who murder children don't do well in jail."

And suddenly I could speak. "Do you really expect me to believe that it was real? It's just another one of your mind tricks. Your mind tricks did nothing to keep me from reaching you, and they won't work now."

The chuckle reached me again, but this time, I felt strong. I could defeat him.

"Perhaps I misjudged you. Perhaps you will find a way to survive in spite of everything. If that is so, then are you certain that you won't live every day in remorse for what you've done, for the innocent blood you spilled? Living like that would be torture."

"I did nothing."

"Your body did… and who commands it?"

"It was all in my head. You know it as well as I do!"

"Was it?" The creature – nearly translucent now, looked down at my hand, and I followed its gaze. The blade was still bright and clean, but my wrist was wet with dark red blood. My heart sank as I watched a single drop fall to the grey earth.

When I looked up again, my tormentor was gone, as though he'd never been there, and the silence of this new, cold Brazil which wasn't Brazil any more echoed around me. I knew what the future held – he'd told me precisely what it held.

The silence was broken by my scream. I screamed hard, and for a long time, but the sound was a weak thing in the enormity of the land.

# Twilight of the Gods

by Jonathan Woodrow

My eyes are bloodshot and stingy and my head pounds like someone jammed a fist into my skull. Tension balls up in the back of my neck and sits there, static. I feel worse than I've felt in a long time and I need to push past it. My wife is still asleep, but the kids are up already. I can hear them leaping around and throwing their toys at the dog just like they always do.

When I get downstairs, I catch the older one holding a busted game controller over his head and he jumps out of his skin when he feels my hand close around his wrist. He thrashes a little before he wises up and looks down at his feet. The old dog hobbles back to her crate. The boy starts struggling again and I realize I've drawn blood with my thumb nail. I let him go and he sinks down to the floor, nursing his wrist like a wounded animal. Serves him right.

Then the younger one speaks. "Breakfast?"

I shake my head. A house full of idiots. "No breakfast, genius. Me go out... have to make some money... buy food... bring back here..." I rub my belly. "Then we eat, mmm."

The older one looks up at me and I can see the question in his face before he asks it.

"Are you doing a transfusion?"

"What's it to you?"

He says nothing.

"I've got too many kids anyway, why not kill two pups with one stone and make some money out of it?"

The boy turns pale and I can't contain myself any longer. I give him a full-on belly laugh and he looks away. I can see his anger return but he's too chicken-shit to say or do anything.

"Relax, little girl. I'm not after you."

He's quiet for a moment, then he opens his mouth with another question. "Well, who's left?"

"What's that, boy?"

"Who else is there? You already got everyone and you're tapped out. Aunt Franny, Uncle Dane, Papa... There *is* no one else. They're all gone. So who's next?"

I frown, a little unsure how to react to this outright defiance. I consider showing him what my fist tastes like when I hear a car horn out front.

"You let me worry about that, boy. Mind your damned business."

I make it to the front door when the boy speaks again.

"Please, dad," he says. All the confrontation's gone. "Don't."

I walk out without another word.

"I appreciate you helping me out with this, Bud."

I climb into the passenger side of my friend's pickup and he puts the truck in drive and pulls away. "Where am I taking you?"

"Just head towards downtown for now. I'll direct you once we get closer."

Bud nods and keeps his eyes on the road. We drive in silence for the first twenty minutes. The radio is on, tuned to an AM talk station, and I hear some lady from down east getting all riled up about upcoming legislation in the transfusion industry. I wince at the mention of the word—the elephant in the car—and change the station. Out of the corner of my eye I see Bud shake his head.

There are so many things I want to explain to Bud, but I don't know how. I want him to understand that I have my reasons for doing what I'm doing—damn good reasons, too—and that for a man in my position there are very few alternatives. With no money, we are facing even bigger problems. The undeniable fact that worse things can happen if I don't do this.

I think of the puppies again.

But no matter how necessary this all is, no matter how good my reasons are, it still doesn't seem right. Not even to me. "But that's life, isn't it?" I say out loud. Bud continues to drive the car and I keep my mouth shut and smile. I'm pretty sure he understands on some level. Life *is* different now. It demands these sorts of bad decisions. It's not like it was before. We were all having too much fun to notice what was happening around us, and then Mom and Dad arrived home early and the party was over.

There had been no fireballs or floods or famine or pestilence. None of that. They had arrived quietly, unnoticed at first until word got around, and by then business was booming. Four Gods in our Metropolitan area alone, and who knows how many more across the globe.

And they look just like us, too. I know that's not so strange in itself, especially since we were always taught that they—or He—would resemble our form, with stories of Him creating us in His own image. But to see one crossing the street or sitting across from you is another thing entirely. Weren't you supposed to feel something more? The divine architect, the Alpha and the Omega, love and forgiveness. Weren't you supposed to sense that you were in the presence of something great? Well, that's not really how it is with these guys. Firstly, they're all men, so the whole "love" thing, at least for me, is a little weird. The only aura they give off is one of complete and utter indifference. None of this should come as a surprise, when you think about it. I mean, why should He or They or whatever give a shit about each and every one of us? How could they? We can't possibly expect them to know us all individually. Even now, the question of whether they had a hand in our creation remains unanswered.

This is all moot anyway, since the reason they came back wasn't out of love or concern, but something closer to cleaning house.

The first time I met one in the flesh was about a year ago. The Gods had recently landed and, naturally, there was a lot of talk. Some

good, some bad, but overall, people were mostly curious. One of the
first transfusions was given to a guy I knew from across town, and this
had caused quite a bit of panic among the other residents of our
community. In an effort to calm things down, our friend Bud had
decided to throw a party at his place. The turnout was huge, and I
always figured this was because people were expecting something...I
don't know, out of the ordinary. What they got instead was a run of the
mill garden party. Barbecue, beer, play area for the kids. But that was
exactly what the doctor ordered. Bud knew that plain-old ordinary was
what everyone needed, and it worked, at least for a while. For a couple
of hours, we were all able to forget about our worries, the changing
times, and remained frozen in an earlier time when our problems
were… I guess, better. I mean, sure, we *had* problems, but they were
pissy little problems nobody would give a shit about today. Isn't that
how it always works? You're not happy with what you have until
something new comes along and shuffles everything around, making
what you had seem fucking peaches, and then you wonder why you
ever complained about it in the first place.

So there we were, sitting on deck chairs on the grass,
simultaneously sunburned and eaten alive by mosquitoes, sipping at
cheap beer from plastic cups, munching on hotdogs, listening to one
of the other neighbors complain about immigrants (because, really,
that's the sort of thing I *want* to be worrying about again), and life was
pretty fucking pristine. Until that prick Dane showed up and had to go
and start spouting conspiracy theories and getting everyone all riled up.
That was when the party ended.

I spent the next day bitching to the wife about her jackass brother and what an asshole he was for ruining the party, and she agreed with me, at least that's what I thought. It was hard to tell what she was thinking, but I'm pretty sure she was angry with him, too. And that was when she said it, the words that would change my life from then on: "He's your best friend, there must be something you like about him."

As soon as she said that I shut the hell up. I had to. With the few beers I had in me, I knew that if I kept talking I would let on what I was thinking, and the whole thing would be blown. She'd find some way to talk me out of it. No, this required a lot of focus on my part. A lot of solitary contemplation. And so, the next day, I drove to see the God in his office on the top floor of the one hundred and fifty story tower downtown. No appointment required, just show up and get it done before you lose your nerve.

The transfusion part was meant to be straight-forward, from what I'd read. Basically, you go there, you offer up someone's life, and the God gives you money for doing it. Piece of cake. There's a little more to it, but that's the gist. So you might ask, what's to stop the nastiest meth-head street scum low-life motherfucker from going back again and again, not a care in the world, killing one person after another after another and making a mint? Well, there's the catch. The financial remuneration is commensurate with the amount of guilt and sadness and mourning the seller experiences in connection with what they're doing. So if you don't give a shit, you don't get paid.

I had my questions, naturally.

"So, what kind of person do you get coming in here, then?"

The God smiled. There was no warmth to the smile, only a certain glee at the opportunity to explain to me what assholes we humans all are.

"The desperate kind, the kind on the edge of their humanity, just about to be pushed over by their own greed."

And my response to this: "Cool."

The God laughed a humorless laugh and tossed a pen across the length of the wide desk onto my lap. The pen moved in between my fingers, warm and alive, convulsing like living tissue, beating through the platinum casing and up through my fingers into my arms and neck.

"You're familiar with the concept of actual cash value, I'm sure," he said. "What I pay is the monetary equivalent to what the victim is worth to you."

It had to be someone close, someone I cared about losing.

"Well, can I get a quote?"

The God sneered and tossed something else into my lap. It was a piece of slate, maybe eight inches by eight inches, and carved into it was the contract. "Sign or get the hell out of here. Your choice."

I nodded and closed my eyes. What did I know about Dane? Well, he was my brother-in-law, and the best man at my wedding. I thought of the good times we'd had together, and asked myself what he was really worth to me. He'd been my best buddy since we were in diapers. We'd battled school bullies, braved the harsh reprimands from our fathers, built forts in the woods, and talked to girls. As adults, we'd got drunk together, worked together, picked up girls together. And best of all, he'd been totally fine when I hooked up with his kid sister. The guy had always been there for me, through thick and thin, and although we'd drifted apart, I had no doubt that ours was a friendship we could pick up again in a heartbeat if it came to it.

Yeah, it was worth a fair price, I'd say.

My hesitation grew, and quickly turned into panic. A part of me wanted to throw down the pen and leave, find some other way to handle things. The God seemed to sense this and he smiled. A real smile this time, genuine hunger. I glanced down and saw that the pen was still in my hand and the dotted line was right there in front of me, so I emptied my head of any further consideration and signed my name. When it was done, I looked up. I was in sort of a daze, and not really sure what was going to happen next or how it would work. But then I saw it.

Dane was standing right there across the table, beside the God, an expression of bemusement on his unshaven face. He looked over at me, at my contract, then raised his hands and ran them over his buzzed head. It was a gesture I'd seen dozens of times before, and it meant he was scared or confused. The God smiled, and I felt my right hand shiver around the pen. It was as though the pen had sprouted nerve endings of its own and was connecting with my whole body. Then, it rose into the air. The nib swelled into a bulging head and pointed in the direction of my best friend.

Dane gave me one final look of desperation. The only words I could squeeze out were, "I'm sorry," before a bright light gushed from my hand and slammed into Dane's chest, hurling him across the room and out through the open window. His cries drifted down and down, fading out gradually until they were simply no longer audible.

I choked, suddenly unsure how to breathe or function as my chest leapt up and down like a fucking jackrabbit. What the hell just happened? I had expected some sort of a bang as he hit the ground; something to mark the significance. But instead Dane got a quiet, meaningless passage, like someone turned down the dials until he was nothing.

Tears filled my eyes and the God stood and walked over to me with a canvas sack in his right hand. The pen was still red hot in my hand as he took it away from me.

"Payment," he said, and dropped the sack onto the desk with a thud. "Pretty good turnout, as it happens. That's just as well, really. There's always a risk of miscarriage, though it's rare on a first try."

As bad as I felt, my attention was caught and I was unable to resist opening the bag to peek inside.

"It's all there. Forty-thousand dollars and change," he said. "That ought to tide you over for a few months. Then, I suppose, I'll be seeing you back here again."

I wanted to tell him that wasn't going to happen, that this was one big dumb mistake that I would never make again, but I wasn't so sure that was true. Instead, I walked out with my loot and drove home.

I spent the next month or so out of work, drinking away the foul memories. I wasn't so great with money, so that forty grand didn't last too long, and I noticed the wife spending more and more time hiding away in the bedroom as we neared the bottom of our funds. Her tendency to hide from her problems instead of facing them was one of her many character flaws.

It was around then I decided to sober up for long enough to consider the next transfusion. Someone had to take responsibility, and we needed money. So I asked myself, what about Papa? Well, my father was still around, though we didn't speak much. I considered how I actually felt about him, and what he was worth to me. This was a tough question, but after much mulling, I figured what the heck, and headed back into the city for another unscheduled appointment with the God. By then I considered myself an expert at the transfusion. A seasoned professional. I was confident in my ability to dig up all the good memories right at the last minute before I signed the contract so as to achieve the maximum cash value.

Papa had netted me only twelve grand, but one of my old girlfriends, a woman named Patty, had yielded fifty-five and change. My remorse was short lived when the God informed me she had been considering a transfusion of her own and had yours truly in mind as a possible candidate. No, that was a damned good payday for me, and that fifty-five lasted nearly six months.

One morning, I got up and the car was gone. Not a biggie in itself, but since the wife was still at home and so were the kids, that missing car got me scratching my head.

"I sold it," she said, no trace of remorse or any notion of what the fuck we were supposed to do without a goddamn car.

"You sold it?"

She nodded, then wiped a tear from her cheek.

"Jesus fucking Christ," I said. "You're still crying? You're always crying. What the fuck for? The last one was my friend, not yours. The only one you're missing is Dane, and you said yourself he was a deadbeat fuckup anyway. What's your problem?"

All she could do was shake her head and point at a canvas bag that sat on the table. I hadn't noticed it before, but I had a pretty good idea what was in it. I picked it up and it felt light.

"What's this?"

"Five grand," she said.

I laughed and shook my head at that. Five fucking grand? For the car? "You know something? I got eleven times that for some worthless bitch I used to bang," I said. "And she was cheap to replace, too. Not like that car."

The wife continued to gaze down at the ground, that pathetic look of defeat on her face. "You do realize I'm just going to have to buy another one, right? I mean, what do reckon you've achieved here? You think we could somehow retire on that five grand? Head off somewhere warm and leave our problems behind?"

She said nothing, which was pretty much what I'd been expecting. I hated her right then. Hated that I still cared about her, but mostly hated that the world had changed and she didn't have the stomach for it. What good was that to her, or to our family? She needed to toughen up, and fast, or she was in for a big surprise as things got darker and shittier than they already were. Because that was the way things were going, I could see that much. Things were still changing, and they were getting really hard. People were dying, obviously, but not just for money anymore. They were dying for no better reason than desperation. They'd seen the greying sunset signaling the end to what had once been a bright, blossoming day, and they weren't so sure whether it would ever rise again in the same way. If you asked me, it probably wouldn't. One way or another, I needed to either talk some sense into the wife, or I'd have to drag her kicking and screaming into reality. It was for her own good.

But she broke my train of thought with a question that came out of left field. "What's a miscarriage?"

"Huh?"

She frowned, concentrating on what she was saying as if the words might otherwise float away. "I heard someone talking about it on the radio. They said it was a growing problem."

I thought about this. Not about the answer, but about why she'd asked the question. What made her think of that, of all things, at a time like this? But I decided not to pick apart her motives for now and just answer the damned question so we could move on.

"I've never experienced one myself, but my understanding is that it's when your remorse and sadness—and that's how they calculate the amount you get paid—is overshadowed by your anticipation at how much you're going to make. And if that happens just at the wrong time during a transfusion, your suffering barely registers, and you're left with nothing. Pocket change."

The wife said nothing, just stared into space and continued

nodding.

The next day I sold her sister Franny and earned back the same amount of money she'd made from the car. When I got home I called her downstairs and dumped the five grand baggie on the table. I grinned. "Have you learned your lesson?" I said. She took a moment to figure out what was happening, but when all the little pieces fell into place, her hands came up to her face and she cried out through her fingers in a way that made her sound like a dying animal. I tried to shush her but it was no use. The kids ran downstairs to see what was going on. It really wasn't what I'd had in mind at all. I wanted to teach her about what it took to survive in this world, and instead the three of them blubbered like babies for the next week or so and pretty much ignored me. I could tell the older one wanted to yell at me, call me names, maybe even hit me. But that spineless pussy didn't have the balls. He knew I would put him down in a heartbeat and exchange him for a few bucks if I had enough of him. No, he was a pansy, just like his mother, but at least he was smart.

Bud drops me off and I thank him for the ride, tell him I'm picking up a new car in a week or so, after payday, and I'll return the favor. I'm about to get out of the car when he grabs my arm. His grip isn't all that hard and I could easily pull away, but I turn to him anyway to see what he has to say. I'm expecting a lecture, but in true Bud form, I get something else entirely.

"What's the going rate these days for a loved one?" he asks.

I'm unsure if his question is genuine or rhetorical but I decide to answer anyway.

"Anything from a couple grand to sixty, I suppose. There's an art to it, more than anything else."

Bud nods. "Yeah, I read about some guy who managed to pull three hundred grand out of an old school pal. I guess it's all a matter of practice, right?"

Well, this takes the wind out of my sails. Three hundred for an old school pal? Course, Bud could be bullshitting me, but I don't think he is.

"I also read they do seminars now on how to maximize the return on your transfusion. They got some former God teaching the program and he tours the country. You ever been to one of those?"

I'm only half listening to what Bud's telling me, but the key points are getting in, hitting me like bowling balls in a way that makes me want to rethink and redo everything I've done over the past year. For a minute I'm actually thinking about going back and trying Dane again, or Papa, or Franny. That's how fucking stupid I am. And that's when I feel it, for the first time: the idea that I might very well be in over my head. My face must've given something away because out of the corner of my eye I can see Bud smile. A real smile, like he's just saved a puppy from drowning or something.

"What do you say, friend. Shall we turn around and head back home?"

I look at him for a second, trying to understand what the hell he's thinking about, but I can't hold back any longer and I burst out laughing at the man. It's a mean-spirited laugh that wipes that fucking smile off his face really fast.

"*Go home?*" I say, incredulous. "To what? You tell me that, Bud. What the fuck am I going home to?"

I was thinking he might lose it, but he's still calm, no trace of anger or frustration.

"It doesn't have to be this way," he says.

This time it's my turn to get frustrated and angry. How could anyone be so naive? I mean, Bud of all people. I shake my head and exhale, muttering something under my breath, though I don't know what it is at first.

"What was that?" he asks.

"I said *you sound like the wife*. You think if you sit at home and pray hard enough all this will get better? It's never getting better. It's too late for us now. We humans are done. Extincto, finito, and this is just the foreplay. This is a gift, don't you see? We're going to die. Every single one of us. And this is their way—I'm talking about the Gods—of letting us hit the snooze button on that. We get a little more time before we're done. That is, if we want it. If you don't, that's your problem. Some of us will die sooner than others, but it's coming. And I can't believe you don't know that, Bud. I thought you were smart."

Bud's face doesn't change, and I don't know how the hell he does that. "And how do you know all of this?" he asks.

"How do I...?" I'm stumped. Not at the question—I haven't even thought about that—but at Bud's stubbornness. "How do you *not* know this?" I say. "Have you been asleep for the last couple years?"

Bud reaches over and takes hold of my other arm, looking me dead in the eyes. "It doesn't have to be this way, friend. It really doesn't. You think it does, but you're wrong. All of you are." He points a finger in the air. "They, up there... they don't control us. We do. Don't you get it? They're not nearly as powerful as everyone believed. And for the first time since man decided to kneel down and talk to the sky, we know this as an empirical fact."

I pull my arms away. "I feel sorry for you, Bud. I really do. The world's changing, and if you don't change with it, you're going to have a big problem. It's the smart people like me who are going to come out on top. You'll see that someday. Hopefully before it's too late."

Bud stays quiet this time. I take it as a sign that some of what I've said has finally stuck.

"And don't worry," I tell him. "I'm not selling you. Not yet, anyway."

Bud snorts. "You're not, huh?"

"You're my ride home."

He gives me a flat wave and I head into the lobby of the tall building for my unscheduled appointment with the God.

"It's you again," he says with his loveless grin.

"Must be some sort of record, right?"

"Not really."

I sit down. "Let's just get this over with, shall we?"

He nods and sits down across from me. "So, who's next?"

For some strange reason I think about the puppies for the second time today. Which is odd, since they haven't crossed my mind in months. There they are, tired and emaciated, their quiet cries of confused suffering, their begging eyes. I try to shake it off, think of something else. And it works.

"I have a question for you, before we start," I say.

The God looks impatient, but doesn't try to stop me.

"What's this I hear about some guy who made three hundred grand from some old school pal he barely knew?"

This seems to pique the God's interest a little. "What of it?"

"Is it true?"

"Yes."

The discussion is moving too fast and I need to slow it down so I can keep up. "So what? You're saying you've been short-changing me all this time?"

The God closes his eyes and sighs, a smile on his face that makes me think of the way a dog owner might consider a retriever who poops on the rug. "Or maybe you've been short changing yourself."

I frown, not sure what to say next. "So tell me what I'm doing wrong."

There's a moment where I think the God is just about to toss me out of his office—maybe his window—but he decides last minute to go another way and humor me.

"You want a quick lesson? Most people pay for that sort of thing. You hear about those seminars?"

I nod.

"Well here's a freebie. You have to delve. Delve deeper into all those juicy, complex emotions. They exist in every human relationship, and that's where all the good stuff is. Take your father, for instance. You got, what, twelve grand from him in the end? Why was that?"

"You tell me," I say, moving on the defensive. "I don't know, maybe it's because he was an asshole and deep down I really hated that fucker. Maybe the feelings I thought I had for him were nothing but my dumb memories playing tricks on me."

The God shakes his head. "Memories are the only real things you have. It's too late now, anyway, but just as an exercise, go ahead and delve, search, dig up all the good complex stuff. Discard anything that's ostensibly good and look for something else."

"But I don't know how."

"Yes," he says. "Yes, you do. Tell me more about the puppies."

I pause, my mouth slightly open, and a chill passes through me. "How do you know about that?"

"It was something I noticed throughout that transfusion, floating just below the surface. I had hoped it would come bursting out at the last minute but you chose to ignore it. So now it's too late, but I want you to explore it anyway. Quickly, though. I don't have all day."

There are very few fond memories I associate with my father. The only ones I could find during the transfusion were when I was very young, and they'd faded over time. There's a reason why I'd only earned twelve grand for him, and that's because, for most of my life, he was a sadistic jerk. The memory of the puppies is no exception to that.

I notice the God checking his watch and I close my eyes and think.

"When I was a boy," I begin, "I had a pet dog named Annabelle. Kind of girlie, I know, but it was the name of a girl at school I had sort of a crush on. Anyway, we never had Annabelle spayed. Could never afford to. So she was confined to the house at all times. Always walked her on a leash, always made sure the doors were closed. Only one time I left the door open and she got out."

The God smiles. "And her impulses got the better of her. You mammals are really not too dissimilar from one another, are you?"

I ignore the spite in his voice and move on. "It took a few weeks before any of us noticed a change. Mother saw it first, and she pulled me aside. There was a look of terror in her face that I only ever remember seeing when Dad was drinking, or if he was having trouble at work. But when we told him what had happened, Dad was fine. He even smiled, said it was one of those things. That this was just a good lesson we could all learn from. It wasn't until the pups were born that I found out mother had been right to be scared.

"I made this enclosure out of some old chicken wire and put the pups in there. There was no way they could get out. Then Dad asked me about food. I sort of shrugged, figuring they'd feed from their mother, and he said that was true, at first, but it wouldn't last forever, and when they were done with that, they'd need real food. And that was the lesson. We couldn't afford to feed any more mouths than we already had. He'd known that all along, and now he wanted me to know that, too."

The God gives me a curious look and I can't help but wonder if he's admiring my father's hard-handed parental approach.

"So eventually, the puppies began to starve. I thought that was one of the worst things I would ever see, creatures that small and defenseless crying out in pain as their bodies shut down from lack of nutrition, but was I wrong about that. Boy, was I wrong about that. When things got really bad, they turned on each other. To cannibalism. They picked off the weakest one first, then moved on, and on..."

The God looks at his watch again, the impatience growing. I start to encounter feelings I didn't even know existed. Images to go along with those feelings. The most prominent being my father's face as he teaches me about what it is to support a family, about taking responsibility, and facing up to consequences. My memory of that day seems harsh, but was it? What if my father had taught me the most valuable lesson of my life?

The complex feelings begin to change, and the ambivalence I thought I'd been holding onto all these years is actually admiration, a deep gratitude for shaping me into the man I am today, and for the first time since the transfusion, I actually mourn my father's passing.

"I haven't got all day," says the God.

I snap out of it. Plenty of time to contemplate that later, but for now, I need to move on, while the lesson is still fresh in my mind.

"Right," I say, putting on my business face. And then, "You're familiar with my wife, I assume?"

The God grins. "You're going after the big fish, I see. You think you're ready?"

"I know I am."

"All right then," he says, and the Pen is in my hand, along with the Slate. I touch the corner of the signature line with the tip of the pen just as the wife appears on the other side of the room. I take a moment to let it all sink in. She doesn't seem to be even the slightest bit surprised at her predicament. Has she known all along? This knocks me sideways a little, but only a little. I think about what the God just told me, going for the complex emotions first, rather than the obvious ones, and I form a mental list.

I consider her inability to grab the bull by the horns, to figure out what she wants and take it. She is weak, and until now, I found this to be an undesirable trait. But she is my wife, and it's my job to look out for her. Those weaknesses make my responsibilities that much more important, like caring for an animal. *A puppy.*

I move quickly through the process, using my newly acquired expertise to dig deep, until my heart aches and I can feel tears pulling at my eyes. The wife notices and her face turns into something resembling sympathy. This causes me to choke up, and I bear down on the slate with the pen, not wanting to waste this glorious feeling of pain and remorse. I dive into the signature with grace and precision, allowing my name to flow through the slate, somehow in keeping with the bittersweet tone of my emotions, and a thought pops inside my head, totally uninvited, and I ponder the full extent of what I'm doing, what it means for my family and me. If some guy can achieve three hundred grand for a mere school pal using the same technique, how much can I expect to make here? A killing! Literally. And my pen swoops down and around, ending at the dot above the 'i', just as the muscles in the corner of my mouth twitch into a grin.

The room turns a dark grey, the wife is absorbed in the dim light that emanates from the tip of the pen, and the God sighs and offers a look of disappointment so inconsequential it's agonizing to watch.

For the first time under these circumstances, I am overcome by pure dread. I look to the God, my eyes begging for reassurance.

He shrugs. "Better luck next time." And my wife is gone.

My jaw drops and I stare at the open window. I wonder if the wife is still falling or whether it's all over for her now. Not that it matters. It was over for her since the day I decided to take part in a transfusion. I lower my head into my hands and try my hardest to weep, scrunching up my face and eyes in an effort to cry, to release some of the horror, but nothing happens. I emit a groan from deep in my chest and I feel like I need to throw up. I'm certain the God's going to send me away at any moment and I consider leaping from the open window after my wife. There is nothing else for me. I am alone, with two kids to take care of, and I have nothing for them. Not anymore. It's all gone. And then a voice brings me back to reality and away from the comforting fantasy of suicide.

*"What did you do?"*

It's my son. The older one. What the hell was he doing here?

*"Dad! What did you do? Where's mom gone?"*

I open my eyes and look up at the desperate sadness in my son's face. He's not yet certain, but he has a pretty good idea what's happened. The most awful thing a man can do to a child: I've taken away his mother. And it was all for nothing.

"I'm so sorry, son," I say, and the impotence of the words is enough to bring back the thoughts of suicide. What could I possibly say to him at this moment?

It's then that the God speaks. "Do we have any other business today?"

I look up and see a curious smile on his face, like he's holding some great secret that would allow us to escape all our troubles.

"A parent's consent is all I need," he says.

I look over at my son, back at the God, and I stand. I walk over to my son and place a hand on his shoulder. "How did you get here?" I ask him.

His face is a swirling ball of anger and sadness. "I hitched a ride on the back of Bud's truck."

I squeeze his shoulder and my soul wretches and dry-heaves, though there is nothing left of it but bile now.

"We're in big trouble now, son," I say.

"Is mom gone?" he asks.

I nod, and then bow my head in shame.

"How could you do this to us?" he asks, his voice cracked and pinched, and it's clear *he* has no problem crying. His emotions are still alive and right on the surface, just as they've always been. I understand now what the God was telling me, and without further thought, I guide the boy over to where I've been sitting and lower him down into the chair. He protests a little, but not much.

"What are you doing?" he says. "Get off me."

I run over to the God and ask, "Where do I sign? As the parent or guardian?"

The pen and slate are in my hands again, and I take one final glance at my little boy before carving out my name for the second time today.

"Look after your brother," I say. "And when you're done here, call Bud and tell him what happened. He'll know what to do. He can help you."

In the background I hear the boy calling my name, calling for his dad, crying out for me to stop whatever it is I'm about to do, but I don't turn around again. Instead, I raise my hand up to the edge of the open window and lean out, feeling the cold breeze blow across my face and ruffle my hair. There's something about the sensation that seems familiar, though I don't know what it is and probably never will.

I hear the whooshing sound of the pen as the contract is fulfilled, but by then I am already gone, descending. I know my son will do well out of the deal whether he wants to or not, and he will be able to take care of what's left of our family far better than I ever could. I watch the sidewalk rush up at me from below, and I wonder if I'll hear a bang or a crash to mark the end, or if I will simply cease to exist.

# Venice Burning

## by A.C. Wise

When R'lyeh rose, it rose everywhere, *everywhen*. Threads spiral out, stitching past to present to future. There are ways to walk between, if you're willing to lose a part of yourself. Most people aren't; it's my specialty.

I stand on a pier, eyes shaded against the water's glare. It's 2015, by the smell - diesel and cooked meat, early enough that such things still exist. It might as well be 2017, or 3051. But this year is where my client is, so I wait, sweating inside a black, leather jacket, watching slick weeds stir below lapping waves.

The sun burns white-hot. Across the water, atop a basilica whose name no longer matters, Mary stretches marble arms over a maze of twisted streets. Legend claims when the basilica was built, the statue turned miraculously toward the water to guard the boats in the canal. The day R'lyeh rose, she turned her back on the water forever and wept tears — sticky and ruby-dark — that weren't quite blood.

A hand touches my arm, nails perfectly manicured and painted sea-shell pink. I'm surprised the Senator came herself. A frightened mother looking for her lost son is one thing; a politician desperate to protect her career is another. I wonder which she is.

From the Senator's perspective, it's only just beginning. R'lyeh is a shadow beneath the waves and there is still hope. But I've seen tendrils

253

slide through the canals of the city, licking the stones and tasting the ancient walls. They want nothing. The Senator still thinks she can bargain with the Risen Ones, strike a deal and become a new Moses to her people.

I focus on the Senator's nails, striking against my black leather. I know this about her: her life will end in a church, green water rising between the pews, light reflecting against the ceiling in shifting patterns. She will die screaming, bound hand and foot, while her blood is pulled through her skin by sheer force of will.

I don't offer to shake her hand. "Do you have a photo of your son?"

The slim case tucked beneath her arm matches her nails, lips, and suit. She hands me a glossy headshot. Her son looks nothing like her. Mr. Senator is an actor, younger than the Senator by at least ten years, dark hair and eyes like his son, but prettier by far.

Marco, the son, has deep brown eyes and the faintest of scars — acne, despite the medicine and cosmetic surgery his parents could easily afford. I hide the edge of a smile at Marco's tiny act of rebellion.

"You understand this is a matter that requires the utmost discretion." The Senator holds out an envelope. She tries for frost, the same control she displays on the Senate floor, but her voice fails.

"I'll be in touch," I say, looking at a point beyond the Senator's left shoulder.

A subtle tugging wraps threads around my spine. I'm amazed at the Senator's self-control, or her talent for denial. How can she not feel what the world has become? How can she resist the temptation to slip into the future? She has the perfect pretense: looking for her son. She could see how it all ends.

I pocket the envelope and Marco's photo, and step past the Senator. Her mouth opens, snaps audibly closed; she isn't used to being dismissed. My boot heels click as I walk away, thinking about her son.

A family vacation in a city of masks and illusory streets — the perfect place to hide, the perfect place to disappear. Twenty-six and vanished — of course Marco doesn't want to be found. Even photographed, the desire to run shines clear in Marco's eyes. Desperation and fear, his expression bring a flicker of memory, which I push aside. There is no place far enough, but he'll still try, fleeing forward to test the notion that the future is infinite.

I start at Harry's Bar. I step forward and slide cross-wise, surrendering to shattered light, burning stars and the aching space between. Tentacles as insubstantial as breath slide beneath my skin. They want nothing, but they take what I have to give. Cold, cold, cold, they grip my spine, caress my skull, and scoop out the heart of me.

If they were beings to be reasoned with, I would ask them to take everything. It doesn't work that way.

Firelight flickers. My scars itch, stretching tight across my back. I hold the memories up as an offering, but the tentacles find their own prize. I don't know what they take from me; I only feel the familiar, hollow ache when it's gone.

It's 2071 when I enter the bar. The light is green, but the waiters still wear immaculate white jackets and ties, a terrible joke. I slide into a seat.

"A double." I don't specify of what; it hardly matters.

Behind the bar, where mirrored shelves used to hold bottles of liquor, pendulous nets hold a jumble of perpetually dripping starfish, conch shells, mussels, and clams. Breathing, wavering things cling to the wall. The air smells of brine. Things at the corner of my eye shift, unfold impossible dimensions, and retreat — deep-sea anemones shy of the light.

The bartender slides a drink in front of me. Misery haunts his gaze. This is our life now, our life then — this is the life to come. His mouth doesn't move when he breathes. His nostrils don't stir. If I didn't know to look, I wouldn't even see the gills slitting his throat, nictating almost imperceptibly. His eyes bulge, moist, blood-shot. I place a bill on the bar and add a stack of coins, a generous tip.

I wait a moment, then place Marco's picture next to the coins. The bartender's skin sweats oil and sorrow. People determined to vanish come to Harry's Bar, and for the right price, the miserable waiters in their starched, white uniforms show them how.

"When?" I ask.

"Can't say." The bartender's voice is frog-hoarse.

I know he means can't, not won't. Everything can be bought and sold here: sugar-sweet cubes that melt on the tongue and bring oblivion; death; pleasure; escape; even answers. The man behind the bar taught Marco how to leave, but didn't ask questions — a good bartender to the last.

"Thanks." I down my drink in one shot.

The liquor unfolds in my mouth, sending a spike through my lungs. My eyes water. I walk back outside.

It's dark. The stars are right. But the stars have always been right.

Where would I go if I was Marco? A useless question. He's running from a suffocating life of expectation. The future reached out blind tentacles, snaring my heart. Marco chose R'lyeh's ways; R'lyeh's ways chose me. But no matter how many times I offer up my memories to those ways, they refuse to take them from me.

Firelight. A horse whinnies. The scent of wet leather and dry hay. Lips trace mine, arching my throat, shivering across my belly. I gather sweat on the tip of my tongue, briny-sweet like the sea. The horse's whicker turns to a scream.

My scars tingle, hot and cold at the same time. Some things can't be outrun, taken, or let go.

Suddenly, I don't give a fuck about Marco. And I have all the time in the world.

I walk along the water's edge, where there used to be a restaurant. Once — after R'lyeh, but before now — the entire city burned. The canals turned to oil and fire swept from rooftop to rooftop, sparing nothing.

Centuries of human existence, wiped out in the blink of an eye. I was there. I will be there again.

Venice, as always, survived. It rose from the ashes, born anew in brick and stone and marble, in deference to the old ways. It was also resurrected in glass and steel, in deference to ways old-yet-new. Finally, it shambled back from the dead with walls that bled and seethed, flickered and writhed, in deference to the way things are now and always will be. Venice: an impossible city, impossible to kill.

I cross a glass bridge. The water creeps, sluggish, beneath it. Lights glimmer on its surface; things sleep in its depths. Venice floats, it sinks, it is drowning, and it is drowned. And it survives. So do I.

I've been to the underwater city where Venice used to be. I've kick-pulled through cathedrals lit by the unearthly, phosphorescent glow of things best left unseen. I've worshiped at unholy altars, caressed by tendrils of night, studded by unnatural stars. I've witnessed the twisted images of saints spider-walking up church walls, their mouths open in silent screams. I've kissed the greened marble lips of the Mary who wept tears that weren't blood. I've seen Venice in all its guises, peeked behind all its masks, witnessed all its states of decay. Venice survives, no matter how ugly its scars.

My feet guide me to a little restaurant off Calle Mandola. It's almost unchanged since the old days, except for the light, and the sick-green smell, and the taste of salt in the air. They still serve a killer martini, though. Inside, the sound hits me like a wall. My heart skitters.

Guilt persists, even when I've given up love.

The place is nearly empty, but Josie sings as if the restaurant is full. Her voice is heartbreak: smoke and burnt amber and chocolate so dark it draws blood. It suits the restaurant's mood, and mine. Waiters move listlessly between tables, bringing baskets of bread, plates of limp vegetables in oily sauce, pasta - everything but meat, which ran out long ago, and fish, which is forbidden.

I tried to bring Josie fresh meat once. She wouldn't touch it. The thought of anything that had been in-between made her shudder and gag.

I remember — as much as I want to forget — how I held Josie's hands. Her moss-green eyes glowed with fear. I asked her to trust me. We stepped in-between.

And just as soon, we were jerked back, as if R'lyeh's ways had spit us out. Josie pulled away from me, the brief touch of *otherness* enough to shatter her already fragile mind.

We were staying in a hotel next to the theatre on Calle Fenice, in a room with walls the color of blood. The shower had stopped working long ago, but the toilet still flushed and, against all reason, the sheets were clean. When I stepped out of the between, Josie lay curled on the floor, clinging to the Turkish carpet as if it were the only thing holding her to this world.

"It burns. Ara, it burns."

I crouched beside her and touched her, feeling the sharp ridges of her spine through clothing and skin.

"Make it stop." She rocked and whimpered.

I lifted her sweater, peeling it as though from a wound. Tattoos, inked long before R'lyeh rose, but woken now, writhed across Josie's flesh. Black ink against skin the color of fired clay, lashing, twisting, moving in ways nothing ever should.

"Make it stop. It hurts. Make it stop." Josie turned her face, just enough to show tears and stark terror.

"I'm sorry," I told her. "I don't know how."

There were so many places I wanted to show her. I wanted to take her deep — somewhere off the coast of Mexico, to another drowned world full of turquoise water and old bones. I wanted to hold her hand, even through thick rubber gloves, and gesture to her through the enforced silence of breathing tubes and masks, hoping she'd understand.

She shuddered at the mere mention, and I went alone. I let the stillness envelop me; I drifted. Vast things floated beside me; an eye the size of Luxemburg opened below me in the deep. I should have been terrified, but I felt only peace as it looked into me and through me.

I used to think there were some sins too terrible even for R'lyeh, some offerings the spaces between would always refuse. But in that moment, I understood: sin is a human concept. So I did what I did to remain human. I buried sin deep at my core. I could walk the ways between a hundred, thousand times, and it would never change the deepest, most fundamental part of me.

In the end, I never took Josie anywhere. For a while, I tried to hold her when nightmares shivered beneath her skin, when her tattoos writhed in their own dreams. My touch only made it worse.

The day I left, she sat on the bed, head bowed. A red-glass heart from Murano lay cupped in her palm, brilliant as blood. I touched it with one finger; the glass was warm from her skin.

"I don't know why I have this," she said.

Her eyes held hurt, raw as a wound. Whatever I'd taken from her, trying to guide her through the between, was something I could never replace. Some wounds never heal. I left. I didn't ask her to forgive me.

Here and now, a ruby spotlight pins Josie — an American girl, singing Southern standards in a drowned and drowning city halfway across the world. Her song cuts knife-deep. I can't help remembering the last time we lay, cooling in each others' sweat, windows open, listening to the crowds leaving the Teatro.

That was the last time salt tasted good.

Josie's voice is sandstone, rubbed against my skin. It is coffee, scalding hot and poured into my lap. In the ruby spotlight and the green light seeping from the edges of the world, she's beautiful.

I sip my martini, slid without asking across the bar by the loyal bartender, Lorence. His skin is damp, his eyes as pained as the poor boy who served me in Harry's Bar. No matter that it hurts him, he still labors to breathe with human lungs, shunning his gills.

The song ends, and Josie leaves the stage. She wears a flower in her braided hair. Once upon a time, I may have given her a flower the same shade - a real one, not a silk monstrosity with hot-glue dew-drops clinging to its petals.

Her eyes meet mine, their moss-green accentuated by the underwater light.

"Ara." Josie brushes her lips against my cheek, making sure to catch the corner of my mouth.

She smells of lily-of-the-valley, dusted heavy to hide the reek of fear. Someone very wealthy must have bought it for her. Scents like that are hard to come by.

Guilt spreads patterns of frost across the surface of my heart, but it doesn't touch the core. Pain flickers in Josie's eyes. I've forgotten; she hasn't.

I tip my head towards Lorence; it's the least I can do. Josie orders something as blood-red as her dress, but with far more kick.

"What are you doing here?" Josie asks.

A tendril of ink slips from beneath the strap of her dress, a questing tongue tasting the air. She shivers. The ink-shadow stains her eyes for a moment, too, turning them the color of lightning-struck wood.

"I was lonely," I say. It may be the most honest thing I've ever said; I don't know.

"Oh?" Her eyes are green again, mocking.

She lifts the long, black braid lying over my shoulder, running it through trembling hands.

"I wish I could do something for you." The words fall, a numb rush over my lips.

Josie is the most breathtaking woman I've ever known. Why can't I feel anything for her? I know what she meant to me, what she means to me, but I don't *feel* it. Not anymore.

"There's nothing you can do." She drops my braid, a soft slap against my leather.

Josie finishes her drink and orders another, her mouth set in a hard line that reminds me of Madam Senator and the case I should be on.

"There's nothing I can do for you, either." Josie steps back, eyes as hard as the line of her mouth.

She's right. There's nothing I can do except buy her drinks. And isn't there a selfish hope that her inhibitions will drop and we'll end up back in that decaying hotel room, listening to the remnants of humanity leave the Teatro while we fuck?

Josie's next words send my pulse into the roof of my mouth. "Do you remember what you told me about your stepbrother and the night you got your scars?"

"No." The word emerges hoarse. I can't remember if it's a lie.

What did I tell her? What if I took her between, trying to make her forget?

Josie leans forward, her lips against my ear, her breath raising tiny hairs on my skin. Her voice is smoke and rough whiskey. "He called you his angel. They're shaped like wings, your scars."

When she draws back, I feel the absence of her breath.

"I don't think you're even human, anymore." Her hips sway as she walks back to the stage.

God help me, I'm wet and trembling. I want to throw her over the bar and nip the soft flesh of her thighs till she bleeds. Maybe she's right about me. Maybe I'm not human. Maybe I'm too much so.

Josie grips the microphone like she wants to throttle it. Her voice is steel wool; her eyes are fixed on me.

The blood-and-seawater light fills my mouth with salt. The world rolls, drowned in memory. Firelight flickers.

"The world is going to end." A voice speaks against my ear.

"It's already ending." I smell wet leather, tangle my fingers through wheat-gold hair, and pull wine-stained lips against mine. Rain drums. Hay prickles bare skin. "So, fuck me,"

I bite down hard, yank fabric roughly over hips; a body pushes into mine. A cry of pleasure and pain, and after, the world burns.

Josie's voice wails. Her smile is blade-edged. Her tattoos slither across her shoulders, chasing the ghost of my fingertips across her skin. Josie tips her head back, throat working. The song becomes a scream, her body shuddering, eyes rolling white between agony and ecstasy.

The bar squirms in murky half-light. Tentacles unfold. They undulate across the walls, wrap my arms, lift my hair. I drift in the green deep and they caress my bones.

I stagger for the door, retch on fire-scored pavement. Chill air slaps my face; I shift without meaning to. The threads binding past to present catch me, hurl me forward in time. My bones nearly shatter.

I brace myself against a wall, trembling. Damp, heavy breezes push air through the narrow, winding streets. My skin cold-sweats with borrowed dew. Where am I? When?

I walk, boots hushing over time-worn stone. I sympathize with Marco. I wonder why I'm hunting him. The Senator's envelope presses against my chest. I want to get this case over with and pretend there's a place I can go to that will feel like home.

Blonde hair, the smell of leather in the rain. I survived; he didn't. Fire scored my back with a thousand whips, tracing the shape of wings.

I walk along the waterfront, fighting memories that insist on surfacing, no matter how many times I try to give them away. I've begged the dark spaces teeming with star-ripe tentacles to take them, but they never do. There are no refunds on the price of survival.

I pass a nightclub. Tentacles — half-seen — lash the night. Shadows obscure the stars and they are just right. The club's beat is a heart-sound, a pulse-thump. The building sways. It shivers. Pigeons weep and mourn in cages embedded in walls of slick, trembling flesh. Overhead, gulls still scream their laughter, but then they would, wouldn't they?

I know where I'm going now. Farther down the wharf is the man I need to see.

Vincenzo sits at the end of a pier jutting out into the water. The piles are ghosts against the lapping dark. Each weed-slicked piece of wood is topped with a creature with too many arms, suckers gripping rotten wood. They *sing*.

The eerie-sweet sound licks my spine, too much like the timbre of Josie's voice. But instead of smoky-hot, the tentacles sing cold. How can things without mouths sing?

Their voices — if they can be called that — are vast, and reminiscent of cavern-glow and waving fronds. Their tears, should they ever cry, would taste of copper, iron, sulfur, and flame.

Vincenzo's arm moves, his brush stroke jerky, involuntary.

"Ara." He doesn't turn.

The scant, pulsing light behind me illuminates the rotting pier. It shows Vincenzo's face and the gaping spaces where his eyes used to be.

I was the one who found him on bathroom tiles slick with blood.

Vincenzo's head rested against the edge of a claw-footed tub. He wept.

Rather — his body shook with sobs and his eyes lay next to the drain in the otherwise-spotless tub, darker than the most cerulean sea and incapable of tears. Blood had spattered where they'd fallen, but otherwise, the porcelain remained white, white, white. His palms were stained rust-dark; so were his clothes. I nearly slipped in the blood covering the floor, but in the vast, arctic space of the tub, there were only a few drops, trailing from the drain back to the eyes.

"I can still *see*." Vincenzo's sobs turned to laughter while I held him.

"Hello, Vincenzo." I can't tell if he flinches or not when I lay my hand on his shoulder.

"You smell like her," he says. Did I tell him about Josie? I can't remember.

"I need information." My soles should be hard after years of running; my soul should be hard after years of leaving myself behind. Some things R'lyeh will never cure. Not in any place — not in any time.

"Watch the painting." Vincenzo's voice holds the same quavering tone as Josie's song.

Pain flickers through the space where his eyes should be, stars shifting through black, bloody caverns. I see blue, crimson-tinged spheres against porcelain-white; I feel him shaking in my arms. It's too late for apologies.

Vincenzo places a fresh canvas on the easel. His arm jerks, spastic. I watch over his shoulder as he paints. Flames. Venice burns.

"Thank you," I say.

Vincenzo's body hitches; he might be bleeding the paint, crimson, saffron, umber. He doesn't stop. I leave him to his colors and his pain.

I shift. Sideways, cross-wise, moving through a cold space as crushing as the deepest parts of the sea. My lungs compress. Tendrils wrap me. They lap my heart, sucker-hold it; they caress every part of my spine. They take a bitter-sweet song sung in a smoky voice like burnt almonds. I shiver as it fades; salt lingers on my tongue. It leaks from my eyes and I don't bother to brush it away.

Venice burns.

Heat batters me. I throw an arm up to shield my face. Inhuman tongues hiss unknown words, shiver laughter, babbling inside the flames. The stars spin. The canal heaves. Angles and rounded nubs of stone-not-stone — worn by untold eons — rise, dripping. The city would shudder in revulsion if it could; instead, it screams as it burns.

Against all reason, I turn toward the city's fire-wrapped heart. Sweat pools beneath my leather. My scars itch, pulling tight.

Marco is here. I was wrong. He wasn't seeking the end of the world, just the end of *his* world.

I find him in the little restaurant off Calle Mandola - Josie's restaurant. The walls are black, curling with smoke-wrought shadows. They don't shift and unfold yet, but they will. Everyone else has either fled or burnt to death. Only Marco remains, belly-up to the bar.

He turns a pock-marked face towards me, unsurprised. Flame makes his already-dark skin ruddy. His eyes shine, and not only with the glow of alcohol. He mimes a toast, lifting his glass, and throws the liquor back, grimacing.

"I knew my mother would send someone."

I don't bother to answer. How long until the flames reach us? I pour myself a drink, and refill Marco's glass. Nothing unfolds against my tongue as I drink. My eyes don't water. It's only alcohol.

"She wants you to come home." I pour again.

Marco slugs the drink in his glass. His eyes shine empty, staring into a middle distance only he can see. When he ran, how far did he go? Has he seen the end of all things? Did he watch his mother die screaming? His eyes are unsettling.

"What are *you* running from?" he asks.

My stomach lurches. I try to pour another shot, but most of it spills on the bar. All this alcohol - we're a Molotov cocktail, waiting to happen. "What do you mean?"

"You wouldn't have chased me this far if you weren't running from something." Marco's eyes fix me.

I shudder. The sensation goes all through me. I don't taste what's in my glass; I taste cheap wine stolen from a funeral table the day we buried our parents — my father, his mother.

My stepbrother.

I saved his life once, pulled him out of the river. He was nine; I was ten. Lying on his back, rocks darkening with the water running from his skin, squinting into the sun, he called me his guardian angel.

I breathe deep, and draw in a lungful of wet leather and hay. Firelight flickers from the old trashcan we dragged into the barn. Rain drums the roof. Our feet hang over the edge of the loft, heels kicking dust-pale wood. A horse whickers softly.

"I hate them," my stepbrother says.

"Who?" I drink straight from the bottle, bitter tannins clinging to my skin, staining cracked lips red.

"All those people at Mom and Dad's funeral. They're all a bunch of fucking phonies."

He takes the bottle from me. A storm hangs over us that has nothing to do with the rain. A weight presses between my shoulder blades; my skin itches. There is something waiting to rise.

Then, there, I am pulled out of myself. I am in Venice, looking at Marco across the bar, watching the world burn. I am floating above the vastness of a star-filled eye. Time means nothing.

I know what I will do to survive.

My stepbrother finishes the wine, tosses the bottle against the far wall where it shatters, spraying glass. A few droplets fall into the fire, making it snap and sizzle. I retrieve another bottle, pen-knife out the cork. We stole a whole armful as we left the funeral.

My stepbrother says, "They're lucky they aren't alive to see what happens next."

I don't have to ask what he means. He feels what's coming, but has he seen the end of the world? Does he know what I'll do to make sure I will?

"What's the worst sin you can think of?" I squint into the dark on the far side of the barn. "Not that Bible shit. Something real."

Shadows shift, fold and unfold. Jason looks down, heels drumming the wood, dust spinning up every time they hit.

"Hurting someone you love and meaning it."

I nod. The stars shift. They've always been right. I know what I have to do to survive. Tendrils reach for me, the color of starlight and as cold as the moon. I have to wrap myself in a sin I can never forgive, the worst thing I can think of, a pain I can never forget or give away. It's the only way to stay human.

I reach for Jason's hand, squeeze fingers as chill as ice.

"The world is ending." Jason's breath is rapid, wine-hot.

I lean close. Our faces almost touch. He understands what's coming and he wants me to save myself because I once saved him. I could refuse his gift, but I don't. My heart beats, cracks, and salty water rushes in.

"It's already ended," Jason says.

"So, fuck me." I pull him close, bite down hard on a kiss. I taste cheap wine and blood.

It would be mercy to say I slid into oblivion, but I felt every minute. I tasted every drop of sweat. I cherished every tear, cradled it on my tongue. After, Jason slept. I drank half the remaining bottle of wine, and threw the rest into the trashcan - a spray of glass, a gout of flame, the horse's soft whinny turning into a scream.

The fire traced wings on my back.

And I flew.

Dizzy, I grip the edge of the bar. "Your mother paid me a lot of money." I force the words out through clenched teeth.

Marco's image doubles, sways. I swam in marble corridors, in drowned-green canals. I tried to let tentacles steal the best of me, the rest of me. It wasn't enough. My sin kept me safe; it kept me whole.

"Your mother..." I try again.

"It doesn't matter." Marco shakes his head.

The ghosted memory of a smoky voice, tasting of bitter chocolate, threads the air and fades away. Scratchy hay presses a pattern of almost-words into my skin. I hold a blind man as he sobs. Shadow tendrils touch the deepest part of me, stripping my bones clean, taking everything except what matters.

I could cash in. I could make the biggest paycheck of my life. I could keep running and test the theory that the future is infinite. Or I could stay this time. I could burn.

Marco's gaze meets mine. Flames reflect between us. Inside the flames, impossible angles rise dripping from the canals. An eerie, piping song needles me with remembrance. Stars draw blood from my skin. Marco lays his hands, palms up, on the bar - an invitation.

There are many possible futures; I see them all. Two charred corpses decorate the remains of Josie's restaurant, one in front of the bar and one behind. One charred corpse sits slumped against the bar, alone. An empty, charred husk of a bar remains, with no one to witness its end.

It will come down to a battle of wills, my will to survive against Marco's will to die. I know what I gave up to survive; what did he give up to run? Which matters more?

My scars itch and stretch tight across my back, shaping wings. Wings for flight, or wings for salvation? Maybe this time they'll stay stitched beneath my skin, folded tight around my body like loving arms.

My wings have always been there; the stars have always been right. R'leyh rose everywhere, *everywhen*. I have always been what I am now. I have always survived.

For the moment, I take Marco's hands. And together, we watch Venice burn.

# *Biographies*

**Glynn Owen Barrass** lives in the North East of England and has been writing since late 2006. He has written over a hundred and twenty short stories, many of which have been published in the UK, USA, France, and Japan. He also edits anthologies for Chaosium's Call of Cthulhu fiction line, and writes material for their flagship roleplaying game. For Chaosium, he has co-written the campaign book *A Time to Harvest* and contributed scenarios to *Blood Brothers III*, *Doors to Darkness*, and a Gaslight Cthulhu book, and contributed technical information and a scenario for the upcoming Punktown sourcebook from Miskatonic River Press. To date, he has edited the collections: *Eldritch Chrome*, *Steampunk Cthulhu*, and *Atomic Age Cthulhu* for Chaosium; *World War Cthulhu* for Dark Regions Press; and *In the Court of the Yellow King* for Celaeno Press. His upcoming books include *Cthulhu AD 1970*, *The Summer of Lovecraft*, and *World War Cthulhu II*.

**Steve Berman** lives all alone in New Jersey, the only state in the union with an official devil.

**Gustavo Bondoni** was born in Argentina, which, he believes, makes him one of the few - if not the only - Argentinean fiction writers writing primarily in English. He moved to the US at the age of three because his father worked for a multinational company that bounced him around the world every three years. Miami, Zurich, Cincinnati. He only made it back to Buenos Aires at the age of twelve, by which time he was not quite an American kid, not quite a European kid, and definitely not Argentinean! His fiction spans the range from science fiction to mainstream stories, passing through sword & sorcery and magic realism along the way, and it has been published in fourteen countries and seven languages to date. Apart from over a hundred short stories, he has published two collections, a short novel, and a novella, with a third collection coming in 2015. His website is gustavobondoni.com.

**Jeff C. Carter** lives in Venice, CA with a dog, two cats, and a human. His latest stories appear in the anthologies Delta Green Extraordinary Renditions, That Hoodoo Voodoo That You Do, A Mythos Grimmly, and issues of Trembles, Calliope, and eFiction magazine. He is currently developing an RPG for Heroic Journey Publishing. You can follow him at jeffccarter.wordpress.com.

**J. Childs-Biddle** lives in Cincinnati, Ohio. She has been writing since a child, starting with a story of a lonely okapi. As an adult, her words about forlorn animals have morphed into stories of Old Gods, anguished spirits, and terribly unfortunate people. She spends most of her free time digging into articles about microbiology, psychology, and cephalopods in wild attempts to piece these elements into dark horror (or designing educational games for children, which is almost the same).

By day, **Evan Dicken** analyzes medical data and studies old Japanese maps at The Ohio State University. By night, he does neither of these things. His work has most recently appeared in *Shock Totem*, *The Lovecraft eZine*, *Analog*, and *Daily Science Fiction*, and he has stories forthcoming from publishers such as Chaosium, Darkfuse, Pseudopod, and Unlikely Story. Feel free to drop by at evandicken.com.

**Jeffrey Fowler** lives in Seattle, Washington and has just recently begun his writing career. Apotheosis is his anthology debut, though he does work as a freelancer writing for role-playing games with companies like By Night Studios and Onyx Path. With an amazingly talented wife, an adorable little girl, and two demonic hell cats for pets, he's a stay at home dad who is becoming practiced at spinning tales for a giggling three-year-old, as well as for publication. Luckily for him, he has an incredibly supportive family, a supremely talented mentor, and a best friend with whom he shares a brain, all of whom are willing to listen to him ramble about ideas and encourage him to write them down with varying degrees of enthusiasm, laughter, and sarcasm.

**Cody Goodfellow** has written three collections and four novels—his latest is *Repo Shark*—and co-written three more with John Skipp. His collections *Silent Weapons For Quiet Wars* and *All-Monster Action* both received the Wonderland Book Award. He wrote, co-produced, and scored the short Lovecraftian hygiene film "Stay At Home Dad," which can be viewed on YouTube. As a bishop of the Esoteric Order of Dagon (San Pedro Chapter), he presides over several Cthulhu Prayer Breakfasts each year. He is also a director of the H.P. Lovecraft Film Festival in Los Angeles and cofounder of Perilous Press, a micropublisher of modern cosmic horror. He "lives" in Burbank, California.

**Andrew Peregrine**'s first writing work was for role-playing games. Over the last ten years he's worked on several lines, including 7th Sea, Victoriana, Doctor Who, Firefly, and Vampire: the Masquerade. His short stories have appeared in Broadsword and Visionary Tongue magazines and he recently wrote for the Onyx Path anthology *Tales of the Sun and Moon*. He hasn't managed to complete a novel yet, but has plenty of unfinished ideas he really means to get around to. He works full time at the Theatre Royal Haymarket as a lighting technician, and wishes he was a lot better at writing bios.

**Peter Rawlik**, a long time collector of Lovecraftian fiction, is the author of more than twenty-five short stories, a smattering of poetry, the Cthulhu Mythos novels *Reanimators, The Weird Company*, and the forthcoming *Reanimatrix*. He is a frequent contributor to the Lovecraft ezine and to the New York Review of Science Fiction. In 2014 his short story *Revenge of the Reanimator* was nominated for a New Pulp Award. He lives in southern Florida where he works on

Everglades issues.

**Joshua Reynolds** is a professional freelance writer. His writing credits include stories in anthologies such as *Atomic Age Cthulhu*, *Challenger: Lost Places*, *New Worlds*, and *Sharkpunk*. He has also contributed to Games Workshop's Warhammer Fantasy and Warhammer 40,000 tie-in lines. A full list of his credits can be found at https://joshuamreynolds.wordpress.com/

**Adrian Simmons** writes, reads, and edits from a well-provisioned base in Central Oklahoma. He has hoofed the Ouachita Trail, the Ozark Highland trail, the northern England coast to coast trail, and a respectable distance of the Camino de Santiago in Spain. His genre nonfiction has appeared in Black Gate and Strange Horizons. His short fiction has popped up in James Gunn's Ad Astra Magazine, Pseudopod, Outposts of Beyond, and Strange Constellations. In 2009. he founded the webzine Heroicfantasyquarterly.com and currently serves as one third of its editorial staff.

**Jason Vanhee** was born and grew up in Seattle, Washington. Raised by a single mother who left him free to explore his imagination, he began to write almost as soon as he could read. His work most often encompasses the speculative fiction that was his reading mainstay in his younger life. Jason lives in Seattle still with his husband Adam. His first published novel, *Engines of the Broken World*, was released by Henry Holt in 2013.

**June Violette** is an agent provocateur, kayaking tour guide, and roleplaying enthusiast from the distant and mysterious city of Seattle, Washington. When not dreaming up terrible ideas unfit to see the light of day, June most enjoys arguing about music and/or soccer, wrangling ferrets, and bearing the battle standard of the mighty Oxford Comma. June's favorite pursuits are those with no practical application in the modern world, a predilection reflected in hir recent decision to study Welsh. Cymru am byth!

**L. K. Whyte** is a Pacific Northwest native, gamer, and academic who loves fantasy, science fiction, horror, mystery, and the macabre. When not teaching or tutoring in colleges or prisons, Whyte enjoys hearty debates, researching gaming as a means of social justice intervention, playing video games, and mapping fictional places. The publication of "What Songs We Sing" marks Whyte's fiction debut.

**A.C. Wise**'s short fiction has appeared in places such as *Shimmer*, *Apex*, *Uncanny*, and *The Year's Best Dark Fantasy and Horror 2015*, among others. Her debut collection, *The Ultra Fabulous Glitter Squadron Saves the World Again*, will be published by Lethe Press in October 2015. In addition to her fiction, she co-edits *Unlikely Story*. Find her online at www.acwise.net.

**Jonathan Woodrow** lives with his wife and three young children in a quiet village on the outskirts of Toronto, Ontario, where he spends his time writing dark, mostly speculative fiction. His short stories have appeared in numerous magazines and anthologies, including *Blight Digest*, *Under the Bed Magazine*, and the terrifying *Cranial Leakage* anthology, along with many others. His debut novel, *Wasteland Gods*, will be released at the end of the year by Horrific Tales Publishing, so keep a look out!

# *About the Editor*

**Jason Andrew** lives in Seattle, Washington with his wife Lisa. By day, he works as a mild-mannered technical writer. By night, he writes stories of the fantastic and occasionally fights crime. As a child, Jason spent his Saturdays watching the Creature Feature classics and furiously scribbling down stories. His first short story, written at age six, titled "The Wolfman Eats Perry Mason" was severely rejected. It also caused his Grandmother to watch him very closely for a few years.

His short fiction has appeared in markets such as *A Mytho Grimmly: A Lovecraftian Fairy Tale Anthology* (Wanderer's Haven Publications)), *Frontier Cthulhu: Ancient Horrors in the New World* (Chaosium), and *Atomic Cthulhu: Tales of Mythos Horror in the 1950s Coins of Chaos* (Chaosium). In 2011, his story "Moonlight in Scarlet" received an honorable mention in Ellen Datlow's List for Best Horror of the Year.

In addition, Jason has written for a number of role-playing games. His most recent projects include *Mind's Eye Theatre: Vampire the Masquerade* (By Night Studios), *Shadowrun: Data Trails* (Catalyst Game Labs), and *Rites of the Blood* (Onyx Path Publishing). He currently holds the position of Developer for the Mind's Eye Theatre line published through **By Night Studios.** Check out his website at http://www.jasonbandrew.com

# *About Simian Publishing*

**Simian Publishing** is a small press company devoted to primal dark fantasy and horror fiction. We're interested in seeing how the old gods, monsters, and Jungian archetypes work in the modern world. We want fiction that touches our souls.

With Print on Demand technology, Simian Publishing is able to take chances on a story or novel that might never see the light of day through a mainstream publisher. Currently, we looking for more direct distributors, but for now you can find our products on a variety of online stores.

www.simianpublishing.org

# *Kickstarter Patron Credits*

Abby Witherell
Adam Alexander
Akule
Al Hay
Alan Stanford
Alexis Perron
Andy Lucas
Annie Zellmer
Ashley Oswald
Brendan Reeves
Brendan W.
Bryce Undy
Caitlin Grace
Carlos Orsi
Chan Ka Chun Patrick
Charlie Rose
Chelle P.
Chris Jarocha-Ernst
Chris Kalley
Chris Miles
Chuck Childers
Craig Hackl
Cullen Gilchrist
Dan Alban
David B.
Drew Biddle
Edward Sizemore
Eric Priehs
Evaristo Ramos
Fabio Fernandes

Herbert Eder
ianquest
IF Collective
James Simons
Jason Aaron Wong
Jason Aiken
Jason Carl
Jason Leisemann
Jeffrey Fowler
Jenni Loopy Smith
Jeremy Hochhalter
Jessica Schulze
Jim Reader
Joe Kontor
Joe Kontor
John D Kennedy
John O'Connor
José Antonio Lambiris Ruiz
Kenneth Hayes
Lauren Phelps
Lee Clark Zumpe
Lisa Andrew
Lisa Kruse
Marc Margelli
Mark Froom
Mark L.
Mark Newman

Martin Tomasek
Matthew Carpenter
Mike Serritella
Miles Britton
Myk Pilgrim
Neil Mahoney
Nick Nafpliotis
Paul Cardullo
Paul Mysliwiec
Proof482
Rebecca J. Allred
Rebecca Romney
Robert Helmbrecht
Robert muncy
Roger Walker
Ron Neely II
Ryan Faricelli
Sandor
Selena McDevitt
Stanley Bowles
Stephen R Myers
T. Mike McCurley
Terry Willitts
The Big BALLER
Tomas
Tore Halvorsen
Tramov
William
Xymon Owain

www.ingramcontent.com/pod-product-compliance
Lightning Source LLC
Chambersburg PA
CBHW071815020726
47502CB00004B/1113

* 9 780979 422133 *